The W
Wit

By Hugh Morrison

MONTPELIER PUBLISHING
2022

Published in Great Britain by Montpelier Publishing.

ISBN: 9798412106908

Chapter One

'My dear brothers and sisters…let us begin.'

Aethelstan Rooksley stepped forward to the table at the front of the little tin chapel and sat down, bowing his head in prayer. There were one or two coughs and throat-clearings from the congregation and then silence. The chapel, despite the bright summer evening light outside, was shrouded in gloom due to heavy blinds at the windows; the only light came from a small red oil lamp on the table. The heat was stifling, and the man theatrically patted a few beads of perspiration from his high forehead with his handkerchief.

Rooksley decided to prolong the silence. Let them wait, he thought. It didn't do to make anything happen too quickly, and after all the hymn-singing and extempore prayers he needed a bit of a rest. All the best performers needed that. He breathed deeply and set his gaze on the middle distance in front of him, a trick which he knew had the effect of making everyone in the room think he was looking straight at them.

He lifted his eyebrows slightly, showing the whites of his eyes above his pupils, another trick which made his gaze seem even more piercing. With his tall, athletic frame and black, swept back hair with its streak of white from an old wound, Rooksley cut an impressive figure even in daylight. In the gloom and with all the apparatus of Spiritualism to call upon, he felt himself almost god-like.

'Is there anybody there?' he intoned. It was hackneyed, and he would not have said it in the type of London seance he was used to, but in a small town like this it seemed to go down well. He repeated the incantation.

'Is there anybody there?'

'Can you ask if my boy, my Harold is there?,' blurted a tearful woman with a strong Suffolk accent, from somewhere at the back of the chapel. There were sharp whisperings of 'hush' and 'don't disturb him' from the others, but Rooksley seized on the opportunity. It was not quite what he wanted, but it would make a good first act before the *pièce de résistance.*

Rooksley leaned his head back and looked at the ceiling. He could just make out the peeling plaster and cobwebs, dark against the white-painted ceiling high above him.

'There is a boy…' whispered Rooksley. He was about to add 'a young boy,' guessing it was probably a death from a childhood illness. Then the woman interrupted again.

'He was only a lad…' she said hurriedly, as if she were worried the connection with the spirit world would be broken before she had finished speaking. 'Tell him he didn't die in vain, tell him we won the war. Tell him his ma and pa still love him.' There were a few shushings but fewer this time. 'I just want to know he's happy.'

Rooksley paused again before speaking. Then he gazed at the back of the chapel, widening his eyes as much as he could. He knew from practicing in the mirror that his pupils would be lit up by the little lamp in front of him, as if they were somehow illuminated by a heavenly vision. The little piece of information the woman had give him made him change tack.

'There is a boy…' he said. 'But he's almost a man. He looks as if he has suffered. He looks older.'

He then stood up walked forward a few steps, fixing his gaze on the pew from which the woman had spoken.

'Did he suffer much, my dear sister?'

'Oh yus,' said the woman with a sniff. 'They said as it took him twelve hours to die.'

'I see him, he is wearing khaki. Lying in a shell hole.'

The woman sniffed again. 'I don't think it can be him,' she said with disappointment in her voice. 'He were in the Navy.'

Rooksley frowned. He should have remembered he was in a coastal town. He changed tack again. He looked down and rubbed his eyes, then looked up again.

'I see more clearly now. I thought it was a shell hole filled with water, but it is the dark sea…he is not in khaki, it is a trick of the light, his uniform appears green, not blue, in the deep water, as he spirals into the abyss….'

There was a gasp from some of the more nervous members of the congregation, but the woman did not respond. Rooksley thought quickly, cursing himself. Twelve hours to die, in the Navy. Probably burns, or a wound of some sort, then. She wouldn't say he took twelve hours to die if he'd drowned. As if to confirm what he was thinking, the woman replied curtly.

'He died of food poisoning. Are you sure it's my Harold?'

Rooksley affected a pained expression as he stepped backward to the table. 'He's fading now…fading…but he says not to worry. Everything is perfect in the hereafter. All is peace. Believe, where you cannot prove.'

There was an audible sigh of relief from the congregation; Rooksley knew that if he could not give them specifics, they would generally be satisfied with vague generalities and platitudes. If he could make it sound like something Tennyson might have written then so much the better. He thought he heard, however, a 'harrumph' from the woman he had spoken to. He decided to move on quickly to another subject.

Things went on in much the same vein for twenty minutes or so. Rooksley was a master at making the vague appear concrete. He did not really think of himself as a trickster or a fraud; he had dabbled in the black arts and the mystic religions of the east for many years, but such esoterica was wasted on a provincial seaside town like this. Here, thought Rooksley, people sought spiritual entertainment rather than any sort of genuine mystical experience.

These seances brought in money, and he needed money before he could move on to better things, perhaps abroad. Things had got a little hot for him in London after he had tried to get some money a little too forcefully from one of his wealthy clients in London, and a looming paternity suit threatened to make matters worse.

An old acquaintance had recommended Eastburgh as a good place to lie low; while idly browsing the properties available in the town, his eye lighted upon the town's Independent Spiritualist Chapel, the rickety prefabricated metal building he now rented. A relic of the spiritualism boom of the eighteen-sixties, the congregation had dwindled and the place was going for a song; the chapel and the adjacent living quarters were just what he needed.

A few months later Rooksley had revitalised the chapel; some of the old congregation had come back and he was happy to let them undertake the more Christian parts of the services such as the tedious, long, extempore prayers and the sentimental Victorian hymns on the wheezy harmonium, while he led the seances.

Rooksley decided it was time to bring on the main attraction of the evening. His new technique. If this did not bring in a small fortune when the plate was taken round, then nothing would. He sensed that the congregation had started to grow restless and so he raised his hands.

'Quiet,' he snapped. 'Up until now I have only seen visions of the spirit world. But now, for the first time I have begun to hear them speaking. The spirits are speaking. Listen, brothers and sisters…listen!'

There was a moment of silence but then, from everywhere and yet nowhere, there came a hissing, scratching sound. There were gasps from the congregation and he saw one or two of the silhouetted women clutch their husbands or friends in fear. Then a reedy, unearthly voice, of indeterminate sex, began to speak.

'We are all here…we are all in the great beyond. It is so beautiful here…please stay, we wish to speak to you…please help the one who is trying to speak to us...'

There was a crash as one of the chapel chairs was knocked over. Rooksley, appearing to be deep in a trance, looked up, expecting, or rather hoping, to see that some impressionable elderly woman had collapsed in a faint. Instead his face flushed with surprise as a heavy-set middle aged man stomped into the aisle and pointed at Rooksley.

'Fraud!' he shouted. 'This man is a fraud, and I shall prove it!'

The heavy-set man was Reg Cotterill. He had been watching Rooksley's performance in the chapel with mounting anger. He was not a Spiritualist but his wife Gladys had always been interested in that sort of thing, and had deserted the parish church when Rooksley had begun to draw large crowds to his seances. The Cotterills had lost a son at Gallipoli, and Gladys had never really got over it; she was always hoping for some sort of sign from what she called the Distant Shore. Cotterill secretly called it 'the Distant Sham' and wished his wife would just let the boy rest in peace.

'He's ever so good,' said Gladys, after returning home one night in a glow of excitement after one of Rooksley's services. 'They say he can do all sorts. Summon the dead, levitate, you name it. A real showman, he is.'

Cotterill had little time for churches or chapels of any denomination, let alone ones such as this which seemed to have only a tenuous connection with formal Christianity, but the word 'showman' had piqued his interest. A retired electrician, he had been supplementing his small pension for a few years with a ventriloquist's act at the little theatre on the end of Eastburgh pier. He had always wanted to be on the stage, but a trade had seemed a safer life than the precarious world of the music halls.

The trouble was, the act was not much good. In fact it was terrible, and even the kiddies who comprised the bulk of his audience could see that. Every matinee one of the little blighters would shout out something about his lips moving, even though he tried to hide them behind a cigar.

He had wondered just what it was that enabled Rooksley to draw a full house in that tin chapel of his. He had been receiving some technical help for his act from a youngster, Les Prior, whose parents ran a wireless shop in the town. What Prior told him about Rooksley had raised his suspicions, and what he had just heard in the seance had confirmed them.

'He's using a gramophone!' shouted Cotterill, his face reddening. Always a short-tempered man, he felt an unstoppable well of anger building up in his chest. The strange, reedy voice suddenly stopped its incantation, and there was silence.

'He's hidden loudspeakers in the chapel!' continued Cotterill. 'Loudspeakers and a gramophone. I'll prove it to you!'

Cotterill stomped forward to the front of the chapel and stood in front of Rooksley, breathing heavily. There were cries of 'shame!' and 'sit down!' from the congregation. At first Cotterill was emboldened by them, thinking they were addressing Rooksley, but when he caught sight of his wife's shocked expression he realised the remarks were intended for him. He hesitated and looked at the medium.

The man fixed him with a malevolent glare and then spoke in a disarmingly polite tone.

'My dear brother, I can see that you are pained. You are grieving. It is easier to deny the existence of the spirit world, to call me a charlatan and a fraud than to face the reality of the soul's persistence after death.'

'Soul's persistence, my eye!' exclaimed Cotterill, though he sounded a little less sure of himself now.

He swallowed hard. He had expected Rooksley to be angry or try to have him thrown out rather than to speak reasonably to him.

'Prove to me you don't have loudspeakers hidden, then!'

'I cannot prove a negative, brother,' said Rooksley, unctuously. 'But shall we look together? Come, let us examine the chapel. "Seek, and ye shall find", as the Name above all Names commands. Is there a loudspeaker or gramophone under here?'

Rooksley raised the damask cloth on the table; there was nothing underneath except a faded, musty persian carpet.

'There is nothing here. Or perhaps I am also a conjuror, who has made the gramophone disappear?'

There were nervous titters from the congregation. Cotterill realised he had gone too far, and began to wonder how he could back down without losing face. Rooksley, however, continued talking in his smooth, calming voice.

'Or is there something concealed in here?'

Rooksley strode to the little door which led to the vestry and hurled it open, switching on the electric light as he did so. The room appeared empty apart from a desk and chair.

'Please, kindly inspect the premises. Go where you will.'

Cotterill hesitated. 'Well…perhaps I…'

Rooksley placed a hand on Cotterill's arm. 'Perhaps you may wish to do so at a more convenient time. We ought not to disturb those who wish to pray and to praise His name for His manifold mercies unto us.'

The churchman-like language made Cotterill remember that he was ostensibly in a place of worship, even if it was of a type he found distasteful. His shoulders slumped with instinctive deference and he sidled back to his seat.

Rooksley smiled. 'My dear brothers and sisters, I fear the spirits have been disturbed, and we will hear no more from beyond the veil this evening. Let us end with a hymn.'

As the harmonium began to wheeze out the opening bars of *Lead, Kindly Light*, Cotterill felt the faces of the congregation glowering at him from all sides.

As the last of the congregation departed into the warm, moonlit summer night, Rooksley locked the door of the chapel and entered his living quarters at the rear of the building. He poured himself a stiff whisky and knocked it back in one gulp, then lit a Turkish cigarette. He felt the weight of the velvet collection bag; it seemed to be mostly coins rather than paper. He suspected the outburst from that man had not helped with the takings, but he congratulated himself on keeping calm and puncturing the man's pomposity, as well as preventing him from finding the secret mechanism hidden beneath the carpet.

What was that fellow's name? He could not think. There was never much need to learn names in this game, he knew, as one could always get away with 'dear brother' or 'dear sister'. He recognised the frumpy wife as a regular attender, but not the man himself. Yet he had seen him before somewhere. He took a deep draw on the pungent cigarette, and realised who the man was. He was the turn off the end of the pier; the one with a ventriloquist's act. He remembered because he had gone there for a lark when he had first arrived in Eastburgh, hoping there might be a few chorus girls on show.

There were no girls— not likely of course in a Nonconformist sort of place like Eastburgh— but he had remembered the ventriloquist act as it was so shoddy. In his mind's eye he saw the poster at the entrance to the pier. It was of the man holding a wooden doll dressed in evening dress, with big eyes and a monocle. 'Reg Cotterill and Lord Harry: every night in season'.

Rooksley decided he would pay a little visit to Reg Cotterill. It was about time, he thought, that the man started thinking a bit more seriously about the Hereafter.

With a clattering, clanking sound the train emerged from the tunnel into dazzling daylight. The Reverend Lucian Shaw, a tall, angular-faced man in middle age with a fine head of grey hair, awoke from his doze, and for the first time on the journey saw the sea; the vast blue plain, shimmering with reflected sunlight, which merged with the chalky azure sky at the horizon in a lemon-coloured haze. Although he knew Holland or Belgium lay only a hundred miles or so beyond, it seemed as if such a vast, empty distance must stretch to the edge of the world.

What was the line from Homer?, thought Shaw. 'The wine-dark sea.' Having never seen the Aegean, he had never quite understood how the sea could look like wine, but he began to understand now. In the strong, almost Mediterranean sunlight, it had a dark, almost purple tone, so different from the usual greyish brown hue that the North Sea had for most of the year. He had never known such fine weather in England, except perhaps in the golden summer of 1914, which now seemed a distant memory and which he had spent far inland anyway.

His wife Marion pulled the window next to her down a little further, fiddling with the leather belt to ensure it stayed in place. It was just enough to fill the stuffy compartment with sea air but not enough to give Fraser, the couple's West Highland terrier, any ideas about sticking his head out.

'Isn't it wonderful, Lucian!' she exclaimed as she breathed in great lungfuls of air and clutched at her straw hat to prevent it blowing away. Her dark hair waved in the breeze; her face, which might have been called handsome rather than beautiful, suddenly looked younger as she smiled.

'So much better than Lower Addenham,' she said. 'The weather was becoming quite unbearable at home.'

'Indeed,' said Shaw, who was himself also glad to have escaped the simmering heat of their village. 'Mind the smuts,' he added as a cloud of soot rushed into the compartment from the engine.

'It's quite all right,' said Mrs Shaw. 'The wind seems to have blown it the other way. How fortunate we are to have a cool breeze. I do hope it keeps up for the whole of the fortnight, like an enormous fan.'

Shaw nodded in agreement. The heat had become unpleasant in recent days. For an Englishman, more than a few days where the thermometer exceeds 70 degrees fahrenheit constitutes a heatwave; and a heatwave for a clergyman obliged to wear a cassock and surplice for much of the time was rather tiresome.

He was looking forward to a few days of being able to dress more casually on the beach, though at present he wore a modified version of his usual attire; black trousers, black shirt-front and Roman collar, but with the addition of a lightweight, cream coloured linen jacket, worn slightly threadbare from several years of holiday outings, and a battered panama hat instead of a black homburg. His was a vocation, and it behoved him to make it known to the world that he was a minister of Christ's church militant here on earth even when on holiday; his clothing was not the overalls of the mechanic or shop-worker to be hung up when the working day was done.

The train began to slow down, swaying and jerking as it crossed a level crossing, then made a peculiar musical sound as the wheels traversed rails of varying thickness over several sets of points. Finally there was a hiss of steam and a moment of silence as the train came to a stop under the little glass canopy at Eastbrough terminus.

Even to someone who lived in a beautiful corner of rural England, away from the modern intrusions of arterial roads, mock-tudor housing estates and industrial sprawl, there was always something special about the moment one opened a railway compartment door by the sea. The salt tang of the air, the fresh breeze and the sense of infinity on one's doorstep were something, thought Shaw, that could not be experienced anywhere else.

The moment of silence passed quickly and then there was a slamming of doors and the sound of cases and trunks dropping heavily on to the platform, and the excited chatter of holiday-makers organising themselves. Shaw managed to summon a porter and their cases were wheeled through the darkened terminus building. From the Smith's bookstall he smelt a smell redolent of his youth; the aroma of hot, fresh newsprint on an array of colourful 'penny dreadfuls' and boys' story papers laid out on the counter.

Shaw always associated that smell with the start of summer holidays. As a boy when he and his parents had arrived at a resort, he was given a penny by his mother to buy an improving paper to read from the station bookstall, such as the *Boy's Own*, but he had always secretly longed to buy one of the lurid yellow-backed half-penny novelettes instead, of which his mother heartily disapproved. He paused for a moment and was surprised to see such booklets had changed little, and one of them even featured a character he remembered from his 'teens, a detective known as Sexton Blake.

He reached into his trouser pocket for a coin to purchase the book, but before he could do so, he felt his wife's arm leading him gently through the doors out onto the station forecourt. They emerged once more into the hot sunlight to see a convoy of motor vehicles driving away in a cloud of blue exhaust smoke.

'Oh dear,' said Mrs Shaw. 'Just as I thought. All the taxis have been taken. You oughtn't to have dawdled by that newsagent's. We'll either have to walk or wait for them to come back. I can't bear walking in this heat with cases. Shall we sit down?'

'Very well,' said Shaw. 'The Excelsior Hotel is, I believe, about a mile from the station. Rather too far to walk, I agree.'

A voice piped up from behind Shaw. 'Carry yer bags for yer, guvnor?'

Shaw looked round to see a small, somewhat dishevelled boy of about ten years of age blinking up at him. The child was holding on to a piece of rope attached to what looked like some sort of home-made trolley or 'go-cart'. Behind him were several other boys with similar looking wheeled contraptions; they were busily engaged in loading the cases of holidaymakers on to them.

'Excelsior's not too far, guvnor, er, I mean, farver,' said the boy. 'Only cost you a penny.'

Shaw hesitated. The boy seemed to take this as an affront.

'Taxi'll cost yer a bob and a tanner at least,' he said. 'Come on farver.'

Mrs Shaw looked doubtfully at the boy and then around the station concourse. 'There don't seem to be any taxis left,' she said briskly, 'and one and sixpence is rather a lot to pay for such a short distance. Very well, please take our cases.'

'Righto missus,' said the boy with a grin, and hoisted the couple's two suitcases onto his barrow. 'Cor, I like your dog,' he continued, patting Fraser's head. 'Wish I 'ad one like that.'

Fraser looked disappointed as the boy stopped patting him and turned his attention back to his trolley. The wheels buckled under the weight of the cases but this did not seem to bother the urchin, and after some initial heaving, he was able to get the little vehicle moving on the pavement.

'Excelsior's this way,' said the boy as Shaw and his wife began to follow him along the road. 'On yer 'olidays are you farver?', he continued.

Shaw smiled. 'That's right. What's your name?'

'Billy,' said the boy, grimacing as he struggled to control the wagon on a slight incline. 'Billy Wainwright, farver.'

'How do you do, Billy. By the way, most people call me Mr Shaw, or vicar, instead of father.'

'Oh,' said the boy. 'I thought all parsons was called farver. Leastways ours is.'

'You are a Roman Catholic?'

The boy laughed. 'Course not. Them's all Irish, ain't they? I go to that church there.'

Billy nodded to a large, flint-walled church on a steep slope.

'Very commendable,' said Shaw.

Billy laughed. 'Well I only do the 'oly stuff— what they calls altar server— 'cos you have to to play in the church football team. Farver Nicholas, that's the parson, he's the referee and lor, you should see him run, even in that black frock he wears.'

Shaw smiled, assuming the boy meant a cassock. He realised the church must be of the High Anglican variety, whose clergy generally refer to themselves as Father.

'And where do you live, Billy?' asked Shaw. 'You do not sound as if you were born and bred in Suffolk, if I may say so.'

'Not likely far…er, vicar,' said Billy. 'I'm not one of them country bumpkins from round here. Me and mother's from London— Befnal Green— but we come up here to live on the Plotlands.'

'Plotlands?' asked Shaw.

'Sort of a village for people what built their own houses,' explained Billy. He pointed to a field about a quarter of a mile away from them, on the edge of the town, where there stood a collection of ramshackle wooden huts and what looked like old railway carriages.

'Mother said we'd be better off out here than in London,' continued Billy. 'She saved up for years from charring, to buy our plot, and now she does cleaning here as well, and we keeps chickens and all sorts.'

Shaw hesitated to ask if the boy had a father, but the child provided the information himself, almost proudly.

'I ain't got no dad. Mother tells everyone he was lost at sea but me older brother told me he gone off and left us when I was a nipper. He's up north somewhere he says. Doesn't bother me. Nobody to give us a belting, and that suits me.'

'You seem a very independent young man,' said Mrs Shaw. 'I trust you go to school regularly?'

'Course I do,' sniffed Billy. 'Got no choice, have I? Us Plotlanders don't mix much with the local kids but we 'as to go to school with 'em.'

'I see,' said Mrs Shaw. 'How fascinating.'

Shaw smiled to himself. He knew his wife subscribed to the idea that children should be seen and not heard, and was not overly keen on conversation with them, especially not strange little street urchins such as this one.

He noticed they were now approaching the Excelsior Hotel; a grey stone building erected around 1890, perched on the low cliffs overlooking the town. As they neared the brick wall around the gardens, Billy stopped and lifted the cases out onto the driveway.

'This is where I stop, vicar,' he said, grimacing as he struggled to unload the cases from his trolley. 'The porters gives us a clip round the ear if we comes any closer than the gate. They can't stand the competition, see. But I reckon that's what they call capitalism.'

'That is quite all right thank you Billy,' said Shaw. 'We shall manage from here.' He pressed a coin into the boy's hand. Billy looked at it, and seeing it was a sixpence, his face fell.

'Ain't you got nothing smaller?' he said. 'I can't make change.'

'You may keep the change, Billy,' said Shaw. 'I have enjoyed our little talk. Perhaps we may meet again sometime.'

'Cor, thanks vicar!' exclaimed Billy, who tucked the sixpence carefully into the pocket of his shorts. 'I'm well known in this town, so if you ever need anyfink, just ask for me and I'll sort it out for yer. Primrose Cottage is the name of our place. 'Cept it ain't really a cottage, and there ain't no primroses neither. But everyone knows it. I'd best get back now as the next train'll be in soon. Cheerio then!'

In a blur of motion Billy turned his little wagon around and, after pushing it briskly, jumped onto it and careered down the hill back to the station.

'What an extraordinary child,' said Mrs Shaw. 'And why on earth did you give him sixpence?' she chided. 'He only asked for a penny.'

'"The labourer is worthy of his hire",' said Shaw, quoting the gospel of St Luke. 'We should encourage such enterprise in our young folk.'

'Don't let the taxi drivers hear you say that,' replied Mrs Shaw. 'They'll say you're cheating a full-grown man out of a job in the middle of a slump.'

She turned her gaze from the sea round to the hotel driveway, from whence came the sound of boots on gravel.

'Speaking of which, here comes a porter.'

Shaw turned and saw a young man in a pill box hat, looking for all the world like 'Buttons' from the pantomime, striding towards them. He then saw something out of the corner of his eye; a blur of orange and then a flash of white; he blinked, and saw what appeared to be a figure draped in a white sheet pass momentarily through a gap in the hedge between the hotel gardens and the roadway.

A superstitious man might have suspected he had just seen a ghost, but Shaw dismissed it as some sort of optical illusion caused by the heat shimmering up from the road, combined with a certain light-headedness he had felt coming on him in the merciless sunlight. It was almost unbearably hot in the shadeless front garden, and he was relieved to enter the cool, dark lobby of the hotel.

He breathed in the peculiar smell common to seaside hotels; an aroma of salt air mixed with wood polish, leather upholstery, boiled cabbage and a hint of some fragrant, hoppy beer from the direction of the bar.

Although not a great drinker, Shaw did appreciate a pint of well-kept ale, and he felt his mouth water at the thought of a dimpled glass mug of mild, with a thin sheen of condensation around its rim. He dismissed such a worldly thought when he remembered it was not yet even lunchtime.

Shaw was woken from his reverie by the noise of 'Buttons' leaving their luggage on the parquet floor and then by a voice to his left behind the reception desk.

'Reverend and Mrs Shaw, I assume?' asked the concierge, who looked at them over half-moon spectacles. 'Good afternoon,' continued the man, as he smoothed his large, drooping moustache. 'My name is Lucas, the hotel manager.'

'How do you do,' said Shaw. 'I trust all is well with our booking? For two weeks, room with sea view and private bathroom.'

'Indeed, indeed,' said Lucas. 'Room one hundred and thirty eight.' He turned to a row of pigeon-holes behind him and took down a large brass key, which he passed to the porter.

Shaw blinked as he saw, again, from the corner of his eye, a figure in white drifting through a pair of double doors at the end of the corridor. Wondering if it was some persistence of vision caused by the bright sunlight outside, he blinked again but he was not seeing things. There *was* a figure in white robes walking towards him. He turned to his wife who, judging by the puzzled expression on her face, had seen the figure also.

Shaw saw that it was a young, pale-skinned woman, perhaps around thirty years of age, bespectacled, without make-up, and her hair tied back plainly from her face. There then appeared another robed figure behind her, a dark skinned man with a shorn head and orange robes.

Both wore sandals on their feet and walked with a silent serenity through the door marked 'lounge and terrace.'

'Ah, you have noticed our guests from the sub-continent,' said Lucas with a smile. 'India, you know. No doubt you will be joining them as part of the conference.'

'Conference?' asked Shaw.

'Yes, you know,' replied Lucas, who stepped out from behind the desk and clutched the lapels of his morning coat as if he were a barrister in court. 'The conference for, er…'— he turned to look at a paper on the reception desk to refresh his memory— the 'Conference of All Spiritual Beings'. I'm Wesleyan Methodist myself, sir, but they do say it takes all sorts to make a world. They are a week into the two-week event and I am pleased to say it all seems most respectable and in order. The next lecture starts shortly, I believe. Are you a speaker?'

'No,' said Shaw. 'I had no idea a conference was taking place in this hotel. We are here on holiday.'

'Forgive me sir,' said the manager. 'I just assumed…what with your…'— here he made a criss-crossing gesture across his throat — '…that you were of the spiritual persuasion.'

'Indeed I am,' said Shaw with a smile, 'but of the Anglican spiritual persuasion. I suspect the conference is aimed at those of a more eastward position.'

'Eastward, sir?' asked the manager, in a slightly confused voice.

'No matter,' said Shaw. 'Perhaps we might see our room?'

'Of course, of course sir,' said Lucas, returning to his place behind the desk. 'The porter here will show you up.'

As they followed the porter up the large main staircase with its dark wood panelling and stained glass, Mrs Shaw, cradling Fraser in her arms, whispered to her husband.

'Who on earth were those people, Lucian? The man looked for all the world like that Mr Gandhi from the newsreels. And whilst one expects robes and sandals and that sort of thing with Indians, the young woman with him was most certainly *not* Indian.'

'I have no idea,' said Shaw. 'Perhaps we shall find out more about them as the holiday progresses. It may even be possible to attend one of their lectures.'

'Oh Lucian really,' chided Mrs Shaw. 'What a thing for a clergyman to say.'

'There is much that Christendom can learn from the religions of the east,' said Shaw, as they reached the top of the grand staircase and turned down a small, thickly carpeted corridor. 'The Transcendentalist movement of the last century— of Thoreau, and Longfellow and so on, did much to reveal eastern religious thought to the west. I find it a rather interesting topic.'

'Oh dear,' said Mrs Shaw, and her husband could tell she was already becoming bored with the subject. 'Well if you want to sit in a stuffy lecture room,' she continued, 'while there is such glorious weather outside, don't let me stop you. I shall be going for healthy walks instead. I just hope there won't be any noisy chanting, or drums and the like. If there are snake charmers, we shall have trouble controlling Fraser. You know he's a splendid ratter.'

At this point in the conversation, they reached their room, and after recklessly giving sixpence to the porter, Shaw and his wife were left alone in their room.

'Oh how delightful, it's got a little balcony,' said Mrs Shaw, who threw her hat on the bed and opened the French doors. She stepped out on to a tiny stone balcony barely big enough for one person, let alone two.

'And there *is* a sea view,' she said, placing a

white-gloved hand against her brow to shield her eyes from the glare. 'Look, you can just make it out behind that tree.'

'If it wasn't for the houses in-between,' sang Shaw, quoting the old music-hall song as he unpacked his case. He placed his battered pocket bible and tiny prayer book, a relic of his days as an army chaplain, on the table between the twin beds.

'Well done you, for finding this place,' said Mrs Shaw as she came back into the room and kissed her husband on the cheek. 'Peaceful and quiet and good value as well.'

Mrs Shaw's face fell as a strange humming sound drifted into the room from outside. She returned to the balcony.

'Oh dear,' she said. 'It's those conference people. They appear to be chanting on the lawn. A lot of noisy fakirs.'

Shaw turned to his wife with a confused expression on his face. 'What did you say, my dear?' he asked.

'Fakirs,' replied Mrs Shaw. 'Indian-looking types in robes. There are several of them on the lawn.'

'Never mind,' said Shaw. 'It is always enlightening to encounter other faiths. How does the hymn go? The one about India's coral strand?' He thought for a moment then quoted. '"From many an ancient river, from many a palmy plain, They call us to deliver their land from error's chain." A rather old-fashioned view in these ecumenical times, but perhaps still with some merits. We have much to learn, on both sides, especially as our Indian brethren move closer to home rule.'

'Well I do hope you don't spend all your time "delivering" people,' said Mrs Shaw as she closed the balcony doors to shut out the noise. 'Remember you're on holiday.'

Chapter Two

The tall, dark-skinned man swathed in orange robes known by the name of Guru Vinda Baba, or simply Guru, pronounced a blessing on the devotees in front of him on the sun-parched lawn of the Excelsior Hotel. His face, topped with a close cropped, almost shaved head of hair, had an eastern handsomeness marred only by a distinctive broken nose and a scar above his right eye.

The demonstration of Vedic chanting had, he thought, gone well, and he smiled benignly at the conference attendees as they came up to him and thanked him before they retired to their rooms for a rest before the afternoon sessions began.

A few of the delegates were Indians adrift in England, most of them undergraduates from Cambridge or London University who now belonged in neither the world of the Indians nor the English; some attempted to be holy men, wearing robes and hoping to become Gurus themselves; others wore western garb with Congress caps, and tried to co-opt Guru Vinda Baba into the cause of Indian nationalism, something in which he resolutely refused to become involved.

Most of the attendees, however, were of the progressively-minded, intellectual English middle classes, interested in all sorts of unconventional things such as vegetarianism, meditation, mesmerism, and the plays of

George Bernard Shaw; their religious beliefs were a broad church but were loosely bound together under the New Thought movement. The combination of respect for Christian tradition and embracing of new, liberating philosophical ideas from the east he knew was a heady mixture for some of his followers, such as his secretary, Mildred Sloan, who he had named Shrutakirti after the princess in the Hindu epic of the *Mahabharata.* At the thought of her name, his heart sank as he realised he needed to talk to her about something rather troubling.

The Guru down cross-legged in a shaded corner of the lawn by a hedge and closed his eyes. The sun was blindingly hot. Such atypical heat had the effect of making the English delegates feel more as if they were in India, he realised, and this was a good thing, but after some time in England he had begun to get used to country's cooler weather, and he suddenly felt tired by the heat himself.

He breathed deeply, attempting to draw energy into his heart *chakras*, in order to dazzle the negative thoughts that had suddenly come upon him. He began to slowly chant under his breath the word *Om*, the name of the First Cause and the sound of cosmic unity, but it was no good. Dark thoughts settled upon his brain, no matter how hard he tried to dismiss them as if they were passing clouds. Thoughts of hatred and revenge.

He felt a cool hand on his bare shoulder and a clear, calm voice from above.

'Guruji? Are you all right?'

The Guru opened his eyes and saw the placid form of Miss Sloan in her white robes bending over him, looking down at him, a look of concern in her eyes behind her heavy-rimmed spectacles.

Dear Mildred…dear Shrutakirti, he thought to himself. Always so concerned. So loyal, even after all that had happened. He knew she harboured feelings of more than sisterly love for him; he had once been worldly and, as a handsome man, was no stranger to the admiration of women, but to indulge such thoughts with Miss Sloan was dangerous. It could drag him— both of them— back to the past, and that was somewhere he did not wish to go. He suddenly remembered why he needed to speak with her.

'I am well, Shrutakirti, but…something troubles me. There has been another letter.'

Miss Sloan's face fell. 'Another, Guruji? From the same man?'

'I believe so,' sighed the Guru.

'And does he want….'

'Yes. This time he asks for fifty pounds. I will not pay.'

'Guruji, you *must* pay him, what choice do we have?'

'There is another way.'

'What other way? If he tells everyone about…'

At this point Miss Sloan stopped talking, her eyes fixed ahead of her beyond a gap in the hedge. The Guru looked behind himself to see a tall, grey haired man in a linen jacket and panama hat, wearing the collar of an English priest, standing awkwardly still on the path, as if he had accidentally interrupted a pair of lovers in a tryst.

Shaw stood immobile for a moment in front of the strange-looking couple, wondering whether to pretend he had not heard anything, or remark on it in some way. He decided the former option was the more suitable.

'I am sorry, I did not realise there was anyone sitting here,' he said. 'I was trying to get through to the beach.'

The man in robes stood up, smiled and pressed his hands together in a gesture of prayer.

'My dear fellow,' he replied, and Shaw was somewhat surprised at the man's accent, which was Oxfordian with a mild, high-caste Indian inflection. 'We were so engrossed in spiritual matters that we neglected the material. Kindly pass through, and accept our apologies for blocking the way.'

Shaw smiled and touched the brim of his hat as he passed.

'One moment sir,' said the man. 'I note you are a clergyman. Perhaps I may know your good name, as a fellow spiritual traveller on life's path?'

Shaw hesitated, wondering whether he was about to become embroiled in something that might be best left alone. His experiences in the last year had made him somewhat wary in involving himself in the affairs of others. Suddenly, he recalled the words of Job from the Old Testament; 'though He slay me, yet will I trust in Him.' It did not behove a clergyman, he concluded, to walk on by when someone might require his assistance.

'Certainly. My name is Shaw, Reverend Shaw, of All Saints' church, Lower Addenham.' Shaw extended his hand, and felt a peculiar tingle of electricity in the strange man's grip.

'Most wonderful,' said the man. 'Truly I am blessed to meet an English holy man. My name is Guru Vinda Baba. This is my assistant, Shrutakirti.'

The woman stood up and offered her hand to Shaw. Despite her thick spectacles and unmade-up face, Shaw could not help noticing she had a steely, somewhat aloof attractiveness about her. He had seen something similar in some women's auxiliary officers during the war. He sensed the woman was a natural organiser and that she was highly protective of the Guru.

'I go by Shrutakirti with our disciples,' said the woman. 'My English name is Sloan, Mildred Sloan.' The woman spoke in a confident and educated upper class accent. Shaw wondered how on earth she had got involved with an Indian 'guru.'

'How do you do,' said Shaw. 'I take it you are involved with the, er, Beings of Spirituality conference?'

'The Conference of All Spiritual Beings,' corrected Miss Sloan curtly. 'We are the organisers, as a matter of fact. The Guru has many speaking engagements across England and the Continent this summer. If you will excuse us, the Guru must now take luncheon.'

The Guru raised his hand and said something in what Shaw assumed was Hindustani; Miss Sloan bowed her head and was silent.

'Perhaps you would honour us with your company at luncheon, Mr Shaw?' asked the Guru. 'Unless of course, you have another appointment?'

'Indeed no,' said Shaw. 'An excellent idea. Having just arrived here on holiday, I was intending to do what, in the army, we called a 'recce', a reconnaissance, of the beach, while my wife unpacked. It is, however, rather hot— for me, at least— and I will be happy to take luncheon. If you will permit my wife to join us?'

'Of course, of course,' said the Guru with a smile, gesturing for Shaw to go ahead of him on the path into the hotel. He looked away as he noticed a sharp glance from

Miss Sloan to the Guru, whose serene expression seemed momentarily tinged with strain.

Twenty minutes later Shaw and his wife were sitting in the hotel's dining room surrounded by some of the most peculiar people he had ever encountered. The Conference of All Spiritual Beings seemed to have block-booked most of the rooms in the hotel and there were very few other non-delegates at luncheon. It also appeared that they were highly honoured to be invited to sit at the table with Guru Vinda Baba, as one of the other guests pointed out.

'The Guru doesn't just invite anyone to the top table,' said a sleek, well-fed man with an American accent on Shaw's left. 'I guess the dog collar is a clear sign you're already on the spiritual path, so to speak.'

Shaw did not quite know how to respond, and he could tell that his wife, as she stroked Fraser in her lap, was feeling distinctly awkward. It was partly the strange company, he thought, and partly the rather odd-tasting vegetarian food they had been given to eat.

'My name's Murray, Mitchell M. Murray,' said the American, extending a well-manicured hand to Shaw across the table.

'My name is Shaw, and this is my wife,' said the cleric. He noticed his wife recoil slightly and then reluctantly shake the American's hand when it was thrust towards her.

'Good to know you, Mr Shaw, Mrs Shaw,' said Murray. 'You may have heard of my magazine, *Mental Magnetism Monthly*.'

'I do not believe so,' said Shaw. 'A psychological journal?'

'You could say that. We're the fastest growing magazine in the field of New Thought. I was in finance before, but the spiritual is the big growth area now in the states, especially since the crash. I'm here to write a series of articles on the Guru. He's starting to make big waves in the world of enlightened beings.'

'Enlightened beings?' asked Shaw.

'That's right,' said a woman to Murray's left. She also spoke in an American accent and, like most of the delegates, wore somewhat bohemian clothing with some strange, oriental looking jewellery.

'I'm Mrs Murray,' said the woman. 'Mary Murray. I'm here with my husband touring Britain and Europe. I run a church too, Mr Shaw.'

'Indeed?' replied Shaw. 'You are a deaconess?'

'Bless me no, Reverend,' said Mrs Murray. 'We don't use fuddy-duddy titles like that at a modern church like ours. That's the First Church of Mental Magnetism, in St Louis Missouri. I'm just known as Pastor Mary to the folks there.'

'How fascinating,' said Mrs Shaw, in a tone that reminded Shaw that she was not comfortable discussing religious matters with strangers.

'We wouldn't normally spend our time in a little place like this, but we just couldn't miss a chance to meet the Guru and Shrutakirti,' continued the woman enthusiastically. 'They're making big waves in the spiritual world and we Mental Magnetists want to claim him as our own before the Theosophists get to him. Some of *them* are even saying he's the Second Coming.'

Mrs Shaw dropped her fork on her plate with a distinctly loud clatter. Shaw saw a look of momentary distaste on her face before she turned to Miss Sloan and spoke brightly.

'What a lovely cool-looking frock you're wearing,' she said, referring to Miss Sloan's white robes. 'So simple and stylish. Perhaps I might look for one myself if this hot weather continues.' She gave a nervous laugh.

'It is the garb of a widow in India,' said Miss Sloan.

There was an awkward pause.

'Oh I'm terribly sorry,' said Mrs Shaw, reddening. 'Since you were called Miss, I didn't think…and one tends to associate black with mourning rather than…'

Miss Sloan cut her off. 'I am unmarried. I dress as a widow to show my renunciation of the world and its carnal desires.'

Mrs Shaw's face was frozen in a polite smile. Shaw, sensing her embarrassment, spoke across the table to the Guru.

'Have you been in England long, Mr, er, Vinda Baba?' he asked.

'Almost two years,' said the Guru. 'Please call me Guru. Titles such as mister are so distracting.' His expression of fixed serenity had not changed, Shaw noticed, throughout the meal.

'And you, Miss Sloan?' asked Shaw. 'Am I correct in assuming you have spent time in India?'

'I lived with my parents in India,' replied Miss Sloan. 'It was while there that I discovered the enlightened path.'

'I see,' said Shaw. 'Which branch of the administration was your father involved in? Missions, perhaps?'

'He was an army officer. Rather a different occupation but still part of the same system of oppression of…'

'Let us not concern ourselves with politics, Shrutakirti,' said the Guru quietly, holding up his hand. 'Suffice to say that I am glad Miss Sloan has inherited the organisational skills of her father. She runs this lecture tour with military precision. Everything arranged to the last detail, and months in advance.'

'Thank you, Guru,' said Miss Sloan, looking down at her plate. There was an awkward silence.

'At any rate, I hope that our English weather is not too

cold for you,' said Shaw quickly. He caught sight of Miss Sloan glaring at him and suddenly wished he had not made such a feeble conversational gambit. Unexpectedly, the Guru laughed briefly before his face returned to its usual placid expression. 'My dear Mr Shaw. I spent many years in a monastery in the Himalayas. The weather there was far colder than yours!'

'And there's no fur coats allowed for the likes of you, eh, Guru?' said Mr Murray, pointing his fork and grinning.

'Coldness and heat are states of mind,' said the Guru, thoughtfully. 'If the mind says "I am hot" then one is hot. If the mind says "I am cold", then one is cold. It is the goal of the enlightened being, therefore, to say, "I am neither. I simply *am*."'

Shaw noticed a look of deep admiration cross Miss Sloan's face as she looked at the Guru. Mr and Mrs Murray looked as if they were gazing upon a religious artefact of great beauty.

'Isn't that wonderful,' breathed Mrs Murray. She then turned to her husband. 'Mitch, I hope you're getting all this down for the magazine.'

'All up here, my dear,' said Mr Murray, tapping his forehead. 'The mind trained in Mental Magnetism is its own dictating machine,' he added, then helped himself to another portion of lentil stew from the bowl in front of him.

Major Ronald Blair, Indian Army (retired), belched slightly as he finished the last of his lunchtime pints of beer. Short and slightly built, he had none of the stoutness of some habitual drinkers, but his ruddy complexion and rheumy eyes betrayed his habits.

He wiped away a fleck of foam from his moustache. The Excelsior Hotel's beer was too fizzy, he found, and he always looked forward to getting out of the hotel and beginning his daily round of the public houses in the town, catching up with the gossip and keeping his alcohol levels safely topped up.

As a permanent resident in the hotel, he kept to his separate table in the corner of the dining room, looking with distaste at the crowds of holidaymakers that filled the place at this time of year. At present there was an even worse lot there than normal, he reflected— the Indian meditation crowd with their soppy English hangers-on, swanning around the place as if it was a Calcutta bazaar rather than a respectable Suffolk seaside resort.

What was the bally world coming to? reflected Blair. When the Indians had first appeared the week before, he thought he was having an attack of the DTs, or that England had all been a dream and he was back on the terrace of that drying-out hospital in Darjeeling. He had seen an Indian in orange robes and a woman— a white woman, mark you— wandering along the high street in the shimmering heat, dressed in mourning as if she was about to hurl herself on a funeral pyre. They were followed by a crowd of admirers— socialists, he guessed, or at any rate, the sort who looked like they spent their time folk-dancing in a garden suburb.

The landlord of the pub he had been sitting outside had told him it was a visit by some sort of Indian guru, that the garden-suburb lot thought was the next Jesus, or some such tommy-rot. It was causing quite a stir in the town apparently, with followers coming to see him from all over the place, some even from America.

Blair knew he should be glad of the visit, as it might benefit his business. He had sunk the last of his savings into buying a cheap war-surplus Sopwith Camel biplane, taking tourists for trips round the bay in the mornings to finance his afternoon's drinking. A lot of wealthy gullible people could be good customers, but he still resented the appearance of the Indians. He had spent the last few years trying to forget about India.

Major Blair had once been something of an entrepreneur, at least when he was sober. When he had found out a bit more about the chap calling himself a guru, a few bells had started ringing in his head and an idea for a money-making scheme had started to form itself. He decided he would think a little more on that, and ordered another bottle of fizzy Watney's ale as a *digestif.*

Blair, by rights, should not have used his military rank in civilian life, as he had only been an acting major and that for a very short time before he was demobilised. But he kept using it as he enjoyed the status it gave him amongst those who were impressed by that sort of thing and who thought it meant he was 'top drawer'.

He was anything but. He had gone out to India in 1912 as a motor mechanic, hoping to make his fortune maintaining cars and aeroplanes for Maharajas, but like so many others before him, Mother India had caught him in her enervating grasp, and somehow the fortune never materialised.

He had, however, begun to carve out a niche by buying a small aeroplane— one of the first in India— and using it to ferry important persons up from the plains to the summer capital of Simla in the Himalayan foothills.

It was only a short hop of half an hour, much faster than the six-hour-long train climb on the little narrow-gauge railway. There were always a few daring young officers willing to take the risk in the plane if they were in a hurry to consummate their latest affair, or if they needed to clear out sharpish when a husband turned up.

When the war came along he decided the chance of flying for the duration was too good to pass up. India did not have an air force so he applied to the Royal Flying Corps back home. They turned him down as too old, and it seemed word had got round the Old Boy Network that he was far too useful ferrying important persons up the mountain to Viceregal Lodge in Simla. His war service, such as it was, had consisted of 'flying a desk' part-time in the Indian Defence Force.

Despite gaining him a commission, the war did not help him much. He was, at best, on the bottom rank of top people. India was run, he reflected, by men who acted as if it was still 1860. They did not want some bounder from a Finchley grammar school in their clubs, and even if he was a major, he would always be a sort of servant.

In 1924 he decided on a final roll of the dice; setting up an air mail service. He had tried to raise capital but had not been successful; the British ruling class did not like him and nor did the Indian mercantile class that was just starting to gain influence in the country. As the drink took ever stronger hold and people trusted his flying skills less and less, he realised it was time to come Home.

Before he had even lost sight of the soupy dawn of Bombay from the steamer, he had made up his mind; he would settle in a small English town and there drink out the remainder of his days. He chose Eastburgh more or less at random, got a room at the Excelsior which he had never left, and used the last of his savings to buy a plane and set himself up as little more than a glorified fairground attraction.

He took a long draught on his beer and caught sight of himself in the mirror over the bar in the corner of the dining room. He was fifty, and looked it; a jowly red face and greying hair receding from his temples, a shirt collar not in its first day of wear, and the frayed Indian Army tie he was not really entitled to wear.

He looked away from his reflection in distaste. The final blow to his ambition and self-esteem had been to read in the *Times* that an Indian— an *Indian* of all people— had beaten him to it and was setting up an airmail service. The newspaper wallah, who had obviously never been further east than the Mile End Road, had even claimed the man was the first to fly an aeroplane in India. A fellow called, if you please, J.R.D. Tata.

'Ta-ta' said Blair, chuckling grimly, as he raised his beer glass to himself in the mirror. He noticed one or two of the diners staring at him, but he did not care.

'Ta-ta to the whole bally lot of you,' he said under his breath in the direction of some Indian undergraduates at the next table. 'If it's home rule you want you can have it. Have the whole damned place and run it into the ground.'

He caught sight of the Indian leader, the 'guru' as they called him. He was pretty sure he knew who the fellow really was, and once he had got round to speaking to a pal in the town about it to make sure, there would be some money in it for them.

'I've got your card marked, "guru",' he said sarcastically under his breath, more quietly this time. 'I think it's time the white man finally got what's due for his burden.'

Rooksley opened his eyes and inhaled deeply. His mid-day meditation was finished, and he looked up at the coastal path, pleased to see that his daily performance had been seen by one or two passers-by. Although he believed in the power of meditation on, and communion with, the spirit world, it did not hurt to maintain his air of mystery in the eyes of the townsfolk and, more importantly, any wealthy tourists, while he was doing it.

He sat cross-legged on North Beach, a long stretch of golden sand about two miles from Eastburgh, out of sight from the more popular South Beach. The beach was accessible only from two paths which led down from the cliffs and the tussocky heath which stretched away towards the dark line of Middlesham Forest on the horizon. It was a lonely, wind-whipped spot, between the primeval vastness of the sea and the gloom of the ancient woodland, which in earlier times would have covered almost the entire country, all the way over to the Irish Sea.

He liked it mainly, however, because of the peculiar archaeological feature in which he presently sat. It was a circle about thirty feet in diameter on the sand, formed by twelve ancient, blackened wooden stumps about two feet high, hewn into rough spikes by the action of the sea over the years, and a larger, central stump with a flat base and a large, jagged timber spike about three times as high as those on the ring's perimeter. It was at the foot of this strange object that Rooksley sat daily, if not exactly to pray, then to at least commune in some way with the elemental forces which he believed could be of some use to him.

The Wooden Witness, the ring was called by the local people, though nobody really knew why. The area was first mentioned on a Tudor map as 'place of ye Esteburghe Ringe, or Woad-Witnesse,' when the land was salt-marsh. As the sea had encroached upon it, the soil had gradually been washed away to reveal the tips of the wood beneath, and in the 1890s it had been excavated by archaeologists to its present height.

Rooksley, who also posed as something of an antiquarian, had read that there were two theories behind the name; the first, that it was originally a large cross surrounded by posts representing the twelve apostles. They were said to have been placed there by St Augustine himself in the sixth century as he preached the Gospel to pagans with woad-smeared faces, who watched the strange foreign missionaries with hostile, suspicious eyes.

The other theory was somewhat darker; that the name derived from the Anglo-Saxon term *Woden ge-witleás*, literally, 'those made mad by Woden', the Norse god of frenzy and death, where those thought to be possessed by evil spirits were offered as human sacrifices.

Rooksley preferred the pagan theory to the Christian one. The Nazarene had His uses, he believed, such as teaching men that the power of the divine was within them rather than somewhere far off in the sky, but the emphasis on love and forgiveness, he thought, had a weakening effect on people.

He smiled and stood up, adjusting his tie and dusting the sand off the black three-piece suit which he wore regardless of how hot it was. It had been a productive morning, he reflected, as he walked back to the his rooms at the tin chapel on the outskirts of Eastburgh. He had delivered a little missive which he hoped would bring him some money, and he had managed to locate where that interfering oaf Cotterill lived.

He had called at the man's house and told his wife he wished to speak to her husband, to help him with his 'spiritual difficulties'. Mrs Cotterill, embarrassed by the previous night's disturbance of the service, was only too happy to let him know where her husband was. He was out on business at the moment, she said, but would be preparing for his evening performance on the pier later. He always liked to prepare alone, as he got such terrible nerves before a show. If, she said to Rooksley, he was to pop in at the theatre this afternoon, he would be sure to find him for a quiet word on his own.

That was exactly what Rooksley had in mind. A quiet word or two to make sure Cotterill stayed quiet about what he knew, or thought he knew— for good.

Rooksley opened the side door of the chapel which led to his rooms, and noticed a letter on the doormat. He saw the name 'Excelsior Hotel' on the envelope and his heart skipped a beat— could a reply have come so soon? He tore open the letter and then his heart sank as he read the scrawled note.

> Dear Rooksley
> Just a line to say you'll never guess who's arrived at the hotel. Been here a few days but I only just placed him. 'A Man with a Past' and one I think you'll remember as well. Can't be sure though, and so would like a 'second opinion' as the doctors say. Come over for a drink tomorrow night around 9 and see if it's him. If it is, it 'Could Be To Your Advantage' as the lawyers say.
> Tootle-pip, (as the youngsters say!)
> Yours,
> Blair.

He stuffed the letter in his jacket pocket and sighed. He had forgotten that that drunken sot, Blair, lived at the Excelsior. Just because they had worked together briefly years ago, the man seemed to think they were old comrades, and was constantly badgering him about money-making schemes, 'dead-cert' racehorses, and so on. The only thing Blair had done of any use was to recommend moving to Eastburgh, and even that, reflected Rooksley, was a dubious favour.

The damned fool had taken a week to identify someone right under his nose, someone who Rooksley had recognised immediately as soon as he had seen the man's picture in the local paper. There was no mistaking that broken nose and scar above the eye, especially as Rooksley had given him them in the first place.

A little digging in the newspaper library in Ipswich had confirmed what he suspected. Now that idiot Blair thought he could queer his pitch, did he? Well, he would soon see about that. He realised that Cotterill was now not the only man in Eastburgh who needed to be dealt with.

Luncheon was over, and Shaw felt increasingly sleepy as coffee was served. The Guru and Mrs Murray were engaged in animated conversation about the nature of something or other— the immortal soul, thought Shaw, but he was not quite certain. Despite the doors onto the terrace all being wide open, the heat in the dining room was almost overpowering and it was the most he could do to keep his eyes open. He could tell his wife felt the same and he resolved to find a gap in the conversation so that they could make their excuses and leave.

He was woken from his reverie by the crash of a glass dropping onto the floor in the corner; there was the murmur of conversation as a waiter hurried over to the table. Then he heard a chair being pushed back and looked up to see a figure walking somewhat unsteadily towards their table.

'Uh-oh,' said Mr Murray, who was puffing on a large, somewhat malodorous cigar. 'Here comes Lieutenant Lush.'

Shaw looked up to see a slightly dishevelled man with a florid face and military moustache approaching. Mrs Murray broke away from her conversation to chide her husband.

'Hush dear,' she whispered loudly. 'He's just a poor, lonely man. I said yesterday he could sure benefit from Mental Magnetism, so we ought to be nice to him.'

'Poor and lonely he may be,' said Mr Murray, 'but he's still a pain in the…'

He did not finish his sentence, as the new arrival spoke with the bright clarity of one doing his best to sound sober.

'G'afternoon, everyone,' said the man. He bowed slightly to Shaw and his wife, extending a hand. Shaw half-rose and shook the man's hand.

'Don't think I've seen you before, Padre,' said the man. 'My name's Blair.'

'My name is Shaw, and this is my wife.'

'Delighted. Interested in flying?'

Shaw could not think what the man meant. Was he about to talk about levitation? He decided it was time for them to leave, but before he could say anything, the Guru spoke.

'Major Blair is the hotel's resident pilot. He takes people on pleasure trips in his aeroplane. He has offered rides to both myself and Miss Sloan, but it is my belief that the soul is the only part of man which should ascend to the heavens.'

'Whatever you say, Guru old son,' said Blair. 'You're the one with the ancient wisdom and so on. Just wondered if the new arrivals might want a spin. Here's my *bona fides*.'

He thrust a small card onto the table in front of Shaw. It had a picture of a small biplane on it and the words 'Travel by Blairways: the only way to see Eastburgh. Trips round the bay from 2/6 per person.'

'Just let me know if you're interested, Mr, er, Padre,' said Blair. 'Room 109. Knock for me any morning for a booking. Sort of a fixture here. Everyone knows me.'

'Indeed they do, sir,' said Murray. 'Now if you don't mind, we'd like to continue our *private* conversation.'

'On my way, on my way,' said Blair, taking the hint. 'Still, it's a shame the lovely Miss Sloan didn't want a spin. Don't suppose you've changed your mind since yesterday, m'dear?'

Shaw expected Miss Sloan to give an angry reply, but was surprised to see a brittle smile flash across her face.

'Actually I would like to have a trip in your aeroplane, Major Blair. I've never flown before and I think it may be of spiritual benefit. That is, if the Guru permits it?'

Shaw noticed a brief look of puzzlement cross the Guru's face, before it returned to its usual benign expression.

'Of course. I trust it will not interfere with our schedule of talks and lectures.'

'No,' said Miss Sloan. 'Would tomorrow morning be

convenient? Perhaps I may call on you presently to make the arrangements, Major Blair?'

'Certainly m'dear, certainly, nothing booked for tomorrow. Well, tootle-oo all. Must dash, bandits at opening time o'clock, what,' said Blair with the confident manner of the drinker who assumes everyone else is as alcoholically inclined as he is.

The man walked away unsteadily towards the door of the kitchens, then corrected himself and strolled across the room to the open French doors.

'Rather you than me, Miss Sloan,' said Mrs Shaw, who up until now had been quiet. 'Aeroplanes always seem somewhat dangerous, and that gentleman, well…'

'I expect he'll be all right when he's sober,' said Miss Sloan quickly. Then she turned to the Guru.

'Guruji, we have the lecture on breath meditation in ten minutes. We ought to prepare.'

'Yes of course, Shrutakirti. If you will excuse us, ladies and gentlemen, I must go,' said the Guru, who looked with a somewhat worried expression at the back of Major Blair as he disappeared from view on the patio.

The Guru and Miss Sloan rose and the Murrays jumped to their feet. Shaw followed suit, with the rather unnerving feeling of having been dismissed from a royal audience.

A few moments later, as they were passing through the lobby, Mrs Shaw turned to her husband.

'I do hope they aren't going to start that chanting outside our room again. I'd rather like to have a little sleep. This heat really is dreadful.'

'Of course, my dear,' said Shaw. 'I shall have a word with the manager. You go on up. I think the best way for me to cool off would be a bathe. I shall be up in a moment to collect my costume. Fraser would like a walk, I expect.'

At the sound of the word 'walk', Fraser's ears pricked

up and he looked expectantly at his master.

'Oh thank you Lucian,' said Mrs Shaw. 'I shall get your things ready for you to collect when you come up.'

Lucas, the manager, appeared to be dozing in an armchair behind the reception desk. There were no other staff around, and so Shaw tried to attract his attention firstly by clearing his throat— which did not work— and then by ringing the bell on the desk, which did.

'Sorry sir,' said Lucas. 'Must have dozed off. The heat, you know. What can I do for you, Mr, er, Shaw?'

'I wondered if you could do something about the chanting,' said Shaw.

'Chanting, sir?' asked Lucas.

'Indeed.'

'Erm…I'm not with you sir. Do you mean psalms?'

'Perhaps I am not making myself clear. Some of the Indian delegates have been chanting rather loudly on the lawn, and my wife would like to rest.'

'Ah, I see what you mean, sir,' said Lucas. 'Don't worry, sir, I shall have a word with the organiser, Miss Sloan. I shall ask them to move away from the building.'

'Thank you,' said Shaw. 'I must say that if we had known a conference was taking place, we probably would have chosen alternative accommodation. We were hoping for somewhere quiet.'

'Well sir,' said Lucas, looking downhearted. 'I would have warned you at the time, had I known. But you made your booking in…when was it now?'

Lucas flipped through the pages of a large diary on the reception desk until he found the page he was looking for.

'Ah yes, you made the booking in May. We did not receive the conference booking until just two weeks ago, at the start of August. A little challenging at high season, but we were able to open up the old annexe and some of these

Indians, well, they don't mind too much what sort of rooms they have, do they? One even hears stories of them sleeping on beds of nails!'

'Quite,' said Shaw distractedly. Something puzzled him, but he could not quite put his finger on what it was. He thanked Lucas for his help, and, fighting the urge to sleep, wearily trudged up the grand staircase to fetch his bathing costume.

Chapter Three

'What did you have for lunch, Lord Harry?' asked Reg Cotterill brightly to his ventriloquist's dummy.

'I had steak, Uncle Reg,' replied the doll.

'How did you find it?'

'It was hiding under the lettuce.'

Cotterill sighed. He had managed to keep his lips immobile for all of the exchange, except for the 'w' in 'was.' W was always a tricky one, he thought. He looked at 'Lord Harry.' The doll stared back at him blankly. He worked the puppet's mouth up and down with his hand and said the word 'was' in his upper-crust voice four times. It came out as 'roz roz roz roz.'

Just as well, thought Cotterill, that he had managed to find a way of improving his act. He was fed up with children, and what was worse, adults, laughing in all the wrong places. There was always some little ragamuffin in every performance, probably from the shanty town up on the hill, who would shout out something like 'gottle of geer' and people would laugh louder than they did at the act.

Well Uncle Reg and Lord Harry were going to give the audience a surprise at today's matinee, thought Cotterill. He looked around the shabby little theatre on the end of the pier, with its faded Victorian decorations and little gilded proscenium arch. He might even be able to get a better booking after this. Perhaps even at Great Yarmouth, he thought. Suddenly a young man with a shock of red hair and thick spectacles put his head through a gap in the the faded velvet curtains.

'R...ready when you are, Mr Cotterill,' said the man, with a slight stammer.

'Right-o Les,' said Cotterill. He made the final adjustments to some wires in Lord Harry's back, which ran down behind the stool on which he and the dummy sat, and which then disappeared under the curtains.

Leslie Prior pulled his head back behind the curtains. He was a good lad, thought Cotterill, if a bit simple. Well, perhaps 'simple' was not quite right, as that usually meant stupid. 'Strange' might be a better adjective. He didn't seem to be able to catch your eye, and talked as if he were reading a railway timetable. He was a wizard at electrical work though, and knew everything there was to know about the wireless and gramophones.

Prior worked in his parents' electrical shop, and Cotterill had got talking to him one day whilst buying some radio valves. An idea about how to transform his ventriloquism act had come to him, but he was not sure about how to carry it out; electrical apparatus had changed so much since he had retired and he just did not know where to start.

The basic idea was to make a recording of himself speaking Lord Harry's part of the act on a gramophone recording machine, what they called a cylinder dictaphone, and then to play it back via a small loudspeaker hidden inside the dummy. It would be the perfect ventriloquism act— he could even drink a glass of water while doing it.

He had had no idea if it was possible, but Prior had thought it an easy task. He had, he told Cotterill, already installed something similar in the little Spiritualist church on the edge of town. Intrigued, Cotterill had asked more about this, but Prior had seemed reluctant to talk about it other than saying he had put concealed loudspeakers in the chapel so that soothing music could be played to the worshippers.

Cotterill felt anger and humiliation rise in his chest at the memory of last night's fiasco in the so-called seance. He decided to put it out of his mind until he had something more substantial to offer the local papers about what went on in that place.

'R...recording now, Mr Cotterill,' called Prior from behind the curtains. 'Just s...speak into the dummy, and I'll p...play it back.'

Cotterill leaned forward to speak into the puppet's mouth. Just then he heard the door of the little theatre open. Some blasted idiot had ignored the 'do not disturb sign' on the entrance which led in from the pier, he thought. He turned to see who it was, and exclaimed in surprise.

'You!'

Shaw pulled his panama hat a little lower over his eyes to shield them from the glare of the afternoon sun, as he and Fraser walked down the hill to the beach, via the centre of Eastburgh. Despite the heat, the streets were busy with holidaymakers and he had to negotiate the narrow pavements carefully. Shaw looked around in satisfaction. The town had been a good choice, he thought. His previous holidays had often been further afield — Scotland, for example, or the Lake District, but this year they had decided to stay somewhere a little closer to home, and Eastburgh fitted the bill. It had a similar charm to the nearby towns of Southwold and Aldeburgh, but was not quite as expensive. With the world economic situation what it now was, Shaw did not think it right for a clergyman and his wife to spend large amounts of money on a holiday.

As they neared the beach he looked admiringly at the elegant parade of Regency town-houses, their white stucco gleaming in the sunlight, and the more recent Victorian villas with knapped-flint walls and neo-gothic timber details. Modern vulgarity had crept in, as in most places, he reflected, with a large new mock-tudor public house with beer garden built close to the beach, and a parade of shops in the modernist style next to it, but he was pleased to see that the seafront was largely unspoilt. He passed through the delightful shade of the Winter Gardens with its palm trees and goldfish ponds, past rows of colourful beach huts, and then on to the wide golden sands of South Beach.

Fraser ran about excitedly on the sand, causing hilarity amongst some children building a large sandcastle, until Shaw brought him to heel. He found a quiet spot in a small patch of weak shade cast by the pier; it was not much but to sit out in the open sun would have been, he thought, inadvisable for someone used to the indoor life.

Then came the awkward moment of changing out of his clothes and into his bathing costume. I must not make a hash of this on my first day, he thought, especially not while wearing a clerical collar. He had tried to book a beach hut without success, and the public conveniences were a long way off, so he had to resort to tying a towel around himself and struggling into the garment, taking care not to confuse the leg holes with the arm holes. Once changed, he folded his clothes into a neat pile and strode down to the water's edge. Fraser barked excitedly and jumped into the water, yelping as a large breaker pushed him back on to the shore. He shook himself and leaped back into the surf again.

Shaw was a strong swimmer, who bathed from April to October in the clear, almost still waters of the River Midwell. The North Sea was a rather different prospect and he found the rolling waves and strong undertow a challenge. The current seemed to drag him along parallel to the beach however hard he tried to swim against it. The hot weather had also given the water a tepid, almost unpleasantly warm feel. After a few minutes he decided he had had enough, and emerged from the crashing foam to return to his place on the beach.

Changing out of his bathing costume was an even greater struggle than changing into it, but fortunately Mrs Shaw had packed a large towel into the side-pack— a relic of his army chaplaincy days— which served as a beach-bag. The heat on the beach was almost unbearable. Shaw decided it was time to find some real shade, and looked up at the nearby pier.

There was a large amusement arcade at the land end of the structure, from which barrel-organ music emanated, and then a smaller one at the sea end, with the words 'Eastburgh Theatre' painted on it in fading letters. A number of shelters with benches were nearby on the wooden planking, and they looked blissfully cool on their shaded sides. He decided he would sit there a while before returning to the hotel, where tea would soon be served. Shaw put Fraser on his lead and negotiated his way carefully through the throng of pedestrians, bicyclists and motor cars trying to navigate their way from the coast road onto the high street, and waited until a policeman on point duty signalled that it was safe to cross the road. Shaw pitied the man in his tunic and white gloves, and noticed perspiration trickling down from under his helmet, also white, like that of a Royal Marine, and presumably the only concession allowed to the summer heat.

Shaw stepped on to the pier and avoided entering the amusement arcade; he had disliked such places, even as a child, when he had preferred to spend his pocket money on books rather than waste it on games of skill and chance. The crowds dwindled as he walked along the pier, and eventually he found an empty shelter close to the little closed theatre. He sat down, lit his pipe and began to puff contentedly, gazing at the hypnotic effect of the sunlight dappling the seawater on the horizon.

Hidden behind the curtain of the theatre's little stage, Les Prior started the recording on the dictaphone. It was an expensive item and his parents were pleased that he had managed to sell it to Mr Cotterill. They were less pleased that he was taking time off from working in their shop, but he had simply told them he was setting up the machine for the purchaser, which was true in a way. He looked down at the list of jokes which Mr Cotterill was going to say. He did not really understand them, but he was interested in the technical challenge of getting the dummy to sound as if he really were talking.

There was a moment of silence, but then he heard the door of the theatre open. He realised somebody had interrupted them— the cleaning lady, he supposed, or the theatre manager who spent much of his time in the little bar by the amusement arcade. Then he felt an icy trembling in his limbs when he heard Mr Cotterill say 'You! — what do you want, Rooksley?'

He forgot all about the dictaphone running, and sat, paralysed by nerves, hoping Rooksley would not notice he was there. He did not like the man; after he had installed the hidden loudspeaker system in the little chapel, he had told him he was not to tell anyone about it, or bad things might happen to him or his family.

He was not quite sure what Rooksley meant by that; at first he had wondered if the man was joking, but he found it almost impossible to judge when people were serious or not as he found facial expressions hard to distinguish. Now, it seemed Rooksley was angry with Mr Cotterill; he listened as the two men argued.

Prior's stomach churned with fear…what was happening? He did not dare emerge from behind the curtain, nor could he leave the theatre without being seen, as to get to the back exit one had to cross through the auditorium. Finally, he plucked up the courage to peek through a gap in the curtain, and what he saw terrified him.

There was a crash as furniture was overturned. He withdrew from the curtain and began rocking backwards and forwards on his heels, with his eyes tight shut, and prayed for Rooksley to go away. Then there was silence.

Although he enjoyed playing the organ at the parish church, and found the ritual of the services comforting, religious belief itself seemed an illogical, unpredictable thing to him. Had his prayer been answered?

His thoughts were disturbed by a scratching noise and then a loud click from the instrument in front of him. He had forgotten that the dictaphone was still running. Then he heard a voice from beyond the curtain, and he realised his prayer had *not* been answered.

'Is somebody there?' said Rooksley darkly.

Prior swallowed hard. Something made him reach forward and uncouple the little recording cylinder from the dictaphone; in his fearful state he fumbled with it and it clattered on the table before he managed to place it in the pocket of his plus-fours.

'There *is* somebody there, isn't there?' said Rooksley. 'Come out, come out, wherever you are…' he added in a sing-song voice. Prior was sure the man was toying with him now. He decided he would have to make a run for it.

Before he could move, there was a crashing, tearing sound and the curtain was ripped down. Prior screamed as Rooksley loomed in front of him, a terrible grin flashing across his face. At his feet, lying on the wooden boards of the stage, he saw Cotterill, his face deathly white and his eyes staring glassily at the ceiling. Next to him on the little table, Lord Harry grinned down at the body with similarly lifeless eyes.

Prior saw Rooksley's smile turn to an expression of anger as his eyes flicked to the dictaphone on the table. Prior had hoped the man might not notice it.

'I…I…d…didn't   s s..,see   any…th…thing…'   he stammered.

'No, but you heard, didn't you?' said Rooksley. 'And I'll

wager that machine heard something as well, didn't it?'

Prior uttered a wordless shriek and pushed the heavy dictaphone off the table at Rooksley; it fell with a sickening thud onto the man's shoes. He inhaled sharply with a long, inhuman gasp and then leapt forward at Prior with a wild yell, like a soldier in some frenzied bayonet charge.

It was too late; the momentary distraction had given Prior sufficient time to jump off the stage and run headlong up the aisle to where he crashed through the main doors onto the brightness of the pier outside.

Shaw decided it was time to go back to the hotel; tea would be served soon and his wife ought to have finished her nap by now. He stood up, pulled his side-pack onto his shoulder and knocked his pipe out on his heel. Suddenly there was a loud bang nearby, as if a shot had gone off. Shaw looked to his left and saw that it was not the sound of a shot he had heard, but the sound of the doors of the little theatre nearby slamming back into their frames.

Before he could get out of his way, a man collided with him, almost knocking him to the ground. Fraser began yelping, and Shaw struggled to regain his balance. Shaw felt hands grip his arms tightly, and looked up to see a bespectacled man with a mop of red hair. On his face was an expression of pure terror, something that Shaw had not seen since the trenches.

'My dear chap, what on earth…' began Shaw, but he was cut off by a stammering shout from the young man.

'H...h….help me!'

There was no smell of drink on the man's breath, noticed Shaw; this was not some deranged alcoholic on a drinking binge. Shaw recognised a look of shell-shock in the man's face, and resolved to calm him down.

'Quiet, Fraser,' snapped Shaw, and the dog instantly obeyed, retreating to his master's heel and eyeing the strange man suspiciously.

'Come and sit down, you've had some sort of shock,' said Shaw, prising the man's hands from his arms with some difficulty. Before he could get the stranger to sit down on the bench, there was another bang, more muffled this time, as if it had come from inside the theatre.

Shaw thought he saw a dark shadow flit momentarily behind the frosted glass of the shelter, which blocked his view of the theatre. The young man looked round the side of the shelter in terror.

'N…no!' he shouted. He pointed to the theatre. 'In there. M…murder!'

He broke free easily from Shaw's gentle grip and ran off along the pier, to be lost from sight in the crowds milling around the amusement arcade.

There was nobody else around at this end of the pier. Shaw decided it was futile to follow the man, and instead strode to the theatre. Cautiously he opened the doors and peered into the gloom. The building seemed to be a miniature copy of a London theatre, complete with a small gilded lobby; beyond that were double doors which opened into the auditorium.

'Is anyone here?' called Shaw. Instinct warned him to turn back; if there really had been a murder, he might be in some danger. But, he thought, somebody might require his help. The higher thought over-rode the lower, and he walked cautiously into the little auditorium.

When he reached the stage, he could see that the man lying there was beyond his help, or indeed anyone's other than the Almighty.

Shaw turned on his heel and ran from the theatre, with Fraser trotting behind him. There did not seem to be any official person around. He saw, about sixty feet away, a boy of about twelve years of age looking over the railing of the pier into the sea. It did not seem as if he had heard anything. Shaw ran over to him.

'I say,' he shouted. 'You, young man.'

The boy looked round and blinked, presumably surprised to see a clergyman with a dog running towards him.

'Me?' asked the boy. 'What've I done?'

'Nothing, my boy, nothing,' said Shaw, who paused to get his breath back. 'There has been an…accident. In the theatre. Can you run fast?'

'Course I can, mister, at school I came first in…'

'Very well, very well,' interrupted Shaw. 'Run as fast as you can to the street. There is a constable on duty at the junction. Tell him to come here immediately. Tell him a man is…has been badly hurt.'

'Cor! said the boy, wide-eyed. 'Leave it to me, mister.'

Shaw watched as the boy's sandals pounded along the wooden planking of the pier. He then hurried back to the theatre to make sure nobody entered the building.

A few moments later he heard a shrill blast on a police whistle, and then the thud of heavy boots coming towards him.

Cabbages, thought Chief Inspector George Ludd, were reliable. Unlike people, all one had to do was plant them well and point them in the right direction, and they came out all right. Not like the ne'er-do-wells he had to deal with daily at the Criminal Investigation Department at Midchester police station.

He looked at the impressive array of the vegetables on the patch of garden at the rear of his little terraced house. His recent promotion had led to a bit more money coming in, and his wife had been dropping hints about a bigger house. It seemed an extravagance, now that the kiddies had grown up and left home, but a larger garden, he decided, might be nice. He resolved to visit the house agent in a couple of months. He would have to wait, of course, until Harvest Home before he could even think about leaving his garden.

Ludd's keen eyes detected a tiny movement on one of the leaves of his cabbages. He turned it upwards and saw a snail about the size of a threepenny bit, its shell as shiny and perfectly striped as a miniature mint humbug.

'Got you my lad,' said Ludd. Deftly he captured the helpless mollusc between his fingers and placed it in the confines of his sealed wooden composting box, there to live out its days where it could do no harm.

Ludd patrolled his garden daily, on the look out for slugs, snails and caterpillars with the same persistence with which he had looked out for pick-pockets, burglars and shop-lifters as a young police constable all those years ago, before the war, when the old king had been on the throne, and the world had seemed a far more intelligible and orderly place.

Before he could indulge in further reminiscence, he heard the telephone bell from inside the house. He put on his jacket and straightened his tie; despite today being his day off, it was bound to be an official call.

It was unlikely to be any other kind of call. Hardly anyone he knew socially was on the telephone, and his wife, Mona, was suspicious of the instrument and did not give out the number to her friends. She had got it into her head that the neighbours could listen in to her conversations; Ludd had tried to explain that it was a private, not a party line, but she did not seem to understand the difference. The bell stopped ringing and he heard his wife answer. She almost shouted when using it, due to another misconception that it was a form of speaking tube which required the user to speak very loudly.

'To whom do you wish to speak to?' he heard her say in that genteel voice she used whenever it was work calling. As if there were anyone else they would want to speak to other than him, thought Ludd.

'I'll take that, my dear,' said Ludd, smiling kindly and taking the instrument gently from his wife, who stepped back and watched intently, biting her lip. She was convinced that any news conveyed on the telephone was bad, and to be fair, thought Ludd, it usually was.

The Chief Inspector's eyes had still not quite adjusted to the gloom of the house's little hallway, and he struggled to find the pad and indelible pencil on the table while fumbling with the two parts of the candlestick telephone.

'Ludd,' he said curtly into the receiver.

He then straightened up to attention.

'Yes, Chief Constable, how may I be of assistance, sir?'

He listened for a few moments, and began writing notes.

'Eastburgh? Yes, I know it. Suspicious death? Can't the local men handle it? I see. No, that's quite all right, sir. Just doing a spot of gardening. I'll get on to it right away. Yes. Oh, mustn't grumble. She's well also. And the same to you sir. Goodbye.'

Ludd hung up the telephone and sighed. It was his day off and now they wanted him to look into a death thirty miles away. Quite why the local constabulary could not deal with it he was not sure, but for the Chief Constable to telephone suggested there was more to it than he was letting on. The annoying thing was that the place was only a short distance from the CID at Great Yarmouth, but that was over the border in Norfolk, out of the jurisdiction.

Midchester CID was, he realised, the nearest detective branch of the Suffolk Constabulary to Eastburgh. His sergeant was off on leave, and he knew for a fact there would be no motor car available at the station. He would have to go by train, but Eastburgh, he remembered from a previous visit, meant two changes and a long wait at Great Netley. Too far to go back and forth every day unless he got up at the absolute crack. He also had a hunch that the case, from what little the Chief Constable had told him, would most likely last a few days, maybe even a week if the doctor and the coroner there had a lot on.

Suddenly he realised he could turn the situation to his advantage. Mrs Ludd had been on at him to book a holiday for some time. He found holidays dull, however, but if he refused, she might go off and visit her sister in Stoke-on-Trent, leaving him to shift for himself.

He was confident he could get Accounts to approve a twin room, as long as he paid out of his own pocket for any extras incurred by Mrs Ludd, and also that he could get the lad next door to water the cabbages while they were away. This would mean he could combine business with pleasure, and give his wife a holiday into the bargain.

He grinned to himself as he realised he would also have the perfect excuse to get away if his wife wanted him to take part in any holiday nonsense like brass band concerts or charabanc trips.

'Pack your bags, dear,' said Ludd to his wife. 'We're going on holiday. And I'm pleased to say, my half of the expense will be courtesy of the British taxpayer.'

Rooksley looked cautiously round the corner of the sea wall into the narrow, dark alleyway which led up from the slimy, seaweed-coated walkway under the pier.

After Prior had bolted out of the theatre, Rooksley had been about to give chase, but he decided against it; although few people were about at that end of the pier, he still might have been seen.

Instead, he had exited the building by a service door at the side of the stalls, which led from the side of the theatre down a steep flight of metal stairs to the walkway used by fisherman at low tide to moor their boats. Only a few inches of water covered it, and he was able to carefully pick his way along, cursing as tepid water sloshed over the tops of his shoes. The strong currents and choppy waves meant that swimmers stayed away, and the deep shadows under the pier enabled him to reach the shore unseen.

He turned onto the esplanade and began to walk casually away from the town centre, intending to take the long way round back to his chapel. As he strode along, he mused on the events of a few minutes ago.

Cotterill, at least, was no longer a threat, he was sure of that. It was unfortunate, however, that Prior had been in the theatre. He could not be sure exactly what he had seen or heard. From what he could tell, it looked as if Prior was installing a similar type of equipment to that which he had set up for Rooksley in his chapel, presumably to give the dummy a voice.

Rooksley chuckled to himself, a low, guttural sound. That fool Cotterill had had the nerve to attack him for using hidden loudspeakers, but was copying the idea for his own ends. Well, he would not be a problem any longer.

Prior, on the other hand, was a concern. He could easily inform on Rooksley, but would he? Nobody, as far as he knew, had seen him there so if Prior went to the police, it would be his word against Rooksley's, and he would deny everything. Of course, some blabber-mouth from the chapel might tell the police that he and Cotterill had had a very public spat, but again, that did not prove he had anything to do with his death.

Then he paused, and slammed his clenched fist onto the brick wall of a gaily-painted seafront villa, causing a black cat sitting on it nearby to hiss at him and jump away. He had forgotten about the blasted dictating machine! He tried to remember if the little recording cylinder had still been in place in the front of the instrument, and realised with certainty that it had not been.

That *might* mean Prior was only setting up the equipment and had not installed it, but it might also mean that he had made a recording of what had been said behind the curtain, and taken it with him when he bolted.

He could not risk that. What was on that little cylinder might be sufficient to hang him.

He decided that he would need to meet with Les Prior again very soon, to get that cylinder and make sure he did not to talk to the police. This time, however, the meeting would be somewhere there would be no chance of escape.

Chapter Four

By the time Shaw returned to his hotel, the shadows were lengthening and the sun had lost some of its power. Nevertheless, he was still hot and tired when he reached his room. Mrs Shaw had already dressed for dinner, and was standing on the little balcony looking out to the small patch of blue sea on the horizon.

She turned when she heard Fraser yelp a welcome and jump into his mistress's arms.

'Oh Lucian,' said his wife. 'Where on earth were you? I was beginning to get rather worried. I thought you would be back for tea but it's almost time for dinner now, or at least, for cocktails.'

Shaw sat down on the edge of his bed and sighed. He explained briefly what had happened, and how he had been questioned by various policemen and made to wait around until finally he was allowed to go home, on the understanding that a detective would call on him later to take a full statement.

'How positively awful,' said Mrs Shaw, biting her lip with concern as she sat beside her husband on the bed and put a consoling arm around him.

'And it had to happen just at the start of our holiday,' she continued.

She paused and then stood up. 'No, that was uncharitable of me. Of course, our first concern must be for the family of that poor man. I shall pray for them. And what about the murderer, do they know who he is?'

'Murderer?' asked Shaw, abstractedly.

'Yes, the young man who ran into you on the pier.'

'My dear Marion, we have no reason to believe he is a murderer.'

'Oh, but I thought you said he shouted "murder" and then bolted.'

'He did, but that proves nothing. A murderer is hardly likely to announce his crime and then run off.'

'Yes of course, Lucian…I say, are you sure you are all right?'

'A little tired, my dear. I think I should like to have dinner and then go to bed.'

'Yes of course. Shall I send for something?'

'Not unless you would prefer to stay here. Having a meal sent up is rather expensive, I believe.'

'You're quite right. Let's put a brave face on things and go down. We've enough time to have a drink before the last sitting. What you need is a long cool gin and It.'

'Gin and what?'

'It. Short for "Italian", meaning vermouth. With lots of ice. Aunt Maude— you know, the one who lived in Tangiers— used to swear by them to calm one's nerves in hot weather. The servants there could be awfully trying, apparently.'

'That sounds delightful, my dear. It certainly has been a rather trying day.'

After they had changed into evening dress— Mrs Shaw in a blue silk dress which matched the strip of sea on the horizon, and Shaw in a black jacket instead of his cream linen one— they walked arm in arm down the staircase into the lobby, with Fraser trotting behind them. Once in front of the reception desk, they were confronted by Lucas, who rubbed his hands together with a nervous motion.

'Ah, Mr Shaw…Mrs Shaw…good evening,' he said. 'You have a, erm, gentleman to see you, sir. From the police, it seems.'

Shaw noticed a look of mild annoyance on the man's face, mixed with curiosity.

'He is waiting in the lobby, over there by the fireplace,' said Lucas, hovering next to Shaw.

Mrs Shaw noticed this and smiled brightly at Lucas. 'I wonder if you would be so kind as to show me to the cocktail bar. I should like to wait for my husband there.'

Lucas looked a little crestfallen, and his eyes searched vainly for a porter, but there was nobody else around.

'Certainly madam,' he said with a slight sigh. 'Come this way, please.'

Once Lucas and Mrs Shaw had passed through the double doors into the deeper recesses of the hotel, with Fraser following at her heels, Shaw walked over to the fireplace, the grate of which was decorated with a summer floral arrangement. He could see the top of a bowler hat protruding from the rear of a leather wing armchair; there was the rustle of a newspaper being folded and the man stood up and turned around. A tall man in his fifties, almost equal to Shaw in height, but heavily built and with a jowly, moustached face. He wore a dark three-piece suit in a thick worsted cloth, and his one concession to the heat seemed to have been the removal of his raincoat, which he had placed over the arm of the chair.

'Good evening, Mr Shaw,' said the man. 'I thought it might be you, when they told me your name and occupation down at the pier.'

'Inspector Ludd,' said Shaw and gave the man a small inclination of his head as a greeting. He did not think it quite correct to shake hands as if it were a social occasion.

'*Chief* Inspector now, sir,' said the detective. 'I got the extra pip after that nasty business* in Lower Addenham last year. Part of the credit goes to you, of course, for that arrest.'

'My congratulations, Chief Inspector,' said Shaw. 'I had rather tried to put those events out of my mind.'

'Of course sir,' said Ludd. 'I understand there was some other nasty business** you— and Mrs Shaw— were subjected to recently. The assassination of King Basil of Fenekslavia.'

'Indeed,' said Shaw. 'Another event I should prefer not to dwell on.'

'Nor me either, sir,' said Ludd. 'Special Branch made it quite clear us local chaps weren't welcome on that case. *Persona non grata*, as the French say.'

'Quite,' replied Shaw.

Ludd stepped forward and lowered his voice slightly.

'I don't suppose…at some stage I might pick your brains on one or two details of that case that weren't mentioned in the papers, Mr Shaw?'

'I fear not, Chief Inspector.'

'Ah, I thought as much,' said Ludd, with a downcast expression, albeit one mixed with a certain grudging admiration. 'Official Secrets Act, or something of that sort, I assume?'

'Something of that sort, yes,' said Shaw cryptically, and sat down on a leather armchair opposite the detective. A hotel waiter appeared next to Shaw and coughed discreetly. He placed a tall glass, gleaming with condensation, on the little table next to his chair.

'Your wife asked me to send this through to you sir,' said the waiter. 'Gin and It.'

*See A Third Class Murder   **See The King is Dead

64

'Thank you,' said Shaw. Then he turned to Ludd, who had resumed his place in his armchair. 'May I offer you something? A soft drink, perhaps?'

Shaw was careful not to use Ludd's title in the presence of the waiter, knowing that gossip could spread like wildfire in a small hotel such as this.

'Thank you indeed,' said Ludd. 'A pale ale will be most welcome.'

'Drinking on duty?' asked Shaw, once the servant had gone.

'Ah, not exactly,' said Ludd with a smile. 'I'll come to that later.' He then looked around to ensure there was nobody nearby to overhear them.

'Perhaps I ought to turn to the matter in hand,' he said. 'I'm sure you'll know what this is about. The chief constable sent me over here as we're the nearest detective branch to Eastburgh. I've had a word with the local constables and the police doctor and so on. I understood you gave them some details but I'd like to hear it straight from the horse's mouth, so to speak. You are, after all, the principal witness, as far as we know at present.'

Before Shaw could reply, Lucas appeared with a pint glass of beer on a silver tray, and placed it on the table next to Ludd.

'Your drink, sir,' said the manager, obsequiously. 'I must say we do not normally entertain police officers on the premises. Er, may I ask…'

'No you may not,' said Ludd brusquely. 'Haven't you got some boots to polish?'

Shaw could not resist a slight smile as Lucas hurried away with a wounded expression, and busied himself at the front desk out of earshot. Ludd swallowed a long draught of the beer and sighed contentedly.

'That's better. The heat is infernal today, eh, Mr Shaw?'

'Let us hope neither of us will have to experience infernal heat, Chief Inspector,' said Shaw.

'Er yes, quite,' said Ludd after a slight pause. 'To the matter in hand,' he continued, and looked down at his notebook. 'You told the officers on the pier that you spoke to a man leaving the theatre, in something of a hurry. Is that right?'

'Certainly,' replied Shaw, after taking a deep swallow of the gin and It. He felt the drink cooling him but warming and relaxing him at the same time. He began to feel more conversational than he had previously.

'I could hardly avoid seeing him,' he continued. 'The man collided with me as he ran along the pier.'

'I see,' said Ludd. 'Could you describe him?'

'I told all this to the constable earlier.'

'I know, but I'd like to hear it directly from you. No offence, Mr Shaw, but some of these bobbies out in the sticks aren't too bright and they don't always write things down proper.'

'Very well. He was young— about nineteen or twenty years of age. Around five and a half feet tall. He wore golfing trousers and one of those, now what are they called…ah yes, Fair Isle pullovers, with a knitted tie. He wore spectacles, and had a shock of red hair.'

Ludd looked up from his book. 'Thank you sir. That fits in with what the constable on traffic duty by the pier saw. The lad ran past him and disappeared into the alleys behind the high street.'

'Has he been identified?' asked Shaw.

'Why do you ask?'

'He was clearly terrified and asked for my help. If possible, I would like to offer it to him.'

'At present I don't advise that, Mr Shaw,' said Ludd, with a frown. 'Rest assured the local chaps know who he is.

Name of Prior, works in an electrical shop on the high street. He wasn't there nor was he at home when we called. But we'll find him soon enough I don't doubt.'

Ludd took another long swallow of beer and then pushed his hat back slightly on his forehead, wiping his brow with a large spotted handkerchief.

'Now Mr Shaw, and this is important, what did he say to you?'

Shaw thought for a moment. 'He said "help me". I tried to get him to sit down. I recognised the symptoms, you see. What they called shell shock in the war. Terror that had almost deprived him of his senses.'

'I saw enough of that myself,' mused Ludd. 'Then what happened?'

'He heard a noise in the theatre, and appeared even more frightened.'

'What sort of a noise?'

'I am not sure. Possibly a door slamming.'

'I see. Go on.'

'He then pointed at the theatre and said "In there. Murder!" and broke away from me. I considered giving chase, but he was too quick and besides, I considered there might be someone in more desperate straits inside the theatre.'

'Yes, quite right,' said Ludd. 'And then you discovered the body.'

'That is correct. I walked into the theatre and saw the man on the stage. He was clearly dead. Mr Cotterill, I believe was his name. The pier manager was sent for to identify him while I was being questioned.'

'Did you notice anything else?'

'It looked as if there had been a struggle. A chair had been knocked over and the curtains had been pulled down. There was some sort of mechanical device on the floor, I assume some sort of theatrical equipment. Oh…and there was a doll on the stage. That is to say, a dummy. The type used by ventriloquists, I believe.'

'And then what did you do?'

'I left the theatre and asked a boy to run and fetch the constable from the road in front of the pier. '

'Why didn't you go yourself?'

'I did not want anyone else to accidentally find the body. And I also thought…'

'Yes?'

Shaw paused. He wondered whether to mention the brief shadow he had seen flit across the frosted glass of the pier shelter as he was trying to calm Prior. He decided it was best to reveal as much as he knew, and that Ludd could make what he would of it.

'I thought that I saw a movement from the side of the theatre.'

Ludd drained the last of his beer and leaned forward in his chair expectantly. 'What sort of movement?'

'I cannot be sure. A shadow, as if somebody had passed quickly behind the shelter in which we were standing. There is a frosted glass partition and I only noticed the briefest of movements from the corner of my eye.'

'Hmm,' said Ludd with a frown. 'Probably just a seagull. They're big brutes round these parts.'

'Perhaps,' said Shaw doubtfully, and finished his own drink.

There was the sound of a dinner gong from the inner recesses of the hotel, and a small crowd of chattering holidaymakers flitted gaily through the lobby on their way to the dining room.

'I think I've taken up enough of your time, Mr Shaw,' said Ludd, and stood up. 'Thank you for your help. Will you be staying here long?'

Shaw rose to his feet. 'We are here for a fortnight.'

'Very good,' said Ludd. 'I'm staying at the Seaview down the road. A little less grand than this place but we can't be seen to be wasting public money.'

'I assumed you would be motoring back to Midchester,' said Shaw.

'Goodness me no sir,' said Ludd. 'There's no spare cars at the moment and the train journey's a little too long. So myself and Mrs Ludd have made a sort of holiday of it. That's why I accepted your offer of a pint of ale. Strictly speaking I'm not on duty.'

'A most ingenious idea,' mused Shaw.

'I thought so too,' said Ludd with a grin. 'Can't stand holidays myself, but the wife likes them, and you know what they say, "happy spouse, happy house."'

'Do they indeed, Chief Inspector?' asked Shaw. He noticed that his own wife was hovering by the door of the lobby and he realised that dinner was about to be served.

'Well I must not keep you waiting,' said Shaw. 'Has the murder been announced to the press?'

Ludd looked questioningly at Shaw, as he shrugged on his raincoat. 'Murder, sir?'

'Yes,' replied Shaw. 'You are treating the incident as a murder, I assume?'

'Bless me no, Mr Shaw. Whatever made you think that?'

Shaw paused before replying. 'Surely there was foul play?'

'I didn't say that,' said Ludd in a warning tone.

'A man was found dead, and a man was seen running from the scene, who cried "murder". That does not a murder make, Mr Shaw.'

'Of course,' said Shaw. 'I just assumed…'

'I know you did, sir,' said Ludd. 'But assumptions are a dangerous habit in *my* profession.'

'I see,' said Shaw, 'and do I take it the lack of obvious injury to Mr Cotterill means it could have been death from natural causes?'

'I won't know until I get a full report from the doctor tomorrow, but it looks that way,' said Ludd. 'There were signs of a struggle but it's possible he suffered a stroke or something, and knocked the equipment and furniture over, pulling the curtain down as he fell. We won't know until I get the report.'

'But why then would Mr…Prior claim there had been a murder?'

Ludd sighed. 'Look Mr Shaw, you were very helpful on the Lower Addenham case and I understand you put up a good show too when King Basil was assassinated. But that doesn't make you a detective.'

'Point taken, Chief Inspector. I ought to go to dinner.'

'That's right sir,' said Ludd, who mopped his brow again and then straightened his hat on his head. 'Enjoy your holiday and leave the police work to the professionals. There'll be an inquest, and you'll be obliged to attend, of course.'

'Of course,' replied Shaw.

'I'll say though that it might make things clearer if you knew a little about Prior,' continued Ludd. 'From what I could gather when I spoke to his mother, he is a bit…peculiar.'

'Peculiar?' asked Shaw.

'Yes. He's a wizard with electrical equipment but isn't quite all there upstairs, if you get my meaning. Lives in a sort of world of his own apparently, and doesn't really have any friends other than a local boy half his age.'

'I see,' replied Shaw, nodding. 'Perhaps he saw the body of Mr Cotterill, and jumped to a false conclusion.'

'Most likely something like that,' said Ludd. 'At the

moment this is being treated simply as a suspicious death until we can find Prior and get things straightened out.' Ludd chuckled to himself and continued. 'If we can't, then the only witness we've got is a wooden one— that little dummy!'

'But what of the shadow I saw behind the shelter?' asked Shaw. 'What if that were another individual fleeing the scene?'

Ludd sighed. 'I can't go around chasing shadows, Mr Shaw. Have your dinner and get a good night's sleep. We'll take care of things and if there are any new developments I shall let you know. Goodnight sir, and goodnight, Mrs Shaw.'

The policeman tipped his hat to Mrs Shaw, who was still patiently waiting near the dining room, and disappeared through the lobby doors towards the somewhat less elegant environs of the Seaview Guest House.

The Reverend Nicholas Frederick James Dewynter, vicar of Eastburgh, or simply Father Nicholas as he preferred to be known, stood silently at the windows of his study looking out at the last dying embers of the sun as it sank somewhere over Middlesham Forest. After a plain supper served by his elderly housekeeper, he was enjoying both of his only two worldly pleasures: a hand-made Virginia cigarette, one of a stock of several hundred sent every month from Dunhill's, and a glass of a very rare and expensive single malt whisky with an unpronounceable gaelic name, ordered directly from a distillery in Perthshire.

These were not entirely vain indulgences; he found that tobacco curbed the desire to eat too much, and the strong, peaty malt whisky curbed the desire to drink too much. Unlike beer or wine, which provoked thirst, it seemed to give one a sense of satisfaction after one, or at most two, glasses.

Dewynter, although of the High Church party in the Church of England, which leans more towards the Roman Catholics in ritual, was not an aesthete like some priests of that persuasion. He did not affect to live like an Italian cardinal, surrounded by marbled luxury and acolytes, supping gin and fine wines. He had a plainly decorated vicarage, kept a frugal table, and wore no other garments except his old, threadbare clerical garb or his cricketing clothes. Of motor cars he knew nothing; he did not even possess a bicycle, and did his parish visiting on foot, wearing little more than a cassock and trilby hat in all weathers.

Admired by some in the parish as an example of monastic discipline, Dewynter reflected, as he puffed on his cigarette, that he had never really had to struggle with temptation. Worldly pleasures, including female charms, held no interest for him. They were not something he had had to try hard to overcome.

In his early thirties and ruggedly handsome, with smooth blond hair and piercing blue eyes, he sometimes found himself in potentially compromising situations engineered by female parishioners, of the type who find handsome, unmarried clergymen irresistibly alluring. These advances he politely brushed off with no more regret than had the women in question proposed they indulge in flower arranging or needlepoint, or some other obscure feminine activity which held no interest for him.

He took a final drag on his cigarette and stubbed it out in his ashtray, then drained the last of his whisky. It was foolish to regret not being tempted, he thought. In fact, it was a form of spiritual pride in itself. He decided to return to the matter he was meant to be thinking about— the death of Mr Cotterill.

Word had spread around the town quite quickly that a body had been found on the pier that afternoon. He did not know Cotterill, and his wife did not attend his church, so he had decided a consolatory visit to her could wait until tomorrow. The more pressing matter was that of Leslie Prior, his church organist. It seemed he had been seen running from the theatre in which Cotterill had been found dead; the police were now looking for him. He had called on Prior's parents and made a fruitless search of the town himself, but to no avail. He decided he would make a special appeal in church tomorrow, and amended his sermon notes accordingly.

He felt sorry for Prior. The young man seemed to live in a world of his own, and spent more time with the youngsters in the congregation than men or women of his own age. Dewynter had something of an interest in neurology, mental disorders and the like, and often wished Prior could be seen by someone in this field. There did not seem to be a name for his condition— if indeed it could be called a condition— and the only doctor of which he had read who had researched anything similar, Hans Asperger, lived in Vienna. He sighed and lit another cigarette, resolving this would be his last before he began his nightly prayers on the little *prie-dieu* in the corner of his bedroom. There was no lamp lit in the study; he preferred to make the most of free natural light as much as possible. Thus there was no glare reflected back at him from the study windows, and he could see outside into the gathering gloom on the edge of the town.

Small paraffin lamps were coming on in the distance, in the little shanty town known as the Plotlands. He felt a wave of love for the inhabitants; good honest ordinary Anglo-Saxon folk, made to be outcasts in their own land due to, as he saw it, unjust property laws dating to the time of King Henry the Eighth, which were now enforced by the representatives of his descendants with almost equal ruthlessness.

The Plotlanders reminded him of his first ministry as a 'slum parson' in the east end of London. Despite being a product of Eton and Oxford, Dewynter felt more affinity with the working classes than the genteel patricians of his parish. He believed the Reformation and the Enclosure Acts had cut them off from the faith of their ancestors, and he strove to return as many to the fold as he could, despite the indifference of most of them.

He frowned as he saw a larger light, an electric one, come on above the porch of the little tin chapel up the lane. He saw a figure by the door and in the pool of light, realised it was Aethelstan Rooksley.

Although the Ten Commandments exhorted him to love his neighbour, Dewynter had great difficulty in this particular instance. Rooksley was actively luring away some of the Plotlanders from Anglo-Catholicism to Spiritualism, a denomination he considered to be the religious equivalent of a 'penny dreadful'.

It was up to them where they worshipped of course, if one could call it worship, but what irked him was that Rooksley was clearly a charlatan. Dewynter had, in the early days, attempted to engage him in friendly conversation, even once inviting him into his study, but it soon became obvious the man knew next to nothing about Christianity. He had, for example, during one chat, confused the term 'eschatological' with 'scatalogical', and had suggested that Dewynter had a liking for dirty jokes.

He looked again at the chapel but the light had gone out. A verse from Romans sprang to mind. 'For they that are such serve not our Lord Jesus Christ, but their own belly, and by good words and fair speeches deceive the hearts of the simple.'

Even Saint Paul, thought Dewynter, all those years ago, had known about the likes of Rooksley. Something, he decided, would have to be done about him.

One of the lights that Dewynter had seen in the distance from his window had been lit by Les Prior, who had quickly hidden it from view in case it should be spotted by anyone in the town. After he had witnessed the death of Cotterill, he had been too afraid to go home or to his parents' shop, in case Rooksley came after him. Instead, he had run all the way to the edge of town, to the little settlement of wooden cabins and re-purposed railway carriages known as the Plotlands. He had run to the safety of the Gang Hut.

Prior was never quite certain if Gang Hut was the right name, as it was only used by two people, and he was not sure if two people were enough to make a gang, but that was what his friend Billy called it. It was a shack made from parts of an old railway carriage, close to the edge of the high downs which overhung North Beach, the remains of a holiday cabin started a few years earlier but then abandoned. Billy Wainwright, the altar server from church, had shown it to him one day after the two had met by chance out on the downs.

He liked Billy, even though his parents said it was odd that he was friends with a lad half his age. He found it hard to make friends with anyone, so age differences did not bother him. He had been teased remorselessly at school for his stammer, his red hair, and his other difficulties, and had given up bothering with anybody's company but his own, but Billy did not seem to mind any of those things.

The boy's face had lit up when Prior had suggested setting up an electrical system for the Gang Hut. He had always been good with electrical equipment and it was no trouble at all to set up some lights using a wet cell battery. He had even managed to incorporate a crystal radio set, and the pair often spent evenings in the hut roaming the airwaves, trying to make sense of French and Dutch broadcasts coming from over the North Sea on waves of static.

Prior could talk for hours about frequencies and bandwidths, valves and capacitors, and sometimes Billy would tell him to stop droning on and listen instead to the snatches of dance-band music which came from the continental commercial stations. They usually went here on Saturday evenings when the weather was good, and Prior had been relieved to find Billy already there when he arrived in the afternoon. He had told some of the story to him and then the boy had disappeared to fetch some food.

He would be safe here, he thought. Nobody knew about this place other than him and Billy, and he could trust him. He could hold out here indefinitely.

He heard a rustling from outside the hut, as if someone was walking stealthily through the long grass. A chill of fear passed down his spine, but then he relaxed as heard the sound of a wood-pigeon's call—the signal.

He cupped his hands as Billy had showed him, and blew through the gap between his thumbs. He clicked off the electric light and unbolted the door, sighing with relief as he saw Billy appear out of the gloom.

'Th…thank goodness you're h…here,' said Prior. 'I'm st…st…starving.'

'Good job I made a few bob shifting cases today,' said Billy, as he placed a sack on the floor of the hut. 'I got you some tins and stuff from the late-night grocer.'

'And a t…tin opener?' asked Prior.

'Course,' said Billy. 'Think I'm daft? It's in the sack. There's one of mum's blankets in there an' all, if you're going to sleep here.'

'Th…thanks Billy. You're a p…pal.'

'Don't mention it,' said the boy with a grin. 'Cor, you should hear what they're saying about you. It's all over the Plotlands by now. You're a wanted man, like in the westerns.'

'I didn't d…do anything!' said Prior indignantly.

'All right, I believe you,' chirped Billy, then added gaily, 'Thousands wouldn't!'

'What do you mean, thousands?'

'Never mind,' sighed Billy. 'Just a joke. I forgot you never understand those.'

Prior began opening some of the tins and they both started devouring peaches in syrup with their fingers.

'W…what are they s…saying about me?' asked Prior.

'That you're wanted in connection with the auspicious death of Mr Cotterill.'

'I told you I d…didn't do anything.' Prior then paused and added evasively, 'It was s…someone else.'

'I know, you said,' replied Billy. 'But you can't say who 'cos he might use dark forces against you like he did against the dead bloke. Can't imagine who that would be. There ain't no witches and wizards around nowadays. Not round here anyway.'

'You won't t…tell anyone, will you, Billy?' asked Prior.

'Course not,' said the boy, wiping peach juice from his fingers on to his ragged shorts. 'I ain't never helped a fugitive from justice before. Fink I'll be quite good at it.'

'Oh th…thanks, Billy.'

'Don't mention it. 'ow long you going to stay 'ere?'

Prior paused before answering. He had not planned that far ahead. He decided to put the thought out of his head and concentrate on getting back into some sort of routine that he could understand. He felt sick at the thought of missing the comforting rituals of church the following day, and to be unable to lose himself in the flow of ordered, predictable musical notes that his hands and feet produced from the organ.

He pulled a ten shilling note from his pocket and stuffed it into Billy's hand, who looked down at the money wide-eyed.

'Just k…keep bringing me f…food and keep quiet,' Prior said firmly, and began opening another tin.

Nobody will find me here, thought Prior. Then the opener skidded off the side of the tin he was holding as his stomach flip-flopped with fear. He suddenly remembered that when he had been given the job of installing loudspeakers in the spiritualist chapel, he had mentioned the hut to Rooksley.

Chapter Five

Shaw woke early, as he always did between the months of May and September when in England the nights are short, and daylight begins to creep in around four o'clock in the morning, accompanied by the raucous sounds of birds as they wake to a new day. Eastburgh was no exception, and Shaw gave up all thought of sleep shortly after 6.00 a.m., as the chatter and cackling of seagulls around the hotel balcony made sleep impossible.

He dressed and took Fraser out to exercise him on the parched lawn of the hotel; the day was already warm with a promise of further heat to come. He returned to the room, bathed in the little adjoining bathroom, and then spent some time in prayer as his wife slept on soundly on the other side of the room.

As it was a Sunday, breakfast was served slightly later than during the week. By nine o'clock the Shaws were seated at the same table they had dined at the previous evening, eating kippers and kedgeree and drinking English Breakfast tea from a silver pot.

As they got up to return to their room, they were passed by the Guru and Miss Sloan. They bade each other good morning.

'Do you have any interesting plans for the day, Mr Shaw?' asked the Guru, as they stood in the hotel lobby in that somewhat awkward way that people who do not know each other well do when meeting by chance in hotels.

'We shall be attending the parish church,' said Shaw.

'Ah,' replied the Guru with a smile. 'What the British call the busman's holiday, no?'

Shaw returned the smile. 'Something of that sort. I find it helpful to my own ministry to experience the layman's point of view from time to time.'

'An excellent idea,' replied the Guru. '"To see ourselves as others see us", as the poet puts it. We are all interconnected; we are all reflectors and all reflected, one and the same.'

Shaw noticed a look of confused boredom cross his wife's face; he was about to change the subject but Miss Sloan interjected.

'What the Guru means is that none of us needs go to a particular place to worship,' she explained. 'The all-in-all is everywhere.'

'Quite right,' said Shaw. 'Although I have always thought that the purpose of church-going is not to bring the Almighty closer to us, but simply to remind us that He is indeed always with us.'

'That is a most noble sentiment,' said the Guru, nodding slowly. 'Then please excuse us Mr and Mrs Shaw; we must not detain you any longer.'

'Morning all!' said a voice brightly from across the lobby. It was Major Blair.

'Morning Padre, Mrs Shaw,' he said cheerfully. 'Off to church parade I suppose? Not much of an attender myself, except for Armistice Day of course, but admirable, admirable.'

He turned to Miss Sloan. 'Now how about you m'dear?' he asked. 'Ready for the off? "Come Josephine in my flying machine," as the song goes, eh?'

'Yes of course,' said Miss Sloan. 'Will you excuse me, Guru?'

'Certainly Shrutakirti,' said the Guru with a bow. 'I wish that you will find one-ness with the elements.'

'No idea what that means, Guru, old chap,' said Blair with a wink. 'Expect aeroplanes aren't your thing. Don't see them much in darkest India, eh?'

The Guru said nothing, but bowed to Miss Sloan and the Shaws, and departed with a rustle of his orange robes.

'I say, I think you're awfully brave going up in an aeroplane,' said Mrs Shaw. 'But won't you be cold, dressed as you are? Would you like to borrow my mackintosh?'

'Thank you but that won't be necessary' said Miss Sloan. 'I have seen Major Blair's aeroplane pass over the bay before, and at that altitude I shan't feel cold.'

'Talking of flying togs, that reminds me,' said Blair. 'Left mine in my room. Give me two ticks and I'll be back down. They've brought my car round the front, jump in and off we'll pop to the hangar.'

Blair bounded up the wide staircase, and Miss Sloan walked serenely out through the hotel's front door, to where Blair's little MG sports car was parked. A few moments later, as Shaw and his wife were walking along the road into town, the car passed them in a cloud of blue exhaust smoke and with a roar which, for a moment, drowned out the ancient sound of church bells drifting across the valley.

Half an hour later, after securing Fraser in a shady spot under a buttress, Shaw and his wife sat in the large, barn-like parish church, surrounded by clouds of incense, as the choir sang Psalm 55.

He could not help his thoughts drifting after he heard the line 'I have seen violence and strife in the city'. Chief Inspector Ludd had not seemed overly concerned about the nature of Cotterill's death, but Shaw felt instinctively that foul play was afoot. Then he mentally corrected himself; it was vain and sinful of him to think he knew better than Ludd about such things. He resolved to put the whole matter out of his mind until such time as he was called to the inquest.

His decision was made just in time; his thoughts were brought back into the present as the congregation rose to its feet with a terrific rumble and creaking of pews for the reading of the gospel. Shaw had never seen such an ornate performance in a parish church; candles were raised, thuribles were swung, and acolytes processed.

Then, amid much bowing and genuflection by those around him, Reverend Dewynter, dressed in ornate golden vestments, raised a heavy gilded bible so high that Shaw was concerned he might topple over backwards. The gospel was intoned, rather than read, something that offended Shaw's sensibilities somewhat, and he could see also a look of slight distaste on his wife's face.

Then they sang the Creed to the Merbecke setting, something Shaw, not a great singer, always struggled with, though as usual he found the sudden tonal shift at 'Who spake by the prophets' to be very moving. It was made more difficult, however, by the organist hitting several wrong notes. Then Dewynter processed once more with his entourage, this time to the pulpit.

There was a moment of quiet and Shaw sensed an air of expectation. He wondered if Dewynter would say anything about yesterday's events. He did not have to wait long. Dewynter cleared his throat and looked down at the upturned faces of the congregation.

'You will by now have heard of the sudden death yesterday of a well-known member of this community, Mr Reginald Cotterill. We shall hold his widow in our prayers; I visited her earlier this morning to pray with her in her hour of sorrow.'

Then there was a pause, as if Dewynter was unsure of what to say. He then continued.

'Some of you may also know that our regular organist, Leslie Prior, is wanted for questioning by the police in connection with Mr Cotterill's death.'

There was a murmur from the congregation, and puzzled looks were exchanged between some of the worshippers.

'I must emphasise that there is absolutely no suspicion of foul play or anything of that sort attaching to Mr Prior. The police merely want to eliminate him from their enquiries. Unfortunately it seems that Mr Prior has gone…missing. He did not return either to work or to his home last night.'

There were louder murmurs this time; Dewynter raised his hand for quiet and then leaned forward in the pulpit.

'If anybody knows the whereabouts of Mr Prior, I charge you to inform the authorities, or, if you prefer, I will do so on your behalf. I repeat, he is *not* in any sort of trouble.'

Shaw noticed that Dewynter turned briefly to look at the two young acolytes sitting near the altar. He paused again for a moment, faced the nave and crossed himself, then spoke rapidly in the manner of one reciting a railway timetable. 'And now may I speak in the name of God, Father, Son and Holy Spirit, Amen.'

There was a murmur of 'amens' and a flurry of genuflections from the congregation, and then Dewynter began his sermon. It was learned and somewhat dry; Shaw felt his mind drifting again, and to his shame, he found he could not fully concentrate afterwards during Holy Communion either.

As the service ended and the organist thundered out a Bach voluntary, with only a few wrong notes, and the clouds of incense began to dissipate through the opened west door, Shaw was still cogitating on the death of Cotterill. It was understandable that Prior might run away in shock after seeing a corpse, or even witnessing the man have a stroke; but why should he now have disappeared?

Shaw smiled politely at the other members of the congregation, leaving the post-service small talk largely to his wife. When they reached the porch, he shook Dewynter's hand, thanked him and made to leave, but Dewynter pulled him gently to one side, leaving his curate to continue with the hand-shaking duties.

'I couldn't help noticing a fellow traveller,' said Dewynter, pointing to his collar to indicate Shaw's clerical attire. 'On holiday, I presume? I hope you enjoyed the service.'

'Oh indeed,' said Shaw. 'Although in my own rather more modest church, alas, we do not have sufficiently adept choristers to attempt such a setting of the psalms. Would I be right in saying it was in F? I always find that key particularly difficult to sing.'

'That is correct,' said Dewynter. 'Our reserve organist coped admirably. Forgive me,' he continued, 'but you're not the man who found poor Cotterill, by any chance?'

'I regret that I am,' replied Shaw. 'My name is Shaw, and

this is my wife.'

'How do you do,' said Dewynter, taking Mrs Shaw's gloved hand in his own momentarily.

'I wondered if it might be you,' said the priest to Shaw. 'When I paid my condolences to Mrs Cotterill this morning, she said the police had told her a clergyman had found her husband's body. The poor woman was rather confused and thought it was me. But then I heard some of the choirboys say in the vestry, that a parson had been seen speaking to the police on the pier yesterday.'

'Are there no other clergymen in a town of this size?' enquired Shaw.

'Apart from myself and my curate, we are the only ones to wear the Roman collar,' said Dewynter. 'There is no Roman Catholic church here, and the Nonconformist ministers…and…others…wear laymens' clothing.'

'Good morning to you Father Nicholas,' effused a matronly woman next to Shaw, as she attempted to draw the priest away with a large, yellow-gloved hand. 'You must let me know about the new bell ringing rota.'

'One moment, Mrs Routledge!' Dewynter smiled apologetically and turned back to Shaw. 'You must excuse me Mr Shaw, Mrs Shaw. "Ask not for whom the bell tolls, it tolls for thee", as Donne puts it.'

'That is quite all right,' said Shaw. 'We ought to be getting back to our hotel for luncheon anyway.'

'Oh, why not take luncheon with me?' asked Dewynter. 'That is…if you do not object to a rather humble table. It would be interesting to talk about…I mean, to converse with another cleric of our denomination for once.'

Shaw had the feeling the man might be fishing for information in some way. Before he could reply, however, Mrs Shaw said brightly, 'Thank you very much for the invitation. We shall be delighted to attend.'

Rooksley got rid of the last of the congregation from the little chapel, and locked the door. He sat down for a moment on one of the benches. He found the Sunday morning Spiritualist services a chore; there was far too much talk about the 'Brotherhood of Man' and 'Personal Responsibility' for his liking. He preferred his evening seances where he could strip the veneer of Christianity away and reveal the occult powers behind all perceived reality.

One good thing was that he had been able to speak with Cotterill's widow, a regular attender at the church, and she did not mention the fact that he, Rooksley, had called on her previously to ask where her husband was. She was probably too stupid, he thought, to make any connection with that and her husband's death. Some of the congregation might remember that he and Cotterill had exchanged heated words the night before he died, but he did not think they were likely to go to the police about it. He breathed out deeply. For the moment, he was safe.

There was, however, the problem of Prior to be solved. He was still missing. Mrs Cotterill had mentioned that the vicar, the one who affected the manners of a Jesuit priest and swanned around the town in a cassock all the time, had visited her to pay his condolences. His condolences! The woman did not even attend his church. She had heard from the police that Prior was wanted in connection with her husband's death, and the vicar had told her he was still missing. That was a good sign as it suggested the police were not looking for anyone else.

Rooksley thought for a moment. It sounded from what Mrs Cotterill had said that the vicar knew Prior quite well, as he was the church organist. Perhaps he should question the vicar; he might know of places that Prior frequented. Then he dismissed the thought—too risky.

Suddenly, he remembered something. It was recalling that Prior was an organist that did it. That was, ostensibly, the reason for getting Prior to install the hidden loudspeakers in the chapel. Rooksley had told Prior that the elderly harmonium in the church was unreliable, and that he wanted to be able to play cylinder recordings of organ music for the edification of the worshippers instead. He did not, of course, mention he wanted to use the system to make people think voices from beyond the grave (his own of course, albeit heavily disguised) were talking to them.

That was it— music! When he had spoken to Prior in his shop about what he wanted, he asked if he had any previous experience of similar work, and he had said he had installed a crystal radio system with a loudspeaker in a hut made of an old railway carriage out on the cliffs near North Beach. He remembered the man had droned on about it like a halfwit and even invited him to see it, saying it was not far from the chapel on the coast road. There could not be many places around there matching that description, thought Prior. Perhaps the man was hiding there? It was certainly worth a try. He decided he would pay a little visit once he had eaten lunch.

'That really was a most delightful meal, Mr Dewynter,' said Mrs Shaw, as she dabbed at her mouth with a plain linen napkin. 'So simple and healthy.'

'Thank you,' said Dewynter. 'Mrs Upton is very good housekeeper.' He smiled up at the grandmother-like servant, who cleared the plates away then left the sparsely decorated vicarage dining room.

'You are lucky to have a reliable servant,' said Shaw. 'We are similarly blessed, with Hettie, our cook-general. But do you not find it lonely out here on your own, as a celibate?'

'Not a bit,' said Dewynter. He drank the last of his glass of claret, a wine which, Shaw reflected, never tasted particularly good in hot weather, even if it were a good vintage, which this was not.

'We are a very busy and lively parish here,' said Dewynter. 'I have no time for loneliness. I am only a few minutes' walk from the bustle of the town, and this house, particularly my study, is in a prime position to observe human life. Perhaps you would care to see my study, Mr Shaw?'

Shaw realised his wife, who was generally more sensitive to social niceties than he, had taken this as a hint that the gentlemen ought to be left alone.

'Fraser needs a little walk,' she said, scooping up the dog from the plain wooden floor where he had been lying, stretched out in an attempt to stay cool. 'Perhaps Mrs

Upton could show me around the garden?'

'Of course,' said Dewynter, and rang a little bell on the carved oak sideboard to summon the domestic.

A few moments later, Shaw and Dewynter were seated in battered leather armchairs looking out of the open windows of the study. A very light breeze blew in from the sea but made no difference to the heat in the room, and barely disturbed the coils of smoke from Shaw's pipe and Dewynter's cigarette.

'I see what you mean about the view,' said Shaw. 'The new settlement, Plotlands, is nearby on that side, and I assume, North Beach is on the other.'

'South Beach,' corrected Dewynter. 'North Beach is further along, in a sort of basin. One can't see it from here, or from anywhere else. If the continental enthusiasm for nude sunbathing ever reaches these shores, it will be an ideal location for it.'

The two men laughed. Shaw was thankful that his wife was not present to hear ribald humour, and hoped that Dewynter was not the type of man to indulge in too much of such talk when in male company. He decided to change the subject. His attention had been drawn, when they had entered the room, to a mechanical device in the corner near Dewynter's desk.

'May I ask, Dewynter,' said Shaw, pointing with his pipe stem, 'what that machine is for? Is it a recording gramophone?' Something stopped him from mentioning that it appeared very similar to the one he had seen the previous day in the theatre.

'Correct,' said Dewynter, as he leant his head back and blew a column of smoke out of his mouth into the still air. 'A dictaphone, to be precise. Bought it from Prior's shop. Along with the telephone and electric light, it is one of my few concessions to the modern world. My handwriting is appalling and after being abandoned by a succession of typing bureaux unable to interpret my scrawls, I decided it would be easier to dictate my sermons.'

'But why use the machine?' asked Shaw. 'Could not a secretary attend to you?'

Dewynter smiled. 'My dear Shaw, a young girl regularly alone in the study of a 32 year-old celibate priest? I may be 'not of this world' but I do know something of how rumours are spread.'

'Of course,' said Shaw, realising he had been somewhat naive.

'I suppose I could have specified a male secretary,' continued Dewynter, 'but those are harder to come by, and expensive. Or some old dragon of an elderly woman— but I could hardly specify *that* to a bureau and in this town I doubt it would make much difference. There would still be rumours. No, the machine is perfectly adequate.'

Dewynter got up and stepped forward to the apparatus. 'I simply speak into this tube here,'— he indicated a horn attached to a tube— 'and my voice is recorded on this rotating cylinder. I then send the cylinder in the post to a typing bureau in Midchester, and it comes back neatly typed and bound in time for Sunday. I intend to publish them one day.'

Dewynter stubbed his cigarette out in the ashtray on his desk and pointed to a shelf of manuscripts next to it.

'An excellent idea,' said Shaw. 'But is one cylinder able to make a long enough recording?'

'That's another good thing about it,' said Dewynter. 'They only record twelve minutes. I have no wish to get into the Low Church habit of interminable sermons.'

Dewynter paused, and returned to his seat. When he spoke, his voice had a more serious tone.

'Look here Shaw,' he said, fixing the cleric with a stern

gaze. 'I've brought you out here on somewhat false pretences. There's something important I'd like to talk to you about and it's not my sermons. Can you spare me a little more of your time?'

Prior had spent an anxious night sleeping on the hard floor of the hut and waking up every hour or so in terror of being discovered. The sun had been up for over six hours now. He looked anxiously out of the grimy window, but as with every other time, he saw nothing but the gently waving tall grass of the downs. He bit his lip and looked at his wrist-watch. Where on earth was Billy? He was supposed to be coming at noon with some food and to tell him if it was safe to leave, and it was nearly half past one now.

Why couldn't people ever do what they said they would?, he thought to himself nervously. For the umpteenth time, he took out his wallet and checked his money. One pound fifteen and six. Not really enough to go on the run with. He cursed himself for giving Billy ten bob, which was far too much for food. He would need every penny from now on.

Calculations of train fares, hotel rooms and meals spun round in his head like numbers on a giant cash register. He could do it, he realised, at least until he could get a job somewhere. Another mental image flashed before him, of an enormous railway timetable. 14.07 to London Liverpool Street, change at Midchester and Ipswich, arrive 16.34. He did not enjoy the cinema much, but on his trips with Billy he had seen enough films to know that people on the run always went to London. He would have to write to Billy and tell him he had gone and was never coming back.

He took a deep breath and opened the door. Instead of bright sunlight, a shadow loomed over him. It was Rooksley.

'Going somewhere?' he said with a malevolent grin.

Prior slammed the rickety door shut, and ran to the opposite side of the hut, forcing his way through a gap into the planks. Once outside, he stood stock still.

He heard sarcastic laughter from behind him at the door of the hut. 'I'll huff and I'll puff and I'll blow your wooden house down.'

What on earth did he mean, blow the house down? thought Prior as he untangled himself from the broken planking, but then self-preservation kicked in and he had no more time to think as he bolted through the long grass away from the hut.

He heard more laughter behind him. Terrified, he looked round to see Rooksley running after him. 'There's nowhere to run to, Leslie,' yelled the man. 'Nobody to hear you shout for help either!'

Prior tried to increase his speed, but he had always been ungainly when running— 'two left feet', his father always said— but Rooksley swept down on him almost as if his feet were not touching the ground.

With a last burst of energy, Prior dashed forward and then staggered back, his arms whirling to retain his balance. He had reached the cliff edge, and for a moment all he could see was the surging, boiling tide a hundred feet below him. He spun round to the direction he had run from, and saw there was no escape that way; he was on a small promontory and Rooksley stood blocking the only way back to the downs. He had his arms folded, and watched him like a cat stalking his prey.

'Hello young Leslie,' said Rooksley. 'Unless you like high jumps, I think you'd better come and have a little talk with me. Come along.'

Rooksley beckoned and made a noise with his tongue as if attempting to coax a recalcitrant pet from a tree.

'I...I...d...d...didn't s...see...anything,' blurted Prior.

'S...s...s...so you said,' mocked Rooksley. 'But I don't b...b...b...believe you.'

Prior's face contorted with the effort of trying to speak. Finally he was able to, in an almost unintelligible rush. 'I w....won't tell anyone.'

Rooksley stepped forward and looked at Prior over the top of his green sun-spectacles. 'Do you know, I think you actually won't. You know what they say about me, don't you, Leslie? That I have special powers.'

Doctor Death, thought Prior frantically. That's what Billy had called Rooksley behind his back when they had once walked past his chapel. The man was reputed to have magical powers and could kill you with a glance, or so Billy said. He swallowed and nodded.

'Good,' said Rooksley. 'I accept your word as a gentleman. But just to make sure, I want something from you. I think you know to what I am referring.'

Prior shook his head.

'Do not try my patience, boy,' said Rooksley, with something approaching gentleness. 'That cylinder recording you made in the theatre. Where is it?'

Prior shook his head again. Rooksley stepped forward; Prior stepped back. His ears were beginning to sing and he could feel a strange pressure rising behind his eyes. He could not speak, and managed only a croaking sound.

Rooksley raised a hand to his ear, and spoke with brittle sarcasm. 'What…what was that? Didn't quite catch it.'

Prior stepped back, and was no longer able to make any sound other than a gasping for breath. Finally he managed to speak.

'G…gave it to someone.'

'Now listen to me, you imbecile,' hissed Rooksley slowly, the sarcasm in his voice replaced with pure malevolence. 'Tell me where that recording is, or I will raise a demon that will take you somewhere so unimaginably horrific that you will beg to be cast into hell instead. For the last time, *who did you give it to*?'

Rooksley raised his hands and Prior felt his eyes boring into him. He stepped back again, and felt the ground under his heels crumble and give way. The singing in his ears was now like a locomotive's whistle. His vision darkened and as he felt himself fall backwards over the cliff edge, he managed to scream one word.

'Vicar!'

Billy picked his way along the rocks at the foot of the cliffs along North Beach. It was a short cut from the town out to the Gang Hut that only he knew about. It was dangerous, because you had to get to a steep path on the cliffs without being cut off by the tide, but it was much quicker than walking along the cliff road on the downs. Not owning a wrist-watch, he was unsure of the time, but he was pretty certain that it was later than noon. He had been held up after the church service by one of the Mother's Union ladies who demanded to know why he was wearing a dirty surplice, and then he had struggled to find anywhere open to buy food.

When he finally found an open tea stall down by the harbour, he decided that offering a ten shilling note for a few buns might attract attention. Instead, he had rushed home and wolfed down his Sunday dinner, and got out of the house as quickly as he was decently able, with a large leg of roast chicken stuffed inside his pullover.

Prior was a stickler for punctuality and might lose his temper if he was late. He would go on and on about it. He did not want to upset his only pal. He knew it was a bit odd to have a friend that much older than him, but the local children did not like the Plotlanders, and most of the Plotlander kids came and went so often he could never get to know any.

He was not sure why Prior was a bit strange sometimes. Nor why he was so upset about the old puppet show man on the pier dying. It was not as if he knew him well. Surely the police would not think he had anything to do with it? The vicar in his sermon had said Prior was not in any trouble, however, and he was keen to tell him that.

Billy jumped sideways to avoid a surge of spray from the rocks which lay between him and the sea. He realised he had only a few minutes to get to the path without getting his shoes and socks soaked. One last leap, and he was above the tide line with the steep cliff path in front of him. Before he could begin his climb, he heard a shout, or a scream, perhaps, he could not tell, from the top of the cliffs about a hundred feet away from him, above the dangerous area of the beach with its mysterious timber circle known as the Wooden Witness.

He looked up, and his eyes widened in horror as he saw Prior, unmistakeable with his shock of red hair and brightly coloured Fair Isle pullover, hurtle through the air from the cliff top and land with a thundering crash on the waves, beneath which he immediately disappeared.

Chapter Six

Shaw's intuition that Dewynter wanted to question him on the death of Cotterill was confirmed when the younger priest leaned forward in his chair and lit another cigarette.

'What do you think,'— here he paused to extricate a small flake of tobacco from his lower lip— 'really happened to poor Cotterill yesterday?'

Shaw saw his wife through the window, looking at a rosebush; she was seemingly engrossed in conversation with the housekeeper. Once on the subject of gardening it was difficult to get her off, so it seemed unlikely they would be leaving any time soon. He decided it might be better, however, to proceed with caution, and so he replied nonchalantly.

'The police seem to think he died from natural causes.'

'But what do *you* think, Shaw?'

'I am neither a doctor nor a policeman. I could see no signs of violence on the man's body, which concurs with the official view…so far.'

'Aha!' said Dewynter enthusiastically. 'Those final two words suggest you have suspicions.'

'Not…suspicions. Reservations, perhaps.'

'Why?'

'Why do you ask?'

'Bless me, Shaw, you're not being cross-examined! All

right, if it is of any interest, I have my reservations as well.'

Shaw refilled his pipe, tamping the Three Nuns tobacco down slowly. He did not, as a rule, smoke more than one bowl in succession in the same pipe, preferring to use a fresh one, but as he had no other and the need for the mental stimulation of nicotine became stronger, he waved a match over the aromatic mixture and puffed a few times as he listened.

'As I mentioned,' said Dewynter, 'I called on Mrs Cotterill this morning before divine service. It was largely a formality, as her parish priest, as she has not attended church here for two years or so, having been lured away by…others.

'Others?'

'Yes, the Spiritualists.'

'Ah.'

'It was that which aroused my interest. According to her, last night she and her husband attended a seance at the Spiritualist chapel up the lane from here. It seems he did not normally attend and had no time for that sort of thing, but on this occasion was quite keen to go. There was a scene.'

'What sort of a scene?'

'Cotterill disrupted the seance and accused Aethelstan Rooksley— I hesitate to call him a minister, let us just call him the leader— of using underhand methods to suggest that voices from beyond the grave were speaking.'

Shaw looked at Dewynter quizzically. 'What…sort of methods?'

'That he used gramophone recordings from hidden loudspeakers.'

'Why did Mrs Cotterill tell you all this?'

'She said that when she and her husband returned home, he was in a terrible temper and she thought he was going to have some sort of seizure— he had heart problems, it seems— and she thought that must have been what "finished him off" the next day, as she put it.'

Shaw puffed on his pipe and thought for a moment. 'I sense that you think there may be more to the matter.'

'You sense correctly,' said Dewynter earnestly as he stubbed out his cigarette with considerable force in the ashtray. 'I believe Rooksley had something to do with it, and not just because he upset Cotterill'.

'You mean…murder?'

'That or manslaughter. There are all sorts of rumours about our Mr Rooksley.'

'Rumours?'

'That he is some sort of magician.'

'My dear chap, you surely do not believe…'

'Such persons are written of in Scripture, and warned against by the Church fathers.'

'Yes,' replied Shaw, 'but those were different times, when men knew less of science. There is evil in the hearts of men, certainly; and such evil, when it takes on a life of its own greater than the sum of its parts, may perhaps be called demonic. But are you suggesting that an ordinary man can somehow harness evil, and use it as he might use electricity?'

'I don't know,' sighed Dewynter. 'You haven't met Rooksley, but he's a rum cove. Something deeply untrustworthy about him. I don't like his denomination either. It's like those mind-cure people dabbling in Indian religion at your hotel.'

'Ah yes. The Church of Mental Magnetism,' said Shaw grandly.

'Is that what they call themselves?' replied Dewynter with another sigh. 'God help us. It's all part of the same problem. It's a reaction to secular modernity, a result of centuries of anaemic low-church Protestantism bleeding out ritual and ceremony and mystery from people's lives. They have become like hungry men craving sweets instead of the wholesome nourishment of the true church.'

Dewynter must have noticed the look on Shaw's face, as he stopped talking for a moment.

'Forgive me, I'm ranting. I expect you're going to say if I feel that strongly I should go over to Rome and be done with it.'

'I think we ought to be careful in our judgements of others,' replied Shaw. 'Especially when we do not have all the facts to hand. And we ought not to be overly concerned about things such as Spiritualism or mind-cures, but rather to see them as a starting point on the road to Christ, a road on which we can help those who travel. They are searching for the truth, and we ought to light their way rather than condemn them for walking in darkness.'

'I say, Shaw, that's very good,' said Dewynter enthusiastically. 'Perhaps I'm being rather morbid and letting personal feelings get in the way of facts. I've always been a bit of a hot-head. After all, Mrs Cotterill did say that Rooksley called on them the next day somewhat apologetically. '

'Did Cotterill accept the apology?'

'No, he was out, apparently, but she told him...I say, I've just remembered something. Why on earth would I have forgotten it? She told him her husband would be rehearsing on the pier later that afternoon.'

An image flashed momentarily across Shaw's mind's eye, of a dark shadow moving quickly behind the frosted glass of the shelter on the pier. Before he could make sense of it, he suddenly heard a commotion from the garden. A woman, or perhaps a boy, was shouting, and Fraser began to yelp. Moments later, Mrs Shaw rushed into the study.

'Come quickly,' she said calmly but urgently. 'There's been a terrible accident.'

Rooksley slammed the worm-eaten door of the chapel behind him and leant against it while he regained his breath. A strange sense of exhilaration and fear was coursing through his veins. Exhilaration, that he had got rid of Prior so easily, and fear that he had been found out.

He was sure that nobody had seen him walking briskly back along the coast road from the cliff's edge to the chapel, but he was less certain that he had not been seen from the beach. After Prior had fallen over, he had gingerly looked over the edge of the cliff. Nobody could survive a fall like that, but he had to make sure Prior was not lying on some ledge or caught in foliage.

He saw nobody caught on the cliff-side and nobody floating in the sea, so in all probability, Prior had drowned. Then he saw, a hundred feet or so away on his right down on the beach, a small boy looking in his direction. The boy then dashed away along the rocks and disappeared from view.

Rooksley hesitated for a moment; could he catch the boy? No, it was hopeless; there was no way down the cliff edge where he was, and by the time he got to the beach, the tide would cut him off. Besides, it would be too risky— he might be seen. He cursed under his breath. He had no idea who the boy was, so would not be able to find him and intimidate him the way he had done with Prior.

There was nothing for it; he would have to disappear. Even now, the boy could have told an adult what had happened. He might even have recognised him. It was only a matter of time before the police arrived and started asking questions; then they would find out who he really was. And if anyone found that cylinder recording, he was done for.

He decided he would head to Southampton and then take the next available ship to some obscure corner of the Empire. A man could never really disappear in England or even on the Continent, but east of Suez, if he knew the language and the people as he did, he could vanish as effectively as any conjuring trick.

He hurried into his living quarters and took down a cardboard suitcase from the top of the rickety wardrobe in his bedroom. He began stuffing items into it; he had very little in the way of possessions apart from his collection of esoteric books. He sighed as he realised he would have to leave them. Then he selected a small, ancient leather-bound book; his only possession of any real financial worth.

Looking down at his clothes, he realised his trademark black suit and hat were too conspicuous. He undressed quickly, fumbling to remove his tie and collar, and then pulled his shirt over his head. He put on flannel trousers, a linen shirt and an ancient sports jacket, the outfit he wore on the occasions that he prowled incognito for low adventure in the back streets of Midchester. He folded the open collar of the shirt over the collar of the jacket, and placed a brown soft hat on his head.

He then rummaged through the pockets of his suit,

placing the little book and the note from Blair along with it in the pocket of his sports jacket. He quickly re-read the note; there was no way he could risk meeting Blair in a public house tonight; the man would have to be warned off by some other method. Telephoning? No, too risky to stand at a public kiosk while some hotel porter tried to find Blair, who might be out or half-cut and passed out in his room. Instead, he hastily scribbled a note, put it into an envelope and put it in his pocket; he would deliver it by hand to the hotel letterbox under cover of darkness.

He then looked into his wallet and frowned. Only three pounds, all the money he had in the world— the church collection was at the Treasurer's home by now, so he would not be able to get hold of that without the man becoming suspicious.

As he looked in the mirror, holding his suitcase, he decided he could pass for a holidaymaker. That was good, he thought. He would walk into town and find a hotel room for the night under a false name. He only needed one night and one morning to finish his business in Eastburgh.

After a somewhat stodgy and unappetising lunch in the gloomy dining room of the Seaview Guest House, Chief Inspector Ludd lay on one of the twin beds in his room while his wife sat on the other, writing dozens of postcards to various friends and relations. She said it was too hot to go out and he was inclined to agree; he lay in his shirtsleeves with his collar loosened and drifted in and out of sleep, thankful that he had been able to stretch to a proper hotel and not some bed and breakfast place run by an old dragon who insisted everyone left the rooms during the day.

It had been a tiring morning; Ludd had risen early and, while his wife had attended the little Methodist church near the seafront, he had wandered the streets and coastal paths of Eastburgh, trying to find evidence, however slim, that pointed to the possible location of Prior. The man seemed to have disappeared into thin air, and that worried him. The local police had assigned two constables to help him, and although they were decent enough lads, he thought, they did not really have the necessary experience and so he preferred to ask around himself.

Sunday morning was not a good time for that sort of detective work, he reflected; most people were either in church or in bed, and he had come up with nothing. It was infernally hot and so he had decided to have a lie-down before going out again. What was it the continentals called it? A *fiesta*? Yes, he would have a little *fiesta*, and then be on his way when the noonday sun had eased off a bit.

He felt himself drifting off to sleep, but then awoke with a start as somebody knocked on the door. He heard his wife open it.

'Is Mr Ludd in there?' enquired a voice. He recognised it as that of the sour-faced, shingle-haired woman who ran the front desk of the little hotel. He had not registered with his official title as she looked, he thought, like a right nosey parker. Ludd got up and straightened his collar.

'Yes?' he enquired, sleepily.

'Somebody on the telephone. I don't normally take messages but he says it's important.'

'Did you take the number?' asked Ludd, now fully awake.

'Certainly not,' said the woman. 'The telephone is not for the use of guests, well, not for outgoing calls anyway. The party is still on the line.'

'Righto,' sighed Ludd, as he shrugged on his jacket.

A few minutes later he stood in the cramped office behind the reception desk as the manageress hovered around, presumably hoping to find out what was going on. Ludd did his best to conceal the real nature of the conversation, which was with the police doctor who had gone in to the mortuary out of hours in order to expedite the post-mortem examination of Cotterill.

'I see, thank you,' said Ludd. 'That's most informative. Send the report to me care of the Seaview Guest House, please.'

He replaced the receiver, and rubbed his chin thoughtfully. His musings were interrupted by the manageress, who deftly wiped a duster over the telephone and adjusted its position on the desk.

'You may like to know for future information that this is not a hotel for commercial travellers,' she sniffed.

'Good,' said Ludd bluntly, 'because I'm not one. Thanks for letting me know about the call.'

He turned to go, but then the telephone rang again. Ludd picked up the receiver.

'Yes?' he asked brusquely.

'What are you doing?' asked the manageress. 'Guests are not permitted to answer the…'

She was not able to complete her sentence, as Ludd had already started speaking rapidly into the instrument in question. This time he did not bother to conceal any potential gossip from the eavesdropping manageress.

'Yes, this is he. Where? Is he dead? No body found?

Then how do you know…oh, I see. Can you get a car round? What do you mean, washing it? Well tell him to rinse it off! Good. Meet me outside as soon as you can.'

Ludd hurried out of the office and went to fetch his hat, leaving the manageress staring open-mouthed after him.

Shaw and Dewynter stood in the vicarage study. They were still slightly out of breath after having run down to the cliff's edge following Billy's gabbled account of Prior's fall. Dewynter had then telephoned to the police and the lifeboat station, and the two men now stood looking at Billy, who appeared very small in the priest's big leather armchair.

He had stopped crying now, and had been given Fraser to hold while they waited for the police to arrive. Mrs Shaw sat on the arm of the chair, keeping a watchful maternal eye over the boy.

The housekeeper had been despatched to find Billy's mother, but it appeared she was not at home; the woman was now scouring the town attempting to find her. Billy sniffed and took a sip of the large glass of lemonade that had been given to him; Mrs Shaw smoothed his hair away from his eyes and tried to console him.

'Did the police say how long they would be, Mr Dewynter?' asked Mrs Shaw.

'They should be here very soon,' said Dewynter.

'Assuming of course they were able to come here by motor car. I believe the local station only has one such vehicle.'

'They ought to hurry,' said Mrs Shaw. 'There may still be a chance…'

'My dear, we have done all we can for the moment,' said Shaw. 'Mr Dewynter and myself have checked the cliff edge and we can see nothing. The lifeboat station has been alerted and said they will also inform the coastguard They…'

Shaw's voice was cut off by the sound of an explosion, like gunfire, in the distance.

'What on earth…?' said Shaw.

'That's the maroon going up,' said Dewynter. 'At the lifeboat station. They use it to signal the men to attend in an emergency.'

'Do you…do you think they'll find him, farver?' asked Billy, who clung to Fraser protectively. The dog seemed to sense the child's nervousness, and his little pink tongue darted across the boy's hand in a calming gesture.

'They will do their very best, Billy,' replied Dewynter. 'All we can do is pray. In fact, as we wait for the police, perhaps…'

Dewynter was interrupted by the crunch of tyres on gravel; Shaw glimpsed a dark Morris Eight saloon car pass the study window and heard it come to a halt outside the front door.

Dewynter went to open the front door and the already crowded study was filled to capacity as Ludd, accompanied by two local uniformed police constables, entered the small room. Ludd introduced himself to Dewynter and then his eyebrows raised in surprise as he saw the other occupants of the room.

'Mr Shaw, Mrs Shaw,' said Ludd with a brief nod. 'Trouble seems to follow you around, if you don't mind my saying so. May I ask what you are doing here?'

'They came as my luncheon guests, Chief Inspector,' said Dewynter. 'I telephoned to the lifeboat station. Is there anything more we can do?'

'We saw the maroon go up just as we came up the road,' said Ludd. 'You did well, Mr Dewynter. We'll handle it from now on. Perhaps I could speak to the boy? I got the jist of it on the telephone but I need to know a few more facts.'

Ludd loomed over Billy. He pushed his hat back slightly on his forehead, and spoke sternly. 'Now sonny, what was it you saw?'

Billy was silent, and he took his hands from Fraser and gripped the sides of the armchair.

'Come on lad, haven't you got a tongue in your head?'

Mrs Shaw patted Billy on the shoulder. 'Come along Billy, tell the Chief Inspector what happened.'

'Mum says I'm not to talk to coppers,' said Billy.

One of the uniformed constables stepped forward from his place by the door. 'Think he's one of them Plotlanders, sir,' he said in a broad Suffolk accent.

'Plotlanders?' asked Ludd.

'London types, most of them,' replied the constable. 'Come up here on holiday or to live in shacks and be a general nuisance.'

'I see,' said Ludd. 'Come on now lad. Out with it. What was it you saw?'

Billy maintained a stony silence. Shaw thought for a moment and then decided to speak to him.

'Billy, are you in the Boy Scouts? Or the Wolf Cubs, perhaps?'

Billy seemed surprised at the question. 'Well, I used to be, back in London. Mum says she can't afford it now. What's that got to do with anyfink?'

'Do you remember the Scout Promise?'

'Course I do,' said Billy. He stood up and raised his right hand in a three-fingered salute, and began speaking mechanically.

'On my honour I promise I will do my duty to God and to the King I will do my best to help others whatever it costs me I know the Scout Law and will obey it.'

He then sat back down and glowered at Ludd.

'Very good, Billy,' said Shaw. 'Part of that promise refers to your duty to the King. That also extends to doing your duty by those placed in authority under His Majesty, such as the police.'

'Well…I suppose so,' said Billy. He looked up at Ludd. 'What is it you want to know, Chief?'

'Chief Inspector,' corrected Ludd. 'Just tell me what you saw, lad.'

'I was on the beach— Norf Beach— about to climb up the cliff path, when I heard a shout, or a scream, from a bit farther up the beach. Up near where them wooden fings is.'

'Wooden…things?' asked Ludd.

'He means the Wooden Witness,' said Dewynter. 'An ancient timber circle in the sands, of unknown origin.'

'I see,' said Ludd, 'and what happened then?'

'I looked up,' said Billy, 'and then…I saw…'

'Come on Billy, be brave,' said Mrs Shaw, patting the boy on the shoulder.

Billy sniffed. 'I saw Les falling off the cliff. He fell into the water and then…he never come up and I never saw him again.'

'Let me just be sure,' said Ludd. 'By "Les", you mean Leslie Prior?'

'S'right,' sniffed Billy.

'Thank you son,' said Ludd. 'Just one thing though.

How did you know it was Prior?'

'By his ginger 'air, of course,' said Billy. 'Everyone knows that carrot top.'

'No, I mean, how do you know him? To recognise him, I mean?' asked Ludd.

Billy appeared confused, and this must have been noticed by Dewynter, who proffered an explanation.

'Billy is an altar server and Prior was…is…our organist. They know each other from church.'

'Hmm,' said Ludd. Shaw guessed the man had remembered that Prior was a little 'unusual' and that this might explain his friendship with a boy half his age.

'All right then, son,' said Ludd. 'Another thing. What were you doing on the beach down there, on your own? Where were you going?'

'Ain't a crime to go on the beach, is it?' said Billy.

'Billy,' said Dewynter, as he lit another cigarette, 'the Chief Inspector is only trying to find out what happened to Leslie. You are not being blamed for anything.'

'Well…all right then,' said Billy. 'I was going to see Les.'

'You knew where he was?' said Ludd angrily. 'Why didn't you….'

'I imagine he did not know that Prior was missing,' said Dewynter quickly. 'I only made the appeal for information about his whereabouts in church this morning, and I assume Billy must have gone looking for him immediately afterwards.'

'Is that right, son?' asked Ludd. 'The truth, now.'

'I…I knew he was hiding out,' replied the boy, nervously. 'He was in our Gang Hut on the downs. He stayed the night there. I was bringing food for him.'

'Why did you not tell anyone about this earlier, Billy?' asked Shaw. 'Was Mr Prior in some sort of trouble?'

Billy swallowed and looked at the three men in front of

him, then the two uniformed constables by the door, and then at Mrs Shaw, who patted him on his shoulder.

'Well, was he, Billy?' asked Mrs Shaw, gently.

'I knew he was wanted by the police,' said Billy. 'It was all round the town. But I couldn't tell anyone because…'

Billy's voice faded away. Ludd looked at the child impatiently. 'Because what?' snapped the Chief Inspector.

'Because…Les reckoned there was a curse on him.'

There was a yelp and Shaw noticed that Billy was squeezing Fraser's back rhythmically with his little fists. The dog yelped again and jumped off Billy's lap, settling down by his feet instead.

'Now come Billy,' said Dewynter. 'You remember that in the Lord's Prayer we ask to be delivered from evil, don't you?'

'Yeah, I suppose so,' said Billy, looking confused.

'Well then,' replied Dewynter, 'do you really think that if we pray— earnestly pray— for such deliverance, that it will not be granted us?'

'Suppose not,' said Billy.

'Who was it who "cursed" him?' asked Shaw. He noticed that Ludd had a puzzled frown on his face as he watched Billy's reactions. The boy was silent for a moment before he replied.

'Said he…said he couldn't tell me who it was. But that it was the bloke who done for the geezer on the pier. Said he'd use dark forces on Les if he ever told what he saw.'

'Have you any idea who it was?' asked Ludd.

Billy paused. 'There's something I ain't told you.'

'Come on son,' urged Ludd, 'We're trying to help you. And your pal, if he's still al…look, just tell us everything you know.'

'After I saw Les fall,' sniffed Billy, 'I looked up and saw someone at the top of the cliff. I reckon he pushed him.'

Mrs Shaw clutched her hand to her mouth in horror.

'Why didn't you say this before?' urged Ludd.

'Can't you see the boy is terrified?' snapped Dewynter. He knelt in front of Billy so that their heads were level.

'Who was it, Billy?' he asked gently.

'Will I…will I get…cursed if I tell?' asked the boy.

'Not a bit of it,' said Dewynter. 'Look here. I shall say something to make sure nothing can harm you. Are you ready? Close your eyes.'

Billy nodded and squeezed his eyes shut.

Dewynter made the sign of the cross as he spoke: 'May the blessing of God Almighty, the Father, the Son, and the Holy Ghost be with you and remain with you always. Amen.'

Shaw echoed the final word and noticed Ludd awkwardly half-raise his bowler hat.

'Now, you're protected,' said Dewynter with a smile. 'Who was it you saw on the cliff?'

'It was…I don't know his real name, but we calls him Doctor Death.'

'I knew it,' said Dewynter eagerly, snapping his fingers. 'You mean Mr Rooksley, from the Spiritualist chapel, don't you?'

'That's right,' said Billy, nodding.

'Rooksley…'mused Ludd. 'Now why do I know that name?' He leafed through his notebook. 'Ah yes,' he continued. 'He's the minister who visited Mrs Cotterill the day her husband was found dead. She said….'

Here Ludd snapped his notebook shut. 'I'm getting sloppy,' he exclaimed. 'She said he was looking for her husband and she told him he'd be on the pier later that afternoon. I was going to question him but I forgot all about it.'

'Why did Rooksley threaten Leslie, Billy?' asked

Dewynter.

'If you don't mind sir, I'll take over from here,' said Ludd as he turned to Billy. 'Come on now lad. The parson's made you safe from any "curses", so what did Rooksley have against your pal?'

'Les said he was the one what done for that bloke on the pier,' blurted Billy. 'He saw him do it and ran off and now the coppers is pinning the blame on Les.'

'Now wait a minute son,' said Ludd. 'Nobody's said that. What you've told us was very brave and helpful.'

'He won't…come after me, will he?' asked Billy. 'Doctor Death, I mean. I know farver give me a blessing against curses and that, but that might not work on a gun or a knife.'

'Hmm,' said Ludd. 'To be on the safe side I'll have a policeman stand outside your house.'

'Muvver won't like that,' said Billy.

'Well she'll have to lump it, won't she?' said Ludd with a smile. 'Perhaps Mr Dewynter will let you wait here until your mother arrives. You'll be safe here.'

'Of course,' said Dewynter. 'There's something else, Chief Inspector, if I may,' said Dewynter, nervously lighting another cigarette and thrusting his matchbox into the pocket of his cassock. 'Rooksley had some sort of *contre-temps* with Mr Cotterill at the Spiritualist chapel on Friday night.'

'Contre…what?' asked Ludd.

'An argument, in the middle of a seance, apparently,' said Dewynter. 'Cotterill accused him flat out of being a charlatan, and I don't blame him.'

'Might have some bearing,' said Ludd. 'Where does he live, this Rooksley?'

'Over at the chapel, up the road there,' replied Dewynter. 'You can see it from the window.' He pointed out of the open casement. Ludd squinted into the bright afternoon. 'That little tin tabernacle, eh? Right, you,'— he indicated the larger of the two constables by the door— 'come along with me to see if we can find this Rooksley character, and you'— here he pointed to the other policeman— 'take the car down to the front and find out what's happening with the lifeboat. I'll be down the station later.'

Ludd made his way out of the study, and turned to Shaw as he passed him.

'Oh, and it might interest you to know, Mr Shaw, that I spoke on the telephone earlier to the police doctor who examined Cotterill's body. He's certain the man died a natural death.'

'Natural?' asked Shaw incredulously.

'Yes,' replied Shaw. 'Not a mark on him. Died of a heart attack. According to his widow he was already taking pills for a weak heart. Doc thinks he could have dropped dead at any time.'

'But what of the disordered furniture on the stage?' asked Shaw. 'Surely there was a struggle?'

'Ever seen a man have a heart attack?' asked Ludd. 'I have. It isn't pleasant. Cotterill most likely kicked and flailed about, pulled the curtain down and knocked the chairs over himself. I'm telling you all this because you can put your mind at rest about it being a murder. I'll leave it to the Coroner to give his verdict, but for now this Prior business is more important.'

'Thank you for letting me know, Chief Inspector,' said Shaw with a frown, as Ludd exited the room.

'Will Les be alright?' called Billy.

Ludd turned and looked back into the room. 'We'll see what the lifeboatmen say once they've dragged the area,' he said. 'It'll be a blooming miracle if anyone survived a fall from…,' He paused and a look of embarrassment crossed his face as he noticed Billy had burst into tears.

'Then let us pray earnestly for just such a miracle, Chief Inspector,' said Shaw quietly.

A few moments later Ludd and the uniformed constable arrived at the tin chapel; Ludd banged on the main doors which shook slightly, but no answer came. 'Get round the back,' he whispered to the constable, who picked his way through the weedy forecourt to the side door.

'This one's open, sir,' he said, pushing the door inwards with a creak of hinges. He stepped in cautiously, and Ludd followed. After a brief search of the small living quarters, Ludd pushed his hat on the back of his head.

'Looks like he's cleared out,' said the constable.

'How do you know that?' asked Ludd.

'Clothes all over the place, stuff scattered about. Door ain't locked, meaning he probably left in a hurry and forgot.'

'Good lad,' said Ludd. 'You've got the makings of a detective.'

'Think so, sir?' asked the constable, with a grin.

'Possibly, but before you get too pleased with yourself, you can go and take that boy home from the vicarage and keep an eye on his house. The kiddie's scared stiff.'

'What'll you do, sir? Knocking off home?'

'Chance would be a fine thing. I'll have a rummage around in here and find out the names of his, what do you call them, church wardens and so on. See if I can get an idea of where he might go. Then I'll walk back into town in this blasted heat,'— here Ludd mopped his brow and pushed his handkerchief back into his top pocket with an expression of distaste— 'and start combing the place for Rooksley. I'll also have to tell that poor lad's parents their missing son's probably at the bottom of the North Sea.'

Ludd looked out towards the sea from the grimy window of Rooksley's living quarters, and just before it disappeared around the corner towards North Beach, he saw the crew on the town's little motorised lifeboat hurl a dragnet into the surging, sparkling waters at the cliff's foot.

Chapter Seven

Once Billy's mother had been found, and she had collected her son (with much scolding for involving her in a police enquiry), Mr and Mrs Shaw set off back to their hotel. Twenty minutes later they arrived on the gravel driveway. Fraser trailed behind them, his tongue lolling and his little legs tired from the long walk from the downs.

Seated cross-legged on the grass a short distance away from the terrace were the Guru and Miss Sloan. They were both motionless under the shade of a pine tree, staring out to sea.

'Oh dear, there are those two again,' said Mrs Shaw. 'I do hope they don't notice us. I'm not really in the mood for polite conversation about the power of positive thought, not after today's events.'

'I am rather tired myself, dear,' said Shaw. 'Perhaps we might spend some time in rest before tea.'

'Peculiar couple,' whispered Mrs Shaw. 'She's clearly besotted with him, but he seems in a world of his own.'

Shaw was always surprised by his wife's ability to discern relationships between people that to him remained undetected.

'I had not noticed,' said Shaw. 'I assumed the Guru was dedicated to the spiritual life, as was Miss Sloan.'

'Oh Lucian,' chided Mrs Shaw. 'You're so innocent

sometimes. We females have an eye for these things, you know. Unrequited love hangs around a woman like an ill-fitting garment, and Miss Sloan is no exception.'

Before he could reply, Shaw almost collided with a figure hurriedly exiting the building. He wore a leather helmet with goggles and had a yellow scarf tied around his face above canvas overalls.

'Padre!' exclaimed the man. Shaw's heart sank slightly as he realised it was Major Blair.

'Sorry to prang you, but in a bit of a hurry,' said Blair. 'How do, Mrs, erm, Padre.' He nodded in the direction of Mrs Shaw.

'That is quite all right,' said Shaw, and stepped aside to let Blair pass.

'Come to think of it Padre, glad I bumped into you,' said Blair. 'Could do with a bit of help.'

Shaw wondered if he was going to be touched for money. 'What assistance do you require?' he asked guardedly.

'Thought you might like to go up in the kite. Just got word from the lifeboat station that some poor blighter's fallen off the cliffs at North Beach and they can't find a trace. They think he might have got washed out to sea and asked if I'd have a look. Done it before once or twice as I'm the only flyer for miles around here. Another pair of eyes would be useful, you can use the binos. Can't hold them while I've got my hands on the stick.'

He thrust a pair of heavy military binoculars into Shaw's hands. Shaw was not overly keen on going up in an aeroplane, especially one piloted by Blair. It was a blessing, at least, that the man seemed to be sober.

'Of course,' said Shaw quickly. 'I shall be happy to help.'

'Good man,' said Blair. 'At least they notified me before opening time, eh, what? By the way I won't charge you the usual five bob the tourists pay, so don't worry about that!'

'Are you sure about this, Lucian?' asked Mrs Shaw, with a worried frown.

'Yes,' said Shaw firmly. 'I feel duty bound to help. There is still a chance he may be alive.'

Shaw kissed his wife, patted Fraser, and set off with Blair in his little sports car in a cloud of dust and exhaust fumes.

A few minutes later they had covered the short distance to the little airfield on the downs beyond the hotel. It consisted of a long strip of mown grass, a ramshackle shed and some oil drums and other mechanical detritus scattered around; a windsock hung from a crooked pole, swaying listlessly in the tepid breeze. Blair brought the car to a halt and jumped out.

'Welcome to Blairways,' he said. 'My little pride and joy's kept in there.' He indicated the shed. 'Got a chap helps me out with it sometimes but he's off on Sundays, matter of fact he's off most of the time down at the Red Lion, so we'll have to bring the old bus out ourselves.'

Blair pulled open the shed doors. Shaw, still slightly queasy, felt even more queasy when he saw what they were about to fly in. It was a small red two-seater bi-plane, somewhat rusty, with various patches and repairs to the bodywork in evidence.

'She's a Sop,' said Blair. Seeing the look of confusion on Shaw's face, he continued. 'Sopwith Camel. Ex Royal Air Force. Two-seater trainer. Got her cheap. Runs well, and the good thing is she's light and manoeuvrable. Come on, give me a hand getting her out.'

'Is it not heavy?' enquired Shaw, as Blair propped open the shed doors.

'Not a bit,' said Blair. 'A girl could push this thing out. Which is handy because old Nobby— that's my

119

mechanic— is half cut most of the time and can barely push the top off a beer bottle.'

Blair laughed uproariously, which did little to instil confidence in Shaw. Once they had pushed the surprisingly light aeroplane out onto the grass, Blair fished out a piece of apparatus from inside the rear cockpit and handed it to Shaw. It was a leather flying helmet with goggles, but with additions that looked like the sort of thing a telephonist would wear; two earphones, and a small horn-shaped tube on the side. A cable led from the device into the cockpit.

'Now this,' said Blair proudly, 'is what makes Blairways unique. Other flyers just take you up in their plane and you can't hear a bally thing because of the noise of the engine. But this is a sort of telephone between the two of us. Soundproofed earphones too, so you don't hear too much engine noise. It means we can talk to each other and hear each other all the time, and I can point out all the bally beauty spots, and so on. The holidaymakers love it, they say it's like listening to the wireless. Runs off a wet cell battery. Clever eh? Chap called Prior fitted it for me. Queer fish but devilish good at electrical stuff.'

Shaw looked aghast at Blair. 'You mean, Leslie Prior?' he said.

'Think so,' replied Blair. 'Works in that shop in the high street. Only got him up here to mend the wireless in the shed, but we got chatting and he came up with this little idea. I ought to patent it, really.'

'But my dear man, it is Prior we are looking for!' said Shaw. 'He fell from the cliffs this afternoon.'

'Good God,' exclaimed Blair. 'Poor bas…ket. They didn't mention a name. Let's get a move on then. There's still a chance he might be alive.'

Blair helped Shaw into the cockpit and placed the

120

headphone set on him, and strapped a belt down over Shaw's waist.

'Whatever you do don't release that,' said Blair with a grin. 'Unless you want to end up with King Neptune when we make a low pass.'

He then jumped down from the wing and adjusted a piece of equipment in the forward cockpit.

'Here's another little unique thing. Normally a plane like this really needs to be started by two people but I've adapted it so that only one person is required. Sort of like putting a brick on the accelerator pedal of a motor car. Then I pull these ropes down here to pull the chocks away. That's the little things holding the wheels in place. Saves having to get Nobby up here to help. Chap I worked with out in India came up with the idea. I ought to patent this as well!'

Blair spun the large, wooden propeller at the front of the plane and there was a staccato roar which partly penetrated the earmuffs Shaw was wearing; his throat was filled momentarily with an acrid taste of petrol as a heavy cloud of exhaust fumes burst from the engine. Blair clambered into the cockpit and the plane began bumping and swaying over the grass.

Shaw uttered a brief prayer for protection, and held on grimly to the binoculars in his hand. The plane gathered pace and, just as he thought he would be shaken from his seat entirely, there was suddenly a feeling of weightlessness, and Shaw realised they had left the ground.

Within a few moments they ascended into a dazzling, roaring, dizzying world, as if they were suspended in a giant glass globe with no fixed horizon. Shaw looked down to see tiny fields and houses below him, like a model village, and specks of boats on the flat, blue plain of the sea;

above him was the endless pale blue of the sky. He felt a sense of transcendence almost akin to that which he had once or twice felt at the elevation of the Host. A sense of oneness with everything, of the tantalising nearness of the secret at the heart of all secrets. He heard Blair's voice crackle through the headphones.

'Quite a sight eh, Padre?'

'Indeed,' replied Shaw.

Then he suddenly remembered the purpose of their mission, and chided himself for his transcendental musings. He must, he thought, have spent too much time in conversation with the Mental Magnetists at the hotel.

'May we go lower?' asked Shaw. 'It is hard to discern anything on the water at this height.'

'Right-o,' crackled Blair's voice, and Shaw felt his stomach lurch as the plane plunged downwards. He struggled to remove the goggles on his helmet, and raised the binoculars to his eyes. He could see the motor-lifeboat bobbing along the shoreline and, further off, two teams of pilot-gig rowers straining at their oars against the current, as their coxswains peered over the sides of their boats.

'May we go further out?' asked Shaw. 'This section is already being searched. The swell I believe heads north, or at least it seemed so as I bathed yesterday. If Prior is being carried on the tide, he will be heading in that direction.'

'Admire your reasoning, Padre,' said Blair, and the plane tilted northwards, heading further out to sea. 'But hate to break it to you, the poor blighter doesn't stand a hope in, erm, Hades. They say he fell off the cliffs at North Beach. Not much chance of surviving that.'

'But there *is* still a chance,' said Shaw. 'We must do all we can.'

'Of course, of course,' replied Blair. 'Not much juice left though. Used most of it taking Miss Sloan out this morning.

We can do another circle round by North Beach then we'll have to head for home.'

As they flew over North Beach Shaw realised just how cut off from view it was; it was in a sort of natural bowl, with cliffs all around, and no houses nearby; the nearest buildings were what he assumed were the Plotlands holiday cabins about half a mile away. At high tide, when Prior was pushed, there would have been nobody on the beach; it was only by some miracle that Billy had been there to see it and fetch help. Shaw prayed that that would not be today's only miracle.

As the plane looped round, Shaw scanned the beach with the binoculars, straining his eyes for a speck of something— anything— that might resemble a floating body. He noticed that the tide had now gone some way out, and had revealed, at the foot of the cliffs, a strange circle of dark shapes with a central shadow, like a miniature Stonehenge.

He suddenly realised what it was; he had read about it in the little town guide he had found in the hotel. It was the Wooden Witness; the ancient timber circle which had been preserved in the sands over the centuries and which had only begun to reappear about 40 years previously. He looked more closely; the circle had a sinister aspect, complementing the darkness on the horizon above it, which he realised was Middlesham Forest. As the angle of the plane increased, he noticed the height of the cliffs above the timber circle and regretfully was inclined to agree with Blair about the slim chances of Prior's survival.

As the afternoon shadows lengthened, Rooksley peered out from behind the chintzy net curtains of his room in the little hotel near Eastburgh harbour that he had booked for the night, posing as a rambler breaking his journey on the way to Norfolk. He had thought for a while what name he should register under. Smith or Brown was too obvious, but it ought not to be anything too noticeable. In the end he decided on something with a respectable, religious feel, and chose 'Christie', with 'Reginald' as his first name in remembrance of the dear departed Reginald Cotterill.

He could just about see the beach from the little dormer window, and had noticed the town lifeboat and some rowing boats plying up and down; that was a good sign because as long as they were there it meant they had not found Prior. A dash out of the town, he decided, was too risky; if the police were checking the roads and the railway station he might get noticed; they would not be expecting him to stay in the town. There was still a chance, albeit a slim one, that the boy he had seen from the cliff top had not actually seen him. Things could be much worse, he decided, and lay back down on the bed to wait until darkness fell.

Shaw and Blair stepped out of the little sports car on the gravel drive of the Excelsior Hotel, where it was whisked away by a porter to a garage. The two men entered the lobby, where stood a little group consisting of Mr and Mrs Murray, the Guru, and Miss Sloan.

'Oh Lord,' whispered Blair, *sotto voce*. 'Not that lot. Can't face those types with a thirst. Thanks for helping out, Padre, I'm off for a quick wash and brush up before the evening's drinking begins. Got a meeting set up with an old pal about a nice little bit of business. Be seeing you!'

He gave a mock salute and bounded up the stairs before he was noticed by the others. Shaw would have liked to have done the same, but he was too late. Murray noticed him and strode up to him.

'Say, Reverend,' said Murray, clamping a large hand onto Shaw's shoulder, from which he recoiled slightly. The American wore a double breasted white Palm Beach suit in a wide cut, with a gaudy tie which made him look even broader than usual. 'I just heard you've been out looking for the fellow who fell off the cliffs,' he said. 'Isn't it just awful?'

'We heard the poor man was quite dashed to pieces on the rocks,' added Mrs Murray. She wore a flowing paisley gown, bedecked with jewellery, and a strange turban hat that made Shaw think of a fortune teller at a church fête.

'But we've been sending out positive thought energy,' she added. '"Thoughts are things", as you know, Reverend. We've been doing so ever since we heard the news down on the boardwalk. Has he been found yet?'

'No body has been found,' said Shaw gravely. 'There is still hope, but I regret it is fading. Major Blair and I called in at the lifeboat station on the way here; the search will be called off when the light fails.'

'That's just too bad,' said Murray, shaking his head. 'Well, to lighten the mood a little, here's some good news. Guru, why don't you tell the Reverend.'

The Guru smiled inscrutably. 'Please, Mr Murray. I am a humble man. The achievement is yours. Be pleased to tell Mr Shaw yourself.'

'Well, all right then,' beamed Murray. He waved a small piece of official looking paper in his hand. 'This here is a cable direct from St Louis Missouri, from the elders of the First Church of Mental Magnetism. On my recommendation they have agreed to fully fund the Guru for a six month lecture tour of the United States.'

'Didn't I just know it,' gushed Mrs Murray, turning to the Guru and Miss Sloan with a rattle of artistic jewellery. 'I told you the Mental Magnetists would sign you up, Guruji, before those Theosophists got to you. And you too of course, Shrutakirti.'

The Guru and Miss Sloan merely nodded; displays of emotion, thought Shaw, seemed somewhat alien to them.

'Well I guess we'd all like to freshen up a little before dinner,' said Mr Murray. 'And I've got to send a cable to our press agency to start spreading the good news. What say we meet up again in half an hour for the second dinner service? Will you and Mrs Shaw join us again, Reverend?'

'I will consult with Mrs Shaw,' said the clergyman. 'We have both had a rather trying day and she may wish to retire early.'

'By all means' said Mr Murray. 'Guru, Shrutakirti, we'll see you down here at 7.30, and I'll be ordering champagne to celebrate— for those that drink it, of course!'

The Murrays disappeared upstairs, chattering with excitement as they went. Miss Sloan turned to the Guru.

'Will you excuse me, Guruji? I ought to practice my evening meditation before dinner.'

'Of course, Shrutakirti,' said the Guru with a bow. Shaw, remembering what his wife had mentioned earlier about Miss Sloan, thought he noticed a fleeting glance of longing in the woman's eyes as she spoke, but it was gone when she turned and nodded to him.

'Mr Shaw,' she said, and left the room silently save for a rustle of her white sari. Shaw himself turned to go but felt the Guru's restraining hand on his arm.

'Forgive me, Mr Shaw. But might I have a few words with you, in private?'

'Certainly,' said Shaw, after a pause. 'I would first however like to see my wife. She was rather worried about my going up in an aeroplane.'

'Of course, of course,' said the Guru apologetically. 'You must go to her. Perhaps we may walk in the gardens in a few minutes' time?'

Shaw, trying hard to conceal his curiosity, nodded. 'Twenty minutes,' he said, and began a slow climb up the grand staircase to his room.

Twenty-two minutes later, the two men strolled in the gardens of the Excelsior Hotel. Despite the difference in their garb, the one in linen jacket and panama hat, puffing on a pipe, and the other in orange robes and sandals, there was nonetheless a strange congruity in their appearance, echoing the centuries-old relationship between England and India.

'You will forgive me acting in a somewhat mysterious manner, Mr Shaw,' said the Guru slowly, once they had reached the far corner of the garden, where the lengthening shadows under a row of pine trees afforded a brief respite from the still, oppressive heat of the early evening.

'But,' continued the Guru, 'I could not help but notice that yesterday, you must have overheard something of a private conversation between myself and Miss Sloan.'

'Well, I…' said Shaw, hesitating. He prodded his pipe with the little tool he carried for that purpose, as he thought of what to say next. What, indeed, could one say to someone one hardly knew, about a conversation involving blackmail letters?

'Please,' said the Guru, raising his hand. 'Do not feel the need to prevaricate out of politeness. You did, am I right, overhear something of our conversation in this very garden yesterday, did you not?'

Shaw felt the Guru's eyes boring into his own. There seemed to be no place for the veneer of English manners in this conversation.

'I did,' said Shaw. 'But as a matter of fact, with everything that has gone on, I had forgotten it.'

The Guru smiled. 'But you would have remembered in time, I think,' he said.

'Perhaps,' said Shaw. 'Nevertheless, I have no interest in prying into other people's personal matters.'

'That is most gratifying, Mr Shaw. Do you believe that everything is pre-ordained?'

'In some sense, yes,' replied Shaw. 'Why do you ask?'

'Because,' replied the Guru, 'I believe it was pre-ordained that you, and not another, should overhear what was said between myself and Miss Sloan.'

'Why, indeed?' asked Shaw in confusion.

'Because it forced my hand,' said the Guru. 'It made me confront a situation I had hoped to avoid. It has, I hope, given me an ally in the form of another man of God.'

'I don't follow,' said Shaw.

'Please, shall we sit?' said the Guru, gesturing to a wrought-iron bench which overlooked the sea, a hazy blue line in the distance which shimmered in the light of the sinking sun.

'I am not merely a drop in the ocean...I am also the ocean in a drop...' recited the Guru wistfully, as he gazed out to the horizon.

'That's rather good,' said Shaw. 'Omar Khayyam, perhaps? My knowledge of the eastern poets is very slight.'

'Jalal-al-Din Rumi,' corrected the Guru. 'A Mahometan, but we need not hold that against him,' he said with a little smile. 'I thought of it because out there, there is one poor soul who may be alive, or may have already returned to the original source of his being.'

'Prior,' said Shaw. 'Yes, we must pray for him. There is still hope.'

'I say this,' replied the Guru, 'because I wish to assure you that I realise my problems are as nothing compared with the great sorrow of the world, and of those chained to the wheel, living and re-living countless lives before their final release.'

Shaw remembered that the eastern religions believed life to be a cycle, a wheel ever-turning, from which *nirvana*, or oblivion, was the only salvation. Or, at least, that was his perception of them. He puffed on his pipe and attempted to lift the Guru's gloomy mood.

'Perhaps,' said Shaw. 'Though of course, in my tradition, we look to the salvation of the world from the One who has already visited us in human form and who has assured us of His return.'

'I did not mean for my melancholy to force you to defend the position of your church,' said the Guru. 'My point was that I am aware I have done wrong action, and require your advice, but if you feel that in the grand scheme of things, I am a minor nuisance, then please feel free to go.'

'You are not a nuisance,' said Shaw. 'In fact quite the

opposite. One does not meet many…gurus…in my profession. But do you not have any spiritual counsellor of your own to turn to?'

The Guru smiled. 'They are a very long way away, Mr Shaw, and out of the reach of letters or telegrams. The delegates on the conference— Mr and Mrs Murray, for example— are well-meaning people, but they are not deeply spiritual. They do not abide within a centuries-old religious tradition, as you do. They are wealthy, worldly people who collect religions and philosophies on their travels, as others collect statuary or paintings.'

'Miss Sloan, perhaps?' asked Shaw.

'Shrutakirti is already sufficiently involved in this matter, Mr Shaw,' replied the Guru sharply. 'I do not wish to concern her further.'

'I see,' said Shaw. 'Then I shall endeavour to assist in what way I can.' He knocked out his pipe on the side of the bench, tapped it against his hand and placed it in the top pocket of his jacket.

'Excellent,' said the Guru. 'In summary, Mr Shaw, I am being blackmailed.'

Prior opened his eyes and blinked; a bright light which seemed to come from everywhere bored into his brain and made him screw his eyes shut again; but the light seemed to be *inside* his head as well. He felt himself floating,

130

drifting backwards and forwards as if rocked in a cradle, and then all was still.

He tried to move his body but nothing happened; his limbs refused to answer the nervous impulses from his brain. Did he even have a body?, he thought wildly, but he could not move his head to look down. He opened his eyes again and all he could see was that blinding light, a low, orange radiance that blotted out everything else. He realised his spectacles were gone, and without them everything was a blur, like one of those modern paintings they showed in the new Pavilion on the front.

He squinted, and looked again; in the distance a figure was approaching. An old man, with a white beard, wearing a long white cloak and carrying a shepherd's crook was walking towards him, with the light radiating from behind his head like the art-deco sunburst designs one saw on the front of wireless sets or on garden gates.

The man stopped, and looked down quizzically at Prior.

'Are you all right, son?' he said.

Prior blinked. He saw other figures hurrying towards him, as if from nowhere. Were they angels? He tried to speak and his voice croaked; finally he got the words out, but to his amazement, there was no stammer.

'Am I...am I in heaven?' he asked.

'No son,' said the man, and bent down in front of him. Prior realised the white robe was a pale coloured mackintosh, and the shepherd's crook a walking stick.

'It's the next best place though,' chuckled the man. 'You're in Lowestoft.'

Chapter Eight

Blackmailed. The word seemed to hang in the air in front of the two men on the bench like a bad smell. Shaw turned to the Guru, folded his arms and sighed.

'I surmised something of the sort, from overhearing your conversation with Miss Sloan yesterday,' he said. 'This is, surely, a matter for the police.'

'I thought you would say that,' said the Guru, 'but we cannot involve them. I cannot risk this matter becoming public.'

'I have an acquaintance in the police force, a member of the detective branch, he…'

'Out of the question,' said the Guru, holding up his hand.

'Very well,' said Shaw. 'But whatever hold the blackmailers have over you, if you give in they may not release you,' said Shaw. 'Your best form of defence is to confess— to humbly confess— your fault, and thus heap coals upon your enemy's head. You will recall the case of the Duke of Wellington, blackmailed by a courtesan, who threatened to tell all in a book of memoirs?'

'Publish and be damned!' said the Guru, with a grim chuckle. 'But my dear Mr Shaw…Wellington could utter such a reply, apocryphal though it may be, as nobody minded a man of the world such as he having had a dalliance of that sort, and nobody cared for the reputation of the woman, as she had none to lose. My own case is somewhat different.'

'In what way?' asked Shaw, bluntly. '*Is* it a liaison of some sort?'

The Guru sighed. 'I wish to keep the matter out of the hands of the police— and the press— because it concerns the reputation of one very dear to me.'

This time it was Shaw's turn to sigh. Why, he thought, were human beings, himself included, so depressingly helpless against sin? Why were they so easily tempted by the hollow, gaudy show of the Prince of Lies?

'You are referring to Miss Sloan, I assume?' asked Shaw.

'That is correct,' said the Guru quietly. 'We had a…liaison. When she lived in India. Miss Sloan's parents hid her away, in disgrace. A child was born, in a nunnery in Delhi reserved for unfortunates, but he died shortly afterwards from a fever. It was kept entirely secret, of course. No Britisher of any standing in India could allow his daughter to become embroiled in a scandal such as that. Her parents agreed not to pursue me for damages on condition that I never attempted to see her again.'

'But you did see her again.'

'Yes, but it was she who sought out me, after she had returned to England and cut off all relations with her parents. I told her that I had changed, that no relationship other than that of pupil and teacher— a spiritual relationship— could exist between us. Attachment to material things, which includes people, only brings suffering, Mr Shaw. She has accepted that.'

Shaw wondered if that were really the case and wished that his wife could advise him on that point, but then again, he was glad she was not present to hear the sordid details of such an affair.

'I have many enemies, Mr Shaw,' said the Guru. 'Not

only among my own countrymen— men who do not wish India to be influenced by what they see as throwbacks to an era of superstition— but also amongst *your* countrymen, the rulers of India, who regard people like me as…what was it your Mr Churchill said of Gandhi in the newspapers? "…a seditious half-naked fakir presuming to parley on equal terms with the representative of a King-Emperor," or some such.

'Many would like to see me exposed and destroyed. That, I am willing to accept. But what I cannot accept is that they should in the process drag Miss Sloan— a noble soul who has great work to do in this world— down with me. Did you know that she studied medicine?'

'No. Is she a doctor?'

'She never qualified. After the scandal she was forced to leave her studies. But it is my hope that she will take them up again and that we will be able to establish an *ashram*— that is a kind of monastery— which will cater for both the spiritual and medical needs of India's poorest people.'

'Why should any scandal affect such a noble project?' asked Shaw, though he had an inkling why it might.

'My dear Mr Shaw. Money, of course. Such a venture requires a large amount of capital. The Mr and Mrs Murrays of this world would not open their purses so readily to those perceived to have low moral standards, I fear.'

Shaw thought for a moment. 'Could you admit your faults, but ask that Miss Sloan's name be kept out of it?'

'You are too trusting, Mr Shaw,' said the Guru, shaking his head. 'Her name would inevitably be revealed. Perhaps by the blackmailer himself, angered by the drawing of his fire.'

'I am at a loss as to how I can help you, Guru,' said Shaw. 'I am happy to listen, to counsel, in any way I am

134

able…but as to practical help, what use am I to you?'

'Mr Shaw,' said the Guru with a wistful smile, 'only a westerner would confuse action and passivity in such a way. A problem shared is a problem halved, as they say.'

'I wish I could be of more help,' said Shaw. 'Criminals of this type need to be stopped.'

'Perhaps…there is some way you could help,' said the Guru. 'It may be possible to resolve the matter peaceably.'

'Go on,' said Shaw.

'I think that if I were to approach the blackmailer, to reason with him, to convince him of the great work that we are undertaking for humanity, that his heart might be turned to repentance.'

'I admire your faith,' said Shaw. 'Personally…my experience of human nature in recent times has led me to be rather less trusting, but of course, there is always hope. How do you propose I may help in such a venture?'

The Guru turned towards Shaw, and placed his hands together in a praying gesture. 'The blackmailer has proposed in his letter that I leave the sum of fifty pounds in a pre-arranged location. He is then to collect it and after that, he will keep his silence.'

'We assume,' added Shaw.

'Indeed,' replied the Guru. 'My proposal is that I speak to this man, as I mentioned. But I do not think it advisable to approach him in the location he has chosen.'

'Where is it?' asked Shaw. His curiosity was increasing, and his initial desire to stay out of the matter had now faded.

'Have you heard of the place known as the Wooden Witness?' said the Guru.

'Yes,' replied Shaw. 'I read about it in the town guide. An ancient timber monument, half sunken in the sands on North Beach.'

'That is correct,' replied the Guru. 'I walked there myself earlier today to look at it. It is a place of…negative energy, I would say. An ideal choice for a moral bankrupt. But it has also been chosen, I believe, for practical reasons. The beach is rarely frequented, and is not overlooked by any houses nor roads, being set in a type of natural depression amid the cliffs. No policeman could stalk the blackmailer without being seen either.'

'I noticed that myself,' said Shaw. 'As for any negative connotations, the guidebook posits that it may have once been a place of Christian worship,' said Shaw, 'and therefore of…positive energy.'

'Perhaps, perhaps,' said the Guru. He looked out to sea again. 'At any rate, the blackmailer has asked…has demanded…that I leave the money in a package in a cleft in the timber of the main stump, or post…call it what you will. At dawn tomorrow.'

'And you wish me to go with you?'

'No Mr Shaw. There will be no money for this man. What I would like you to do is identify him.'

'Why me? Could you not go yourself?'

The Guru chuckled. 'In these robes? On a deserted beach, where anyone approaching may be seen for miles around? He would think it a trap.'

'Could you perhaps wear…less conspicuous garb?'

'Oh Mr Shaw, I am a poor *sadhu*; a wandering holy man. I possess no other clothing and it would be a betrayal of my calling to do such a thing even if I had the means. Besides,' he chuckled, 'a face as black as mine on an English beach would be conspicuous whatever I wore.'

'Very well,' said Shaw. 'What would you have me do?'

'I propose,' said the Guru eagerly, 'that you walk along the beach in the guise of a clergyman walking his dog—you have a dog, I think? Good. In the guise of one walking his dog early in the morning. No detective would dare dress in so obvious a disguise, so the villain will not suspect anything amiss. You pass the man at the Wooden Witness, you perhaps even bid him good morning and raise your hat as English gentlemen do. Do you have a camera, Mr Shaw?'

'No.'

'A pity. You might have taken his photograph, clandestinely. But your memory will be sufficient, I think. You must take full note of his description, which you will then give to me as soon as you can afterwards. I will do the rest.'

'But what good will a description do you?' asked Shaw in a puzzled voice. 'He could be anyone.'

'I believe the man will be one of two possible suspects, Mr Shaw. One of whom you have met, the other I think you have not.'

'May I know their names?'

'I would prefer that you did not at this stage, Mr Shaw. If my suspicions are wrong about his identity, I will have slandered his good name unnecessarily.'

'But why do you suspect it may be two different people?' asked Shaw.

'I have received two letters, written in different hands, and with a different style of expression. The first letter is the one which refers to tomorrow's date. The second makes no specific demand, but rather, veiled threats, and he says he will write again in future.'

'May I see the letters?'

'I would prefer it if you did not, Mr Shaw,' said the Guru, guardedly. 'They contain information which I would rather not have revealed to others.'

'I see,' said Shaw. 'Very well. But why can you not confront the man directly, on the beach? I shall be willing to accompany you if wish.'

'I do not think it would be the right place,' said the Guru. 'Who knows what desperate lengths the man may go to if thwarted in his nefarious scheme. He may be armed, for example.'

'In England?' exclaimed Shaw.

'I understand a pistol may be bought quite easily in England,' said the Guru. 'I think it better to confront him in a public place, that is to say, a populous place where a desperate act cannot so easily be carried out, as it might be on a lonely beach at dawn.'

'Yes, I see,' said Shaw. 'Well, I am willing to assist you. I see no harm in taking a stroll along North Beach at dawn. What time would that be, may I ask?'

'He has stated 4.00 a.m.,' said the Guru.

Shaw thought for a moment. 'But what if he is watching from a hiding place, and sees that nobody has placed the money in the tree-trunk earlier? Will he not simply escape without being seen?'

'You have an eye for detail, Mr Shaw!' exclaimed the Guru. 'A most admirable quality. I have also thought of this— or rather, it was Shrutakirti who thought of it— as she is my confidante in many matters. First light is just before 4.00 a.m, as I know myself from rising for early meditation. If the blackmailer has concealed himself in a vantage point, he cannot be sure that someone— such as myself— has not already visited the tree-stump under the cover of darkness to place the money therein, and will be thus obliged to check, and reveal himself.'

'Very well,' said Shaw. 'I shall endeavour to be there at the appointed time, and shall report any findings to you immediately afterwards. But I shall not indulge in any amateur detective work, Guru. Please do not expect me to confront the suspect, or follow him. I am not a policeman and I do not wish to be sued for harassment.'

The Guru laughed and took both Shaw's hands in his own. 'Of course, I do not expect such behaviour. You will be merely on a morning stroll, observing. I will do the rest. You cannot know how much this means to me, to us, Mr Shaw.'

The Guru looked to his left, beyond Shaw, and a smile crossed his face. 'Ah,' he said. 'Here is Shrutakirti.'

The pallid, white-clad Miss Sloan approached the bench almost like a ghost which had appeared out of nowhere; Shaw and the Guru stood up.

'Shrutakirti,' said the Guru, 'Mr Shaw has agreed to our plan.'

'Thank you,' said Miss Sloan to Shaw, then turned to the Guru. 'But Guruji, I still think it is risky. What if you cannot talk the man round?'

The Guru raised a hand. 'Please, Shrutakirti. Trust in the Power that drives all things, from the planets in their courses to the smallest insects of the air. It will not fail those who humbly honour it. Now, shall we go in to dinner?'

They passed into the lobby of the hotel which felt oppressively stuffy after the growing evening coolness of the garden. As they passed the front desk, Lucas, the manager, stepped out in front of Shaw.

'I understand you were out searching with Major blair for the gentleman who fell off the cliff earlier today sir,' he said in an admiring voice.

'That is correct,' said Shaw. 'But alas…'

'You won't have heard then?' said Lucas excitedly. 'The man's been found. Alive. Washed up further up the coast. The assistant porter's a lifeboatman and has just got back with the news.'

'O praise His holy name,' said Shaw under his breath,

then shook Lucas warmly by the hand.

'That is most welcome news,' said the Guru. 'All things work to the good, Mr Shaw. As we say in India, "everything will be all right in the end. If it is not all right, it is not the end"'.

'Well thank the Lord,' said Lucas, 'and I mean that sincerely, sir. Of course you know what they're saying in the town about it, don't you?'

Shaw made to leave the lobby in order to fetch his wife down for dinner. 'One ought not to listen to rumour, Mr Lucas. Good evening to you.'

'They're saying he didn't *fall*,' called out Lucas, as Shaw, the Guru and Miss Sloan walked towards the grand staircase. 'They're saying he was *pushed*. By that spiritualist fellow— Rooksley.'

As they walked into the dining room, Shaw could not help noticing a worried glance pass momentarily between the Guru and Miss Sloan.

Rooksley lay on the bed in his little hotel room, waiting for night to fall. The heat in the attic chamber was intense, and he had the sash window wide open. It was one of those still English summer nights where the outdoors seems but a vast extension of one's home, and when one could, if one wished, simply lie down on the ground and fall asleep, as warm and dry as if it were one's own bedroom. Rooksley cursed as he opened the packet of cigarettes in his pocket, to find he had run out; there was unlikely to be anywhere open now to sell them and anyway he could not risk going outdoors any more than he had to.

He lit the electric lamp and sat down at the small desk, where he had left the letter he had written earlier, addressed to Major Blair, care of the Excelsior Hotel. He tapped it thoughtfully against his palm, then he walked to the window to assess whether it was yet dark enough to go out.

On a night such as this, conversation travelled far, and Rooksley could hear voices in the street below, almost as if they were in the room with him. He peered down to see a group of working men— fishermen, he guessed— in shirt-sleeves, some of them wearing only their unbuttoned vests over their trousers. They were walking up from the harbour. He did not have to strain his ears to hear them, and within moments he got the jist of their conversation. Prior had been found alive. Not only that, it seemed common knowledge that he, Rooksley, was a wanted man; one salty old sea-dog, with a large black beard, declared he would 'find the blasted witch-doctor that did it', and vowed he would 'give 'im a dose of the same medicine, and if 'e comes up, I'll put my foot on 'is 'ead.'

Rooksley withdrew his head quickly from the window, as the men passed by below. He thought quickly. If people in the town knew he was wanted, it would soon be in the newspapers— by tomorrow, he imagined— and everyone would be out looking for him. They may even, he thought, have procured his photograph from somewhere, and be circulating it on one of those posters one saw on the notice boards outside police stations.

He had not expected Prior to be found alive. It was all the more vital now that he found that cylinder recording, as that, along with Prior's testimony, could well be enough to hang him. He did not think the authorities would find him once he disappeared abroad, but he would have to risk being caught before them; a false passport would have to be procured and that meant money, and a visit to someone he knew in London.

Money! If only he'd had enough to get up to London and onto a ship, he thought to himself, he could have left this dismal town and got away scot-free. He was no armed robber or burglar, and even if he were, it would be madness to attempt something like that with the whole town looking for him. He had no choice; he would have to risk the pick-up on the beach tomorrow. He could not pass up the chance to get an easy fifty pounds.

Then there was the note for Blair. Could he do that some other way? No; he could not risk telephoning the man's hotel, being seen in a lighted kiosk; and anyway, he had no change. Besides, the man would probably be tight by now and might not remember the call. No, a note was best, making it clear to the man that dire consequences would befall him if he breathed a word of what he knew to anyone.

Although he had told the party in question that the demand would be final, that fifty pounds, he hoped, would be the first instalment of many. He knew from experience that a man could live in the east quite well on fifty pounds, say, every quarter, with a servant or two and perhaps even a native mistress. With the new airmail system and money-transfer services, he would not have to go any further than the local post office in some quiet colonial outpost in order to continue his lucrative little sideline indefinitely.

He made a mental note that once he had picked up the money tomorrow and got clear of the town, he would write to his victim again and set out clear demands for regular future payments. He smiled to himself. Documents would be lodged with solicitors— yes, that was the way to do it— with strict instructions to send them to various newspapers should regular deposits to a certain bank account not be made. He would not even have to bother sending letters to the man.

Rooksley grinned to himself, wolfishly, and placed his hand on the little leather-bound book beside him on the desk. He felt the will to power coursing through his veins. It was not just the physically strong that triumphed, he thought; one also had to be mentally strong to rule in this world. That was the advantage he had over half-wits like Prior. The will to power. He could out-think everyone. He looked out of the window again and decided it was time to begin the night's work.

Dinner at the Excelsior was over, and Blair rose to his feet unsteadily from his separate table in the corner of the dining room. He pushed down the stiff front of his evening dress shirt back in to his waistcoat, from which it had popped out as his stomach swelled in size during the meal. As he passed through to the bar, he kept well away from the Guru and his various admirers; it would not do to have Rooksley walk in and see them together, but he kept an eye on the man to make sure he knew where he was so that he could point him out. He made a mock salute at Shaw and his wife as they left, presumably on their way to an early night after the exertions of the day.

He had noticed the Guru usually went out on to the terrace after dinner and held court with his acolytes, talking, Blair assumed, a lot of tommy-rot about Indian philosophy or some such.

'Philoso…philso…' he tried to say the word aloud, but the bottle of hock he had consumed with dinner had made it difficult to form his lips in the correct shape. 'Philosofiddlesticks,' he concluded, and sat down in a corner of the lounge bar to wait for Rooksley.

After half an hour, and two large glasses of brandy, Blair began to feel a little uneasy. Had the fellow stood him up? Had he got the date wrong? He checked his little pocket diary, but there it was, clear as day. 9.00 p.m., Rooksley, hotel bar.

He called the waiter over and caught hold of the man's wrist.

'I say…what's your name…' he squinted up at the waiter. 'Wait, wait, don't tell me…been living here long enough…Johnson!'

'Thompson, sir,' said the waiter with a sigh.

'Any callers come for me this evening?'

'Callers, sir?'

'Yes. Fellow called Rooksley. Dresses in black.'
The waiter appeared shocked, and swallowed hard.

'What's the matter, old chap?' asked Blair. 'Seen a ghost?'

'Erm…haven't you heard the news sir?'

'News? Never listen to it. BBC ought to be shut down if you ask me. Bolshies, most of 'em.'

'No sir, I mean the news from the town. Rooksley is the fellow the police are looking for. They think he pushed that man off the cliff.'

'Good God!' exclaimed Blair. 'Why didn't someone tell me this bef....' he stopped short, suddenly realising it might be better to keep quiet. Despite his brain being clouded by drink, he was still able to function in a crisis, and he thought surprisingly quickly.

'Must have been thinking of entirely the wrong chap!' he said with a laugh. 'That's it. 'Course I heard the news, had the cove's name in my head and repeated it without thinking. No...no...the chap I'm supposed to meet is called, erm, erm, Rakesby.'

'Very good sir. There's been nobody asking for you though. Of that name nor any other.'

'Very well, very well,' said Blair, taking a stiff draught of brandy, and dismissing the waiter with a slight shove.

Blair breathed out heavily. That was, he thought, what they call a 'close shave'. What on earth had Rooksley got himself mixed up in now? Why should he have pushed that young man off a cliff? He frowned as he took another swig of brandy, and swallowed hard. The fellow had always had a nasty temper, he remembered. Thrashing servants and so on. Out east that sort of thing was tolerated up to a point, but even over there, Rooksley had gone a bit too far.

If he was capable of pushing someone off a cliff...Blair took a deep breath. This whole scheme had been a stupid idea, he thought. He wracked his brains to remember what he had written to Rooksley in that note he had sent him when he had invited him to the hotel. He was pretty sure he had put nothing incriminating in it.

He drained the glass of brandy and bit his lip, deep in thought. Through the French doors, open to the summer night, he could see the Guru sitting on a bench at the end of the terrace, holding court with that bunch of ghastly

Indian undergraduates and the American couple. Probably talking to them about peace and love, he thought, after which they would scuttle back home to India to throw bombs at the Viceroy. He was awoken from his reverie by Lucas, the hotel manager, who cleared his throat and passed a letter to him on a silver tray.

'This just came for you, sir,' said Lucas.

Blair tried to focus on the letter. He picked it up and noticed it was still sealed, but the handwriting on the envelope stirred something in the depths of his brain. He inserted his little finger under the flap in order to open it, then stopped.

'Thank you Lucas, old man,' he said, trying to sound affable. 'Carry on.'

'May I be of any assistance in the matter, sir?' asked Lucas.

'No you may not. Now run along.'

Blair made a shoo-ing gesture, then stopped. 'Oh wait a moment, Lucas. There is something you can help with. Who gave you this note?'

'I don't know, sir,' said Lucas. 'The party just left it in the letterbox at the front door. I heard it rattle and looked out to see him dashing off down the drive, about ten minutes ago.'

'What did he look like?'

'Nothing special that I recall sir. I only saw him for a brief moment in the lamp-light. Tall-ish. Had his hat down over his eyes.'

'Yes, he would, wouldn't he?' whispered Blair under his breath.

'Come again, sir?' asked Lucas.

'Nothing, nothing,' said Blair, heartily. 'Now run along, there's a good fellow.' He waved Lucas away, and the man retreated through the bar doors to his perch behind the front desk. Blair read the contents of the letter hurriedly, and swallowed hard.

> Blair
> If you meddle in my affairs, you will regret it. I know all the details about the 'party in question' and have no intention of sharing any proceeds with you.
> Say anything to anyone, and it will be the worse for you.
> You will not see me again, but I will be watching you.

The last four words had been underscored to drive the point home. The letter was unsigned, but Blair did not have to guess who it was from. It had been bally silly, he decided, to send that letter to the Guru hinting he might want a bit of cash in exchange for his silence. At least he had had the sense to keep it anonymous. He had intended to send another one making it clear what he wanted, but he now decided to call the whole thing off.

He knew better than to try to milk the cash cow of someone like Rooksley. Especially now that the man was, presumably, wanted by the police. He was better off staying well away from him, he decided. He ordered another drink and decided to celebrate his new-found honesty.

On the terrace of the Hotel Excelsior, Shaw and his wife sat at a table overlooking the gardens, admiring the slim crescent moon which left a faint reflection on the glassily calm water of the North Sea in the distance.

'You're rather quiet, dear,' said Mrs Shaw, as she swallowed the last of her post-prandial coffee. Shaw had lit his pipe and was puffing on it reflectively, staring ahead into the gathering dusk, his hand resting on Fraser's back as the little dog sat on the wooden terrace chair between them.

'I'm sorry,' said Shaw, turning to his wife. 'I'm rather tired. '

'Of course dear,' said Mrs Shaw. 'But one also feels a sense of levity, doesn't one? All's well that ends well. Just imagine how awful it would be to have to go bed knowing that Mr Prior had not been found.'

'Yes, we must be thankful,' said Shaw. He had, as his wife mentioned, felt a sense of levity at the news that Prior was safe, but this was overshadowed by the conversation he had had with the Guru. He had not wanted to get involved, but his vocation, as he had reflected at the start of the trip, was not something that could be discarded and, if somebody came to him in need, he was duty bound to help.

He could not help feeling, however, that there was something not quite right about his involvement in the business of the Guru being blackmailed, and it was not something he wished to discuss with his wife; he would just have to ponder the matter alone.

Especially troubling was the fact that the Guru had said that extortioner was known to him, or at least he— Shaw— had met him. Who on earth could it be? The whole thing, he concluded, felt like one of those detective stories he sometimes borrowed from Boots' library in Midchester, but unlike the story books, he could not put this one down and forget about it until he picked it up again.

Chapter Nine

In his spartan bedroom in the vicarage, Dewynter lay in a profound slumber after the exertions of the day.

After Billy's mother had been found, he had hurried down to the quayside and volunteered as an oarsman for the lifeboat crew. He had been a rowing Blue at Oxford, and despite that being over a decade previously he could still keep up with the lifeboatmen with ease. The cigarette habit had not yet affected his lungs so in addition to rowing he was also able to keep the men's spirits up by leading choruses of *Pull for the Shore, Sailor,* and *Will Your Anchor Hold?* as they plied up and and down the coast searching for Prior. The words of the latter hymn seemed particularly apt.

> It will surely hold in the floods of death
> When the waters cold chill our latest breath
> On the rising tide it can never fail
> While our hopes abide within the veil.

Dewynter had clung to the words of that hymn as the exhausted rowers had finally moored the boats as the light began to fail. His despair was short-lived; as they dejectedly hauled the boats up onto the sands an excited fisherman ran towards them, shouting that Prior had been found alive in Lowestoft. There was then much back

149

slapping and hand shaking, and the men, including Dewynter, cheered as they heard that the nearby pub, despite not having a licence for Sunday opening, was standing them all drinks. 'No law against giving it away,' beamed the landlord as he passed mug after overflowing mug of beer down the chain of men on the beach.

'How about a prayer, vicar?' said the coxswain of one of the boats. 'We're mostly chapel, not church, down here, but I reckon you'd say it better than any of us.'

'Very well,' said Dewynter, buttoning up the top of his cassock, which was soaked in perspiration from the exertions of rowing. 'Let us pray.'

The men removed their caps, apart from a few standing awkwardly on the edge of the group; some sniggered nervously and nudged their fellows, but then fell silent as Dewynter's clear voice recited from memory the General Thanksgiving from the Book of Common Prayer as he looked out to sea. The ancient words seemed to ripple out on the air in mystical union with the gentle waves which gradually ebbed away from the shore on the tide.

'...we bless thee for our creation, preservation, and all the blessings of this life; but above all for thine inestimable love in the redemption of the world by our Lord Jesus Christ, for the means of grace, and for the hope of glory...'

Dewynter woke with a start; a noise downstairs. He listened carefully, unsure whether he had dreamed it. No further sound came, and he began to drift back to sleep. Then another, similar noise came. A scratching, metallic clinking, as if someone was rummaging through a drawer of cutlery. A burglar stealing the silver perhaps, thought Dewynter, and chuckled sleepily at the thought of a hapless thief finding only the few cheap tin spoons that he kept for his daily use. He thought it more likely to be a fox outside, emboldened by the fact it was not the hunting season and because the warm weather gave the dustbin an enticing smell.

Another sound came, this time the opening and closing of a door. Dewynter felt his heart begin to pound and became fully awake; foxes did not, he believed, open and close doors.

He was alone in the house; his housekeeper was only a daily. There were no other houses near enough to hear him shout for help, and the only means of summoning assistance was by the telephone, which was in his study — the place where the sounds seemed to be coming from.

He decided it would be cowardly to wait in his bedroom; crime, he knew, had to be confronted head-on; to do otherwise was to condone sin. That did not mean taking reckless action, however; he decided he would make enough noise and light enough lamps to scare off the predator— or predators— before a confrontation became necessary.

He shrugged on his dressing gown and put on his slippers. He remembered a piece of advice from his old churchwarden in the east end of London, a veteran of several burglaries; if someone breaks in, make as much noise as you can and if you are alone, call out to someone else in the house as if he were there with you.

'There's someone downstairs,' shouted Dewynter along the landing, as he flicked on the light switch. 'You telephone for the police and I'll go down with...James.'

James, he thought, sounded the sort of name a butler might have. He hoped the ruse of making it sound as if *three* people were in the house would work even more effectively. Taking a deep breath, he clattered down the stairs and shouted again. 'I'm going in to the study!'

Hoping this would have encouraged the intruder to make a quick getaway while he still could, Dewynter threw open the study door. He was about to reach for the light switch, but realised the room was already bathed in light. He looked around to see the room in disarray — drawers flung open and objects strewn across the floor. He cursed himself for his stupidity as he saw the window which he had left open before going to bed; that must have been how the burglar had got in.

He turned to leave the room and check the rest of the house, but when he did so, his vision was obscured as some rough material was hurled over his face, and he felt his knees crash into the rug with agonising force as he was pushed to the floor from behind.

The Morris Eight saloon car sped south along the coast road from Lowestoft. There was little traffic about at this time of night, and the constable at the wheel was able to maintain a steady fifty miles an hour for most of the way. Chief Inspector Ludd sat next to him in the passenger seat, staring ahead at the myriad moths and insects which flashed towards the car's head-lamps, like some strange mid-summer snowstorm. Through his open window, he could hear the rhythmic hissing of grasshoppers in the fields, a sound, he realised, one only heard in England on the warmest of summer nights.

Ludd yawned; it had been a long day, but he thanked his lucky stars the Eastburgh force had been able to spare a motor car to take him to and from Lowestoft cottage hospital to interview Prior. The last train south from there went at 9.00 pm and without the car, he would have been stranded. It had also enabled him to get Prior's parents and take them with him to the hospital and get them digs for the night.

He had been surprised to see Prior awake when he arrived, ushered into the ward by a starched, rustling Matron who admonished him to be quiet before he had even said anything.

When he had spoken on the telephone to the Lowestoft police they seemed to think Prior was at death's door but it turned out he was just exhausted, bruised and sun-burned; all he needed was a good rest, plenty of water to drink and lots of calamine lotion on his skin. These little country-bumpkin police stations, he reflected, must have so little to do that when anything happened they exaggerated it out of all proportion.

He could tell Prior wasn't quite right in the head though— he was one of those chaps that couldn't look you in the eye and seemed to talk at you rather than to you, but what he had said seemed perfectly rational.

He had passed out when he hit the water and had come to a long way out from the shore. He had tried to swim inland but the current had swept him northwards along the coast. Exhausted, he had eventually stopped swimming and had expected to sink beneath the waves but he did not— it seemed that in the fall, his shirt had been forced full of air and this had kept him afloat. Eventually he blacked out again and the next thing he knew, he was washed up like a beached whale at Lowestoft with half the town running towards him.

It seemed Rooksley had not pushed him off the cliff after all. Prior had been reticent at first but after being told that Rooksley had been spotted on the cliff by Billy, he conceded that they had argued, he had run away from Rooksley but then had a funny turn of some sort and fallen over the edge.

Ludd had asked why he had run away from the pier where Cotterill was found dead, and Prior had said he had panicked after he witnessed an argument between Cotterill and Rooksley, but no blows had been exchanged, and Cotterill had just dropped dead in front of him. That, thought Ludd, at least tied in with the doctor's report.

Prior, it seemed, had then realised that he had recorded the argument between Cotterill and Rooksley accidentally, while preparing a recording for Cotterill's show. When asked where the recording was, he said he had given it to a vicar on the pier, but he had no idea who the man was.

Ludd frowned; it all looked as if it was just a series of misunderstandings and nasty accidents. He sighed; he would not know the full story until they got hold of Rooksley. The man sounded a piece of work all right, probably guilty of threatening behaviour, but that was not enough evidence for him to be wanted on suspicion of murder. 'Wanted in connection with a suspicious death' was about all Ludd could justify at this stage, he thought, and that might not get much interest from the public.

The car decelerated with a soft whine as they reached the outskirts of Eastburgh, its head-lamps picking out the glossy black and white paint on a finger-post sign at a junction. Ludd decided to keep an open mind about the case until they could find the elusive Mr Rooksley, or 'Doctor Death'— a name which, Ludd thought, was starting to sound more and more apt.

Winded and unable to see, Dewynter fought wildly against his assailant. His arms broke free momentarily and he tore at the material on his head. Suddenly he could see again; it was a tweed jacket that had been pulled down over his head. In front of him he saw the attacker; a man in shirt-sleeves, wearing a soft hat, with a large handkerchief tied across his face. He regained his vice-like grip on Dewynter's arms and pushed the man against the floor.

'Stop struggling and you won't get hurt,' he hissed.

'Who in God's name are you?' growled Dewynter. 'I know your voice.'

'Never mind who I am. Where is it?'

Dewynter was genuinely confused. 'Where is what?' he asked.

'Don't fool with me, priest,' said the man, and cuffed Dewynter across the face with the back of his hand. Dewynter saw stars in front of his eyes and felt blood well up in his mouth, but anger and adrenaline prevented him from feeling any great pain.

'You know what I mean,' continued the man. 'The cylinder recording. The one Prior gave you.'

'Prior?' shouted Dewynter. 'Then I know who you are, fiend!'

Using all his strength he was able to break free again from the man's grip, and tore at the silk handkerchief obscuring his face; in the process the man's hat was knocked from his head. While his opponent was momentarily distracted, Dewynter was able to get to his feet and charge at the man, sending him crashing heavily into the side of the desk. Pages of next Sunday's sermon notes fluttered down over the man's head as he scrabbled to regain his balance.

'Rooksley!' exclaimed Dewynter. He pushed home his advantage, crushing the man's face against the battered mahogany desk. Although shorter than his opponent, he had the advantage of youth and boxing experience on his side. In his Stepney days he had run a fight club and had gained something of a reputation with the local lads as having a devilish right cross and a short temper to go with it.

'What the blazes are you talking about?' demanded Dewynter. 'What cylinder recording? Don't you know you're wanted by the police after what happened to Prior?'

Rooksley laughed, the sound harsh and distorted as his mouth was pressed into the side of the desk.

'Speak, man,' urged Dewynter.

'Prior gave you a cylinder recording, before he died,' said Rooksley. 'He told me himself that he had given it to the vicar. What did you do with it?'

'You're in no position to ask questions,' said Dewynter. 'And I've already said I have no idea what you're talking about. Prior didn't give me any recording.'

Dewynter thought quickly. He was not sure if he had the right to carry out a citizen's arrest, but he could not let the man go either. He wondered what to do with him until he summoned assistance. He decided locking him in the kitchen broom cupboard was the only workable solution, and devil take the legal consequences.

'On your feet,' said Dewynter, and pulled Rooksley up. 'You can cool off in the kitchen while I call the police.'

'Very well,' said Rooksley. 'I concede. Perhaps we can discuss this like gentlemen, if you would be so good as to let me go.'

'Perhaps we can,' said Dewynter, suspiciously. He decided to chance it, and let go of his grip on Rooksley's arms. He immediately regretted it. In a flash Rooksley grabbed the heavy glass ashtray on the desk and struck Dewynter on the temple with it, scattering cigarette ends and ash everywhere as he did so.

Dewynter fell to his knees, clutching at his temple; he was momentarily paralysed by pain. He blinked cigarette ash out of his eyes and saw Rooksley scooping up the cylinders which were stacked next to the dictaphone by the desk; he stuffed them into his jacket pockets, shrugged the garment on and pushed his hat on his head.

'See what happens to those who oppose me,' spat Rooksley. 'And to make sure you don't call the police, you can have another dose.'

He picked up the ashtray again and approached Dewynter, who was swaying on the point of collapse.

Seeing the man approach again, Dewynter felt a sudden surge of rage through his body. The old righteous anger he had last felt as a slum parson, when a local trouble-maker— a hoodlum and wife-beater— had thrown beer at him while he passed by a public house, cursing him and daring him to turn the other cheek. Dewynter had snapped, grabbed the pewter mug from the man's hand and struck him across the face with it, knocking him out cold. The man had left the area after that, all reputation lost, and even the local beat constable unofficially congratulated him on 'doing a job that ought to have been done a long time previous'.

Before Rooksley could raise the ashtray to strike what could have been the fatal blow, Dewynter countered with his left, sending a spasm of pain up Rooksley's arm as his fist connected with the nerves on the man's wrist; he dropped the ashtray and howled in pain. Dewynter followed with a right uppercut to Rooksley's jaw, silencing him; the medium's eyes bulged in fear and he turned to clamber over the windowsill and then through the open casement, scattering recording cylinders and papers as he escaped.

In one bound Dewynter passed through the window and began to run after Rooksley, shouting as he went.

'You won't get far, Rooksley! Prior has been found— alive! God is not mocked!'

Rooksley turned to look briefly behind, a horrified expression on his face. I have him now, thought Dewynter.

'Back, fiend!' yelled Dewynter at the top of his voice. 'Back to your master! Back, Gadarene swine!'

Rooksley looked behind again, his face contorted in panic, and ran towards the cliffs. Dewynter could make out in the moonlight the man heading towards the rising greensward which led up to the hidden edge of the cliffs over North Beach. Yelling all the way, Dewynter began to gain ground but as they approached the edge of the cliffs, Rooksley suddenly disappeared from view.

Dewynter slowed slightly, and that was sufficient to end the surge of adrenaline through his body; the wound on his head was now pouring blood into his eyes and he felt nausea surge up from the pit of his stomach. Something caught at his ankle and in one fluid motion he collapsed on to the dusty, sheep-trodden path and passed out.

Hours later, the sky, which had never really completely darkened, began to lighten over the sea; a milk-coloured mist rose from the ground as the temperature slowly rose with the approaching sun. Rooksley, whose nature inclined more to the cold north and the long darkness of winter nights, normally disliked this time of year. Now, however, he was grateful, in as much as he could feel gratitude, for the warm weather, since he had had to pass the night huddled in a depression on the cliff path under some gorse bushes.

Once Dewynter had suddenly gone quiet, he had assumed the man had turned tail and gone home to telephone the police. He had expected before long the night sky to be lit up by battery torches, and the air to be filled with the sound of police whistles and barking dogs. He dared not attempt to get back to his hotel in case he was seen by some constable on the beat, who would be bound to ask questions of a bruised and bloodied man walking the streets in the dead of night.

He had decided the best option was to hide until any search died down, then pick up the blackmail money and walk north, perhaps as far as Lowestoft, posing as an itinerant labourer, then get a train to London. He wondered briefly what he would do if the money was not there, but put the thought out of his mind. Those with the will to power did not worry about consequences, they moulded reality to their own ends. He breathed deeply, trying to channel energy through his body. His face and arm ached where Dewynter had punched him, and he was desperately thirsty.

After two hours or so crouched under the gorse bushes, he began to wonder if the police were going to arrive. By now they should have been here. He cursed himself for failing to cut the telephone wires to the vicarage; something he had been attempting to do when Dewynter had disturbed him. He decided the police must have put the search off until daybreak, not wanting to risk clambering over the cliffs in the dark; either that or something had happened to Dewynter and he had not been able to summon help. He had fetched the man a pretty tidy blow on the head with that ashtray. Perhaps the effect had been delayed, and the man was now lying dead or mortally injured somewhere on the greensward. I can but hope, he thought with a sickly grin.

He felt the recording cylinders in his jacket pockets, stuffed in beside the little leather-bound book, and hoped one of them was the one he wanted. He wished he had not bothered now; he had tried to be clever by wiping out any possible evidence against him and in the process had nearly got himself caught. Well, he thought, it won't happen again. Any policemen foolish enough to attempt to arrest him were going to have a fight to the death on their hands. He fingered the book and thumbed through it, his poor Latin enabling him to just about understand the chapter heading at which he stopped.

He peered at the pages through the gloom, and smiled vulpinely as he recited a paragraph. He then marked the page with Blair's letter and replaced the book in his pocket. A lone bird started singing in the distance, and before long others had joined in in that cacophony known as the dawn chorus, the bane of insomniacs all over England.

Rooksley looked at his watch and realised it would soon be time to collect the money from the hiding place. He cursed as he realised how awry his plans had gone. He had intended to hide in a thicket close to the Wooden Witness before dawn so that he could make sure he could observe anybody placing the money in the hiding place. Instead, he had run around wildly in the dark and had lost his bearings; only now with the dawn did he work out where he was and it would be too late to observe anything now.

He looked at his watch again; 4.00 a.m. The money, if it were there, would have been left there by now; he would just have to take his chance and expose himself. Cautiously he rose from his hiding place and made his way down the rough cliff path to the beach. Once there, he turned to walk northwards to the Wooden Witness, almost out of sight at the far end of North Beach. His shoes sank crisply a half inch or so into the sand as he walked; the tide was coming in, a few feet away from him, which meant, he realised, that anybody attempting to lay a trap for him would also have left footprints. He smiled at his own cleverness, and trudged on.

The sounds of the wakening sea-birds and the crashing waves filled his ears as he walked. Then, from everywhere yet nowhere, they were drowned out by another sound, one which, he thought, could not possibly be made so close to him on a deserted beach. He turned swiftly, realising that the sound came from behind him, and his face, tinged with the first rays of dawn sunlight, was suddenly obscured by an enormous shadow. It was the last thing he ever saw.

Shaw awoke with a start, and looked at the little travel alarm clock on the night table. He cursed mildly; it was well after the time he had intended to get up, and he realised that he had failed to push in completely the little button on the back of the timepiece which set the alarm.

He dressed hurriedly, remembering that the Guru had suggested he wear clerical garb; he grabbed his knapsack with his towel and swimming costume inside to give himself the appearance of, he hoped, an ascetic clergyman who enjoyed early morning dips in the sea, rather than an amateur detective engaging in a mission he was increasingly beginning to think of as ill-advised.

He scribbled a note to his still-slumbering wife, who had already been warned of his early departure (but not the full reason for it) and attached Fraser's lead to his collar. The dog was clearly delighted at the prospect of a morning walk and panted eagerly as he trotted down the large staircase at his master's heels.

They passed the front desk, unobserved by the dozing night porter, and hurried out into the hotel grounds and on to the road which led to the downs. Despite his trepidation over the task in hand, Shaw could not help noticing the beauty of the dawn; the air of Eden, he thought, could not have smelled better to our first parents than the air of the Suffolk coast on a summer's morning.

He looked at his watch again and realised he was very late. He wondered about running, but decided it would appear suspicious, and anyway, he doubted he could manage such a thing for more than a few minutes. A brisk walk, he concluded, was the only alternative.

Twenty minutes later, somewhat out of breath, he and Fraser reached the bottom of the cliff path which led down to the hidden sands of North Beach. Up ahead, in the early morning mist, he could just make out the Wooden Witness. He trudged rapidly across the sand, assuming the pace of a man out for a brisk morning walk. Fraser strained at his lead and he looked to see what was attracting the animal's attention.

Laid out in the sand, emerging from the seaweed strewn base of the cliffs towards the far end of the beach, he saw clear, fresh footprints. A man's shoe, with the little details of metal segments on the heel and toe clearly marked. Shaw swallowed hard; he would now need his wits about him. He scanned the beach without looking too obvious about it, but saw nobody. Had the man already disappeared? Then he heard Fraser yelp and saw him stop, looking up expectantly at his master. The footprints had ended.

The last pair were smudged and enlarged, as if the man had marked time, or perhaps turned around, and then…nothing. What had happened to him? The sea, gently soaking the sand, was still a few feet away; it would have been an almost impossible feat to jump into it from a standing position. The man could not have got into a boat, as there were no marks on the sand. Shaw's mind whirled. Could he have somehow erased his tracks, as Red Indians— or was it Arabs?— were said to do, by sweeping the sand behind him as he went? That might have been possible on dry dunes, but this sand was firm and damp, the consistency of fresh icing on a Christmas cake; it was utterly untouched from this point on.

Shaw frowned and carried on walking; there was something, he thought, very strange going on. There was no sign anywhere of another human being on the beach, but as he came closer to the Wooden Witness, he began to think he could see somebody. He strained his eyes but the last of the morning mist still shrouded the sinister edifice.

Fraser barked once, then began a chorus of yelps interspersed with the whining, whistling sound a frightened dog makes. Shaw tugged on his lead, forcing the reluctant animal forward and preventing him from shying away.

He began to jog along the sand towards the Wooden Witness; there was now clearly visible a figure atop the central pillar of the circle, leaning backwards with his arms outstretched in what Shaw immediately thought was some grotesque parody of the Crucifixion.

He reached the monument; Shaw had seen enough of the hurriedly printed 'Wanted' posters placed around Eastburgh by the police the day before to know that the man, with his distinctive white-streaked hair, was Aethelstan Rooksley.

As he gazed in horror at the grim scene before him, he realised that Rooksley had not been nailed to the tree as the Lord had been, but had been impaled through his chest on the blunt tip of the blackened, glistening wooden spike. His sightless eyes stared upwards, as if imploring the heavens for some deliverance which had never come.

Chapter Ten

Some time before Shaw had made his grisly discovery, Dewynter had come to on the rough sheep-track which led to the cliffs. For a moment he was disorientated and thought he was in his own bed, but the hard ground beneath him, and the severe pain from his temple suddenly brought him into full wakefulness and a recollection of the previous night's events. He pulled himself to his feet and then sat down again, retching into the soft grass by the track.

Having no watch on his person, he had no idea how long he had lain semi-conscious, but judging by the light he thought it must have been several hours. He recited the Lord's Prayer and the Gloria under his breath until he felt able to stand, and then gave thanks for the warm night; had it been winter he might have perished wearing only his night-clothes.

Rooksley would be long gone by now, he thought, but he must still alert the authorities. The man was a dangerous criminal and there was still a chance he could be apprehended. He got to his feet and half walked, half staggered back to the vicarage where he immediately put through a telephone call to Eastburgh police station.

Shaw breathed deeply and tried to remain calm. Rooksley was beyond help, but it was vital that such a grisly sight should not be seen by others— families and children who might soon be out on early morning walks. He had seen worse as a chaplain in the war, but somehow a violent death on a peaceful English beach seemed more horrific than those that had occurred on the blasted, hellish landscape of Flanders, where such sights had been commonplace.

His eye was caught by the upturned soles of Rooksley's shoes; each heel had a metal segment nailed to it, conforming to the pattern Shaw had seen in the footprints on the sand. He looked down below Rooksley's feet and saw several objects on the sand at the base of the blackened, slime-covered wooden pillar; a man's hat, Rooksley's presumably, sat on its crown and swayed slightly in the breeze.

Beside it was a little book, and scattered all around were about half a dozen small metal objects which Shaw at first did not recognise. Then he suddenly remembered what they were— recording cylinders, of the type he had seen in Dewynter's study. As he looked further away he could see the sand was completely undisturbed. Neither Rooksley nor an assailant could have got to the Wooden Witness since the tide went out, unless perhaps…he turned and looked behind at the towering bulk of the cliffs soaring above, obscured in deep shadow, with the rising sun just beginning to illuminate their base. He realised this was the point at which Prior had fallen from the cliff. Prior, however, had chanced to fall at high water; from the tide marks on the cliff Shaw could see that the central timber spike of the monument would be fifteen feet or so underwater at that point. Even if Prior had fallen directly above it, he would probably not have been injured as the water would have slowed his descent.

If Rooksley had fallen from the same place, when the tide was out, however, he would have landed right on top of it. But why on earth was Rooksley on the cliff? Had he been pushed? And how did that explain the disappearing footprints on the sand further down the beach?

Shaw was shaken out of his train of thought by Fraser, who was whining and crying, pulling on his lead to get his master to move away. Shaw looked down to see small trails of water entering the wooden circle. He realised that before long, the entire beach would be cut off by the rising tide. He was a fool, he thought, for not having checked the tide times properly before walking here; there appeared to be some bottle-neck effect which was causing the water to rise far more quickly than it did on South Beach. That would explain, he realised, why the place was generally avoided by swimmers and walkers.

His thoughts moved rapidly as he tried to calculate the rate of tidal flow. It would be impossible for him to move Rooksley's body on his own, and he did not think he ought to anyway before the police arrived. There would probably be enough time to get help and remove Rooksley from the spike before the area was submerged, but the objects around the base of the timber would have to be moved. He picked up the hat and wedged it between Rooksley's legs and the wooden pillar, then lifted the flap of his knapsack, which he habitually kept unfastened, and picked up the little book. As he did so, the volume fell open and a slip of paper with writing on it fell face-down onto the sands.

Shaw gasped in frustration as he saw the paper had landed on one of the small tidal rivulets which had begun to encroach on the timber circle. He picked up the paper but the ink had already begun to run. All he could make out, before the seawater soaked the entire text into a blue smudge, was the following:

Dear Rooksley
Just a line to say you'll never guess who's arrived at the hotel. Been here a few days but I only just placed him. 'A Man with a Past' and one I think you'll remember as well. Can't be sure…

Shaw replaced the paper, which had now almost disintegrated, back where it was in the book and placed the book securely down inside his knapsack. His fingers touched on an unfamiliar object, and he rummaged about in the bag to see what it was. His eyes widened as he realised it was a recording cylinder, identical to the ones scattered at his feet on the sand. How on earth had it got there?

There was no time to speculate; the tide was now pouring in to the timber circle, and he felt seawater trickle over the tops of his shoes. Fraser was yelping in alarm now and tugging with all his might on the lead. Shaw bent to scoop up the recording cylinders which were now bobbing about on the water. He shoved them into his trouser pockets and picked up Fraser, then splashed through the incoming tide along the underside of the cliffs.

There was supposed to be a path near here, he thought, as the boy, Billy, had climbed it after he had seen Prior fall. Shaw scanned the cliff side but could see nothing but a sheer rock face. He turned to look back at the beach but no sands were now visible; the water had risen to the cliff edge. To attempt to go that way would be dangerous; it would mean eventually having to swim, fully clothed, against the strong current which ran northwards along the beach.

There *must* be a way up, thought Shaw. He continued scrabbling along, and suddenly his eyes discerned a rough, impossibly steep path a hundred feet or so to his right. Then, to his amazement, he heard the shrill of a police whistle and saw a red-faced constable gingerly picking his way down the path towards him. Shaw saw the man's head turn towards the horrific sight on the Wooden Witness; he took out his truncheon from his trouser pocket, and pointed it at Shaw. He called out with a Suffolk accent so broad it was almost unintelligible.

'Now you come over here quietly like a good chap,' he shouted, glancing up as another constable carefully made his way down the cliff behind him, 'and you keep your hands where I can see 'em.'

'What I don't understand, Mr Shaw,' said Chief Inspector Ludd, 'is what you were doing on the beach that early in the morning.'

Shaw was seated in the vicarage study with the detective and a number of uniformed constables standing around. They drank tea from plain cups and saucers, administered by Mrs Upton, the housekeeper, who had recently arrived and who was now fussing about the house in a state of subdued shock. Fraser lay under an armchair dozing, seeming to have lost interest in the unfolding drama.

On the ancient leather sofa in the corner of the room sat Dewynter, still in his dressing gown and pyjamas. He was being attended to by the town's only police doctor who, after announcing he was satisfied there was no concussion, was applying a bandage to the swelling on the side of the priest's head where he had been dazed by the glass ashtray.

Shaw thought for a moment before answering. Once Ludd had appeared on the cliff path and recognised Shaw, the grisly task of removing Rooksley's body from the incoming tide had begun. It had taken three constables to get the corpse up to the top of the cliff path, where he had lain under a police raincoat until the doctor could be summoned and the remains removed. It was only now that they were in the vicarage that Shaw was able to gather his wits and assess the situation more calmly.

Ludd's question caused Shaw something of a moral conflict. To reveal why he had been walking at that particular time and place would cause him to betray a confidence. It could result in ruin for the reputation of the Guru and Miss Sloan. He decided, at this stage at least, to simply state what he had been doing on the beach rather than the full reason for it.

'I was on an early morning walk, Chief Inspector,' said Ludd. 'I had also hoped for a bathe, hence I brought my swimming things.' He tapped the knapsack that lay at his feet.

'All right, Mr Shaw,' said Ludd, taking a slurp of his tea. 'I believe you— Lord knows I don't suspect *you* of anything— it's just that I'd like to get things clear in my mind and I'd like both you and Mr Dewynter to answer a few questions while I have you both together.'

He consulted his notebook, and turned back a page.

'Now, Mr Dewynter, are you well enough to speak?'

Dewynter waved away the doctor, who had just made the final knot on a bandage around the man's head.

'Yes, yes, I'm quite all right thank you,' said Dewynter.

The medical man snapped his bag shut and made to go, but Ludd touched him on the arm. 'Don't go too far, doctor, will you? I'll need you again in a few moments.'

'Very well,' replied the doctor, 'but I would rather begin my examinations of the body as soon as possible, Chief Inspector. There is no refrigerator at the…facilities here in Eastburgh.'

'Refrigerator? What are you on about?' asked Ludd impatiently.

The doctor sighed. 'For the, ah, deceased. In this hot weather…'

Shaw heard a little sob and saw that the housekeeper, Mrs Upton, had heard the last remark. Ludd did not seem to notice.

'Oh, of course,' nodded Ludd. 'Stupid of me. He'll go off like a dead fish in this heat. Right you are then, carry on. Let me have sight of your report the moment you finish it. Have it sent to the Seaview Guest House, not the local station.'

'Very well,' said the doctor briskly, and with that was gone.

Ludd nodded as the man left the room. Dewynter reached forward to his desk and took a packet of cigarettes, offered them around but received no takers, then lit one for himself.

'Ask away, Chief Inspector,' said Dewynter, exhaling a

171

plume of smoke which appeared bright blue in the morning light slanting through the open study windows.

'As you know,' said Ludd, 'I got here a little later than the others, on account of having to be turned out of my bed by one of the lads here, but I understand from the pair who arrived here first, that you disturbed an intruder around 1.00 a.m.'

There was a clattering of tea-cups from the corner of the room as Mrs Upton let out a sob into her handkerchief.

'Mrs Upton,' said Dewynter tactfully with a smile. 'I wonder if you would be so kind as to prepare some of your excellent sandwiches in the kitchen for the Chief Inspector and his men. I'm sure they must be famished.'

'Very good sir,' said the elderly lady in a choked voice, as she hurried out of the room.

'You lot can go home,' said Ludd to the constables. 'Make out a full report marked for my attention and then knock off, you've been on duty since late turn, I'll wager.'

There was a mumbling of 'thank you sirs' and tired salutes as the three constables shuffled out of the room.

'Where was I?' asked Dewynter when they had gone. 'Ah yes. The intruder. 1.00 a.m. I know it was then as I could see my alarm clock in the moonlight.'

'There was an altercation and you discovered the identity of the man,' proffered Ludd.

'Yes, it was Aethelstan Rooksley. He tried to disguise himself with a handkerchief over his face but I made sure to pull that off.'

'Did he say anything?'

'He demanded to know the whereabouts of a cylinder recording that he claimed had been given to me by Leslie Prior.'

Shaw felt his eyebrows raise involuntarily, and remembered what he had found next to Rooksley's body.

He decided, for the moment, to keep quiet.

'And had such a recording been given to you?' asked Ludd.

'Most certainly not,' said Dewynter, taking a long draw on his cigarette. 'I had no idea what the man was talking about, and told him so. Violence was then offered and I was obliged to disregard our Lord's commandment to turn the other cheek.'

'Looks like you copped some of it though,' said Ludd, looking at the bandage on Dewynter's head.

'My mistake was to assume my opponent would observe the Queensberry Rules, as I did,' said Dewynter with a smile. 'However, he must have decided it was better not to stay for the full round, and made his escape out of the open window.'

'And you followed him.'

'Quite right. I must confess I lost my temper and was not thinking straight. While giving chase I tripped and, I assume, knocked myself unconscious on a gravel path. I did not awaken until morning.'

'Any idea where he went?'

'None. I had somewhat lost my bearings myself. When I came to, I realised he must have been making for the cliff path.' Dewynter stubbed out his cigarette angrily. 'If I had known he was going that way I would have let him go without pursuit. Then perhaps he might still be alive.'

'Now, now sir,' said Ludd. 'Don't go blaming yourself. A man has a right to defend his own property. It's not your fault if a miscreant ends up falling over a cliff while you chase him away.'

Shaw bit his lip. 'May I ask, Chief Inspector…?'

'Yes, what is it, Mr Shaw?' asked Ludd.

'You are quite sure that Rooksley died in the fall from the cliff?'

'Seems plain enough to me,' said Ludd. 'The doctor says his injuries are consistent with a fall from a great height, and the soil at the cliff edge directly above is disturbed; he was running that way in the dark in a blind panic. Why, how else do you think he got there?'

Shaw frowned. He thought of the disappearing footprints on the sand. Should he mention them? But what on earth did they mean? And the note in Rooksley's book? Neither thing even existed any more— the footprints were washed away by the tide without anyone else having seen them, and the note was now a sodden mess of paper and ink. He decided that for the time being, it was better to keep silent.

'Of course, Chief Inspector. It does seem the most obvious answer.'

'I take it you didn't see any footprints around the body?' asked Ludd. 'It was under a foot of water by the time we got down there— my blasted socks are still wet— but I'm guessing you must have been there before the tide came in.'

'I...' Shaw paused before continuing. 'There were no prints anywhere...near the body. The sand was undisturbed.'

'Just as I thought,' said Ludd. 'So he must have fallen, otherwise you would have seen his footprints, and perhaps that of an assailant also.'

'Quite so,' said Shaw quietly.

'It seems to me obvious how he died,' said Ludd, nodding. 'What I *don't* understand is why he broke in here. You said he claimed Prior gave you a cylinder recording, Mr Dewynter. Any idea why?'

'None whatsoever,' said Dewynter. 'As you can see, I have a dictaphone here,'— he indicated the apparatus by his desk with a wave of his hand,— 'but all I have are my own sermon recordings. Rooksley grabbed most of them on the way out. I don't suppose…'

'I'm just coming to that,' said Ludd. 'You'll be pleased to hear that Mr Shaw recovered them on the beach from around Rooksley's body. He mentioned it to me briefly while the doctor was examining Rooksley. Mr Shaw?'

'Of course,' said Shaw, extracting the cylinders from his pocket and placing them on the desk. 'I do hope the water has not damaged them.'

'My dear chap,' said Dewynter. 'How splendid of you to have the presence of mind to do that. I rather think I would have run away screaming from the sight, from what the Chief Inspector has told me about the body.'

'Mr Shaw was in France during the war,' said Ludd. 'I imagine he's seen worse, though I agree it wasn't a pretty picture. You're better off not having seen it.'

'I got my commission as soon as I left school, just before the Armistice,' said Dewynter gloomily. 'The only action I saw was the regimental ball at Aldershot. By the time I got over there it was all finished.'

'Yes, well, you think yourself lucky, sir,' said Ludd. 'Now, back to this recording cylinder. Mr Prior says he gave it to a vicar on the pier. Have you any idea who…Good God!'

Shaw noticed Ludd's head turn sharply towards him. 'Why on earth didn't I think of it? A vicar, on the pier — that must have been *you*, Mr Shaw.'

'I?' asked Shaw in confusion. 'But Prior did not give me anything. He bumped into me, and…of course!'

Shaw picked up his knapsack from the floor and rummaged through it. He produced the recording cylinder he had found earlier.

'I found this in my bag and completely forgot about it,' he said excitedly. 'I could not think how it got in there but of course, Prior must have placed it in my bag. I always keep the flap open, you see. It would have been quite easy.'

Ludd snapped his fingers. 'And Prior told Rooksley he gave it to a vicar. That was all he managed to say, apparently, before he blacked out and fell. Rooksley must have thought he meant *you*, Mr Dewynter. I assume you're the only vicar in the town?'

'Yes, that's right,' said Dewynter, his eyes widening. 'And Rooksley knew I had a dictaphone — at any rate, he would have seen it when I invited him over here.'

'You invited him here, sir?' asked Ludd.

'Oh, it was years ago,' said Dewynter. 'I extended the hand of friendship at first, but it soon became clear to me the man was a charlatan, if not downright dangerous. Do you know, when he was in here I asked him what he thought of hermeneutics, and he said "Herman who?"'

Shaw laughed out loud and then stopped quickly as he saw the look of blank confusion on Ludd's face.

'Ought we to listen to the recording?' asked Shaw.

'If you please, gents,' said Ludd, gesturing to the apparatus by the desk. 'The recording device in the theatre that Prior was operating looked much the same as this one.'

Dewynter nodded. 'It's a common model I believe.' He took the little cylinder from Shaw and examined it. 'Same type. Should fit all right.'

He flicked on a switch and there was a low electrical hum. He then placed the cylinder in a little cradle at the top of the device and turned a knob; the cylinder began to spin and a crackling sound emerged from the small horn attached to the dictaphone.

Shaw, despite the heat of the morning, felt a chill run down his spine as he heard the recording.

'You caused a considerable disturbance in the house of God last night, Cotterill,' said a menacing voice from what sounded like a long way off.

'That's Rooksley,' said Dewynter, who was leaning forward in his chair, his face rapt in concentration.

'House of God, my foot,' said another voice. 'You're a charlatan, Rooksley, and I intend to prove it.'

'That's Cotterill, I think,' said Dewynter.

There then came what sounded like boots on wood, then that of a chair scraping on a floor; presumably, thought Shaw, as Cotterill got up from his stool.

'I will tell you this once, and once only,' said Rooksley. 'Stay away from my church, and stay out of things which you do not understand.'

'Oh I understand all right,' said Cotterill, and Shaw could tell the man was almost apoplectic with rage. 'I understand you're a cheat and a liar, taking money from people and giving them false hope to…don't you come any closer!'

'Look at you, ridiculous man with your child's puppet show,' hissed Rooksley. 'With a click of my fingers I can harness elemental forces sufficient to destroy someone as weak as you, Cotterill.'

'Don't…talk….daft….' said the other man in a choked voice. He sounded as if he were struggling to breath.

'Look at you now, worm,' said Rooksley with a laugh. 'I already have mastery over you. Without even touching you I have reduced you to…'

Rooksley's voice was cut off by the sound of a heavy crash on the floorboards. Then there was a moment of silence after which Rooksley said slowly, 'Is somebody there?'

Then there was a click and then silence, except for the whirring sound of the cylinder. The three men listened intently until the device finally stopped spinning. Dewynter reached forward to switch off the dictaphone, and sighed heavily.

'If ever evil had a voice, that was it,' he said. 'Poor Leslie, having to witness that. No wonder he panicked.'

'I've heard a few villains in my time but that sends shivers down my spine,' said Ludd, as he pushed his hat a little further back on his head. 'I can't say I'm sorry to see him packed off to the mortuary. Still, that concludes matters pretty neatly, I'd say.'

'Concludes matters?' asked Shaw.

'Yes, I'd say so,' said Ludd. 'Of course, it'll be up to the coroner, but it looks clear enough to me now what happened. Cotterill and Rooksley argued, and the strain was enough to bring on Cotterill's heart attack. Rooksley, after the recording ended, presumably found Prior spying and threatened him; Prior made a run for it and dropped the cylinder into Mr Shaw's bag, possibly fearing for his life. Rooksley managed to find Prior, and demanded to have the cylinder. Prior had one of his funny turns and fell off the cliff, but not before he'd blurted out he'd given the recording to a vicar.'

'Whom Rooksley, logically enough, assumed was me,' said Dewynter.

'Quite,' replied Ludd, 'but who in fact, although you did not realise it at the time, was *you*, Mr Shaw. But as far as Rooksley was concerned, there was a potentially damning piece of evidence on a recording cylinder in the possession of Mr Dewynter, and that's why he came here looking for it. '

'But he didn't find it, and instead I drove him to his death,' said Dewynter, shaking his head.

'Now now sir,' said Ludd. 'We'll have no more talk like that. You heard the dictaphone just now. That man was a nasty piece of work judging by his voice, and I should know; I've met a few characters in my time. He got what was coming to him when he fell off that cliff, if you ask me.'

'"Vengeance is mine, saith the Lord",' quoted Dewynter. '"I will repay". To think of it. A murder, here in Eastburgh.'

'We're jumping ahead of ourselves, sir,' said Ludd. 'I can't say until the inquest, of course, but as far as I can see, no murder has been committed. Indeed, not really any crime at all, other than threatening behaviour. Cotterill died, as far as we can tell, from natural causes. Rooksley says in the recording he didn't touch Cotterill and that ties in with the doctor's report. Prior has confirmed that also. Even if we'd caught him alive we'd have been lucky to make any charges stick.'

'There is one thing I ought to mention,' said Shaw. He wondered just how much he ought to reveal; he decided withholding physical evidence would be a step too far. He reached into his knapsack and produced the little book.

'This,' said Shaw, handing it to Ludd. 'I found it by Rooksley's body.'

'Oh yes?' said Ludd, eyeing the book without much interest. 'Bible, is it? Or do those Spiritualists use something else?' He flicked through the contents and handed it back to Shaw.

'Looks more like Italian than English. What's he doing with an Italian book?' asked the policeman.

'Not Italian, Chief Inspector, Latin,' said Shaw. 'It is, from what I could tell from my brief examination, a volume concerning the use of what, for want of a better term, we might call… black magic.'

'Hmm. From what I've heard of Rooksley that sounds like his sort of bedtime reading,' said Ludd with a frown.

'May I see that?' asked Dewynter.

'By all means,' said Ludd. 'Means nothing to me, but I expect you speak Latin like a native.'

Ludd handed Dewynter the book and he examined it carefully. After a few moments Dewynter looked up. 'I have studied some similar works, as part of a dissertation on medieval heresies. These are what we might call in common parlance, magic spells. There were all sorts of odd chaps around in the middle ages who fancied themselves as magicians. Alchemists and the like.'

'I thought as much,' said Shaw, 'although my Latin is rather rusty. I have not made much use of it since university days.'

'This is all very interesting, gentlemen,' said Ludd, 'but I don't see it has much bearing the case.'

'What's this paper doing here?' asked Dewynter, as he gingerly handled the note, used as a bookmark, that Shaw had found earlier.

'I found that with the book,' said Shaw. 'Unfortunately, I dropped it on the beach and the writing has been obliterated.'

'Did you get a chance to read it?' asked Ludd.

'I did, but now you mention it, I am struggling to remember the exact words, and part of it was already smudged. Something about meeting an old acquaintance that might be to Rooksley's advantage.'

'Hmm,' said Ludd. 'Could be anything. I don't see it makes much difference now anyway. No, I'll get the local lads to ask around on the off-chance that anyone saw Rooksley fall over that cliff, but it seems pretty clear to me what happened. You'll both have to appear at the inquest, of course.'

'You are closing the investigation?' asked Shaw.

Ludd took his jacket from where it hung on the back of

Dewynter's study chair, and shrugged it on with a chuckle.

'You sound like you've been watching the new American talkies,' he said. 'Mrs Ludd drags me along to the kinema to see them sometimes. Detective films. They always end with the case closed, all ends neatly tied up. Unfortunately real policing isn't like that, though it would be nice if it were. No, Mr Shaw, I'm not closing the case, but realistically there's little else I can do here now, and I've a dozen other investigations on the go back in Midchester. That's another thing the films don't show you. The 'tec grappling with more than one case at a time.'

'I understood you were working whilst your wife was here on holiday,' said Shaw. 'Will she not be disappointed if you depart?'

'No,' said Ludd dismissively. 'Mrs Ludd? Disappointed? She's already thick as thieves with a widow woman from Macclesfield she met in the hotel. I won't be missed by her for a few days. Mind you, I can't say the feeling will be mutual— I shall be eating police canteen food until she gets back. Oh and by the way, I shall try to get the coroner to combine the inquest for both Coterill and Rooksley. Hopefully it will be next week sometime, when you will still be here, Mr Shaw.'

Shaw nodded but Dewynter did not look up from the little book.

'Did you hear me, Mr Dewynter?' asked Ludd. 'You'll be obliged to attend the inquest as well.'

'Yes, yes,' said Dewynter, distractedly.

'Something interesting in that book, then?' asked Ludd.

'Perhaps,' said Dewynter, with a worried expression on his face. 'The note was used to mark a chapter concerning spells for the raising of *ales daemonium*. A winged demon.'

Chapter Eleven

Word travelled quickly around Eastburgh about the death of Rooksley; a local journalist who had already managed a 'scoop' for one of the county dailies about Prior's fall and subsequent rescue, had got hold of sufficient information from his sources to hammer out a quick piece for the early edition of the evening paper entitled 'Horrifying Death of Suffolk Satanist'.

By late afternoon it was the talk of the town, and some of the more intrepid holidaymakers had ventured out to the Wooden Witness, where one local entrepreneur had started whittling off pieces of the ancient monument with his penknife and selling them for a shilling each, until a constable was despatched to protect the site.

Shaw had seen the evening news headlines outside a newsagent's stand close to the pier, and he sighed as he tapped out his pipe into a little heap of ashes on the sand, which he then buried with his foot. He and his wife were seated on deckchairs on the beach in the shade of the promenade; he had had no energy nor enthusiasm to do anything else after the events of the morning, and instead let the sound of the waves and the shrieks of happy children playing by the shoreline wash over him.

'At least it wasn't a murder this time,' said Mrs Shaw, as she fanned herself with a copy of the evening newspaper.

Shaw grunted. 'What was that, my dear?'

'I said at least it wasn't a murder this time.' She counted off on her fingers. 'Cotterill, died of natural causes; that young man, what was his name, Prior, thought to have been pushed off the cliff, but it turned out he wasn't, and isn't dead now anyway, and now this Rooksley person *is* dead, but it was an accident. It all has the makings of a splendid murder story, except nobody has actually been murdered.'

'You sound almost disappointed, Marion,' said Shaw. 'I would have thought by now that you would have realised detective stories and the talkies are nothing like real life. Surely we have seen enough of murder to last us all our days.'

'You are right of course, Lucian,' said Mrs Shaw. 'But you do sound rather down in the dumps about it all. I put it down to the shock of finding that poor man on the beach. And this dreadful heat of course. Eighty-one degrees and set fair, it said on the hotel barometer. When *will* it end?' She sat back in her chair with a long exhalation and continued to fan herself with the newspaper.

'I am sorry,' said Shaw. 'I did not mean to sound angry. You are right. It was rather a shock finding Rooksley in that…condition.'

He fell silent and stroked the head of Fraser, who was lying prostrate under Shaw's deckchair in an attempt to keep cool. It was not, he thought, merely the shock of finding Rooksley that troubled him. He had seen worse in France, and Rooksley had at least, he assumed, expired quickly, unlike some poor souls he had seen die after agonising hours on barbed wire.

What troubled him were those strange footprints on the sand, which were now as lost as the passing moment. If only he had had a camera! There must have been a logical explanation for those prints to end so abruptly, he thought.

But what? The words of Cowper's hymn suddenly formed before his eyes:

God moves in a mysterious way
His wonders to perform;
He plants His footsteps in the sea
And rides upon the storm.

'He plants His footsteps in the sea…' that must have been it, thought Shaw. The only rational explanation was that somebody walking along the beach had somehow managed to get into the sea. Some fluke of the tide, a freak wave perhaps, had then erased the prints, making it appear as if the man had disappeared into thin air. It was probably, he concluded, a fisherman who had picked up a mate from the shore in a little boat, and a wave had washed away all trace of the encounter.

Such a thing was entirely possible, he thought, on a beach with such strange tides and currents. He breathed a sigh of relief and was glad he had not mentioned it to Chief Inspector Ludd.

He was still troubled, however. An uncomfortable feeling in the pit of his stomach, which had been growing all day. He would, he realised, have to speak to the Guru about the matter. If, as seemed likely, Rooksley had been a blackmailer, this surely threw some suspicion on the Guru himself. Could he have…no, thought Shaw. The idea was preposterous. To put his mind at rest, he decided he would speak to the man this evening; and if he was not satisfied with his answer, he would tell all to Ludd.

'Why don't you have a little nap, Lucian?' asked Mrs Shaw. 'You must be awfully tired after such an early start, and all the…excitements.'

'I am quite all right, my dear,' said Shaw. 'Shall we

perhaps walk back to the hotel? Tea will be served shortly.'

'What a good idea,' said his wife. 'I feel rather like having a nap myself, but it always seems indulgent. "O wretched man, that I should sleep in the daytime," as Bunyan put it.'

'Bunyan took it from Revelations, I think, but I agree,' said Shaw, and his thoughts began to drift again. He did not think it likely that the Guru had been involved in the death of Rooksley, and yet…No, he thought, it was too fantastic; a product of an overwrought mind, brought on by the shock of the morning's events. What was the Greek term the alienists used for it? Paranoia, that was it. He was indulging in paranoia, and that must stop. He stood up and dusted sand off his trouser cuffs.

'Come along, my dear; let us go back,' Shaw said, as he breathed in a lungful of sea air. 'I am quite parched; a pot of Earl Grey will be most refreshing.'

As the worst of the day's heat began to wane, Chief Inspector Ludd folded the last of his clean shirts into his battered old suitcase and pushed the lid shut. He realised his wife would not be back home with him until after next washday, which meant he would have to scrub his combinations and collars out in the sink every night before bed. At least they'll dry quick in this blasted heat, he thought.

He put his hat on and walked down to the hallway, where the sour-faced manageress eyed him suspiciously.

'You're leavin'?' she asked, her voice more 'common-prim' than usual.

'That's right,' said Ludd, placing his suitcase on the tiled floor of the little hallway. 'Would you telephone for a taxi cab, just to the station?'

'I wonder you don't go straight through and use it yourself.'

'That was official police business on those occasions, madam. This is only a personal call, but if it's any trouble I'll use the box in the road.'

'That's quite all right, I shall do it,' sniffed the woman. 'I understood you was wanting tea for two this afternoon. Shall I cancel it?'

'Tea?' asked Ludd in a confused voice.

'Yes,' said the woman. 'Your wife ordered it just before she went out with Mrs Throakby-Marlow.'

'Ah, well that's all right then. Mrs Ludd is staying on here. The tea'll be for her and her new pal Mrs, whats-her-name. I'm off back to Midchester, see.'

'I see,' said the woman, with an arched eyebrow, and Ludd got the unpleasant feeling that the harmony of his marital situation was being subtly called into question.

'I hate to leave such a *friendly* little establishment,' said Ludd, 'but I'm needed elsewhere on police business. Send the account to my address, and see that it's properly itemised, won't you?'

'Of course,' said the woman, with pursed lips, as she turned to go into the back office to telephone for a taxi. She stopped, and turned back to Ludd.

'Oh, I almost forgot,' she said. 'This came for you a few minutes ago. I was about to bring it up. When I had the time, of course.'

'Of course,' said Ludd dryly.

She proffered an official-looking brown envelope to Ludd. He frowned, turned away from the woman and opened the envelope. It was from the police doctor. Quite the busy bee, thought Ludd; he must, he realised, have done the whole thing as soon as he got Rooksley's body back.

What Ludd saw in the report made him frown even more.

'Why the devil didn't he tell me that before?' he said under his breath, then turned to the manageress.

'On second thoughts,' he said to the woman, who was pretending not to be interested in the report from over Ludd's shoulder, 'make that tea for three. I'm staying on.'

After tea, while his wife was reading in their room, Shaw resolved that he would speak to the Guru. He had hoped, in that peculiar English way, that he might just 'bump into' him rather than seek him out directly, but he was not to be found by accident. The function room used by him as a lecture theatre was empty; the little board by the door indicated that the final lecture, on 'the Breath and the Spirit' had ended some time ago.

Finally Shaw could wait no longer and asked Lucas, the manager, if he might know the Guru's room number as he wished to speak to him on a personal matter. Surprisingly, the man consented, and a few moments later Shaw knocked on the door of room 335, on the top floor of the hotel at the end of what, Shaw assumed, must have been a servant's corridor when the hotel was built.

A voice answered his knock and Shaw walked in. The room was tiny and sparsely furnished, and the Guru sat cross-legged on the floor. It was intensely hot under the eaves of the building, despite the window being wide open, and some sort of pungent incense— sandalwood, at Shaw's guess, was burning in an ashtray.

'My dear Mr Shaw,' said the Guru. 'What a pleasant surprise. I have just finished my afternoon meditation. Please, sit down. I expect you would prefer a chair.'

The Guru stood up and moved a plain upright chair into the middle of the room, motioned for Shaw to sit on it, then sat on the metal-framed bed.

'My apologies for the sparseness of the room,' said the Guru. 'It is intended for the man-servants of wealthy guests, and the like. It is perfectly adequate for my taste, although Miss Sloan has a better-appointed room directly below this one. She booked it for me, but I insisted that she take it instead. I am born to asceticism, but she only came to it later in life and one cannot expect her to be devoid of material attachments as I.'

Shaw was not particularly in the mood for polite conversation. 'I will come to the point, Guru,' he said, sitting bolt upright on the hard chair. 'It is about Rooksley.'

At the mention of the name, the Guru's impassive smile did not change and Shaw did not notice any glimmer of recognition in the man's deep-set, dark brown eyes.

'You will have heard the news,' continued Shaw.

'Mr Murray told me of it at luncheon,' said the Guru, 'and the evening newspaper mentions it, so Miss Sloan tells me. It is quite the talk of the town. Some say it is "black magic"'. He leant forward and gave a mischievous chuckle.

'I fail to find it amusing,' said Shaw. 'The man died a hideous death.'

'Forgive me, Mr Shaw, I did not intend to imply levity. I was merely amused at the superstition, in a supposedly advanced culture, that ascribes the quality of magic to something as simple as the motion of gravity.'

'I have read the newspaper report myself also,' said Shaw, 'which gives the official explanation that the man died after falling off the cliffs following an attack on the vicar of this parish.'

'A sad business,' said the Guru, shaking his head. 'But fate, or what we call in the east, *karma,* is inescapable. How is it your Bible puts it? "For all they that live by the sword shall perish by the sword", I think?'

'I will be frank, Guru,' said Shaw. 'Yesterday you asked me, in confidence, to attempt to identify a man you believed to be blackmailing you. At the pre-arranged time and place, I find the body of a man battered to death in the most horrific way. You will pardon me if I do not become somewhat suspicious that this happens after you have strongly implied the man was blackmailing you.'

The Guru rubbed his temples and took a small medicine bottle from the bedside table. He poured a small amount into a teaspoon and swallowed it.

'Forgive me, Mr Shaw. A sedative prescribed for a nervous condition with which I am afflicted. Unlike Mr Gandhi, I have nothing against western civilization, particularly modern medicine.'

'I am sorry to hear that,' said Shaw. 'Please continue.'

'Nobody was more shocked than I to learn of Rooksley's death,' said the Guru, with no trace of a smile this time.

'But I can assure you *I* had nothing to do with it.'

'But do you not see how bad this looks for you,' replied Shaw, 'if the police pursue certain lines of enquiry? You have obliged me, if not to lie directly, then to keep certain matters quiet from the authorities. It is only because of my acquaintance with the investigating officer that I am above suspicion myself.'

At this last remark, Shaw thought he saw a glimmer of surprise in the Guru's implacable expression.

'I understood that what I told you was in confidence, Mr Shaw. If that is no longer acceptable, you must do as your conscience dictates.'

'I would rather you spoke to the police yourself,' said Shaw. 'It will look better for you and may enable you to keep Miss Sloan's name out of things.'

'But why, Mr Shaw?' asked the Guru plaintively. 'From the newspaper report, it appears the authorities are not looking for any killer. The man fell from the cliff and died, with no suspicion of, what is the English phrase? "Foul play".

*Because I don't believe that...*Shaw was about to say, then checked himself. He saw in his mind's eye the disappearing footprints in the sand...the strange, half obliterated note...there was something more to the whole thing than a fall from a cliff. But what?

Before Shaw could answer there was an urgent knock at the door. The Guru bade the enquirer to enter, and Lucas appeared.

'Beg pardon sir,' he said to the Guru, then looked relieved as he saw Shaw. 'Glad I've caught you Reverend Shaw— I tried your room but your wife said she didn't know your whereabouts. Then I remembered you'd asked for this room number.'

'What is it?' asked Shaw.

Lucas looked at the Guru and back at Shaw. He seemed uncertain of what to say.

'Ah…an urgent matter of some delicacy, sir. Might you step outside?'

'I'll make this brief,' said Ludd, as they walked in the gardens of the hotel a few moments after Lucas had fetched Shaw. The 'matter of some delicacy' referred to by the manager had, of course, been the arrival of Ludd.

'This isn't official,' said the Chief Inspector, 'but all the same I'd rather not discuss it in the lobby as we did before. Walls have ears, and so on.'

Ludd paused as they crossed the lawn, and looked at a pair of Indian undergraduates, dressed in the peculiar hybrid costume of *lungi*, or male skirt, topped with an English cricket blazer. They sat in earnest conversation with Miss Sloan on the grass.

'Seen a few of these…dusky-hued gentlemen around the town,' said Ludd. 'Some sort of cultural exchange, is it?'

Shaw explained about Guru Vinda Baba's conference, and the Church of Mental Magnetism; Ludd responded with a professionally raised eyebrow.

'But who's the woman?' he said with some suspicion. 'Surely she's not Indian?'

'That is Miss Sloan, assistant to the Guru.'

'Hmm,' said Ludd. 'Not sure I approve of this sort of

thing. "East is east, and west is west, and never the twain shall meet", in my book, but it's a free country I suppose. Anyway, that wasn't the reason for the visit. I'm here on a police matter.'

'I was under the impression that you were on holiday,' said Shaw. 'Shall we sit down?'

He motioned to a bench under a cypress tree, and the two men sat down in the delicious relative coolness of the shade.

'*Working* holiday,' stressed Ludd. 'I was intending to go home this afternoon but something in the doctor's report on Rooksley's death has made me reappraise the whole thing.'

Shaw felt a slight unease in the pit of his stomach. He was certain now that he should have revealed what he knew to the Chief Inspector, and, having informed the Guru of this course of action, he now prepared to take it.

'Chief Inspector,' said Shaw, slowly filling his pipe, 'may I explain…'

'Just a minute, Mr Shaw,' said Ludd. 'You don't know what I'm going to say yet.'

'I think I have some idea,' said Shaw as he lit his pipe and puffed fragrant blue clouds of tobacco smoke into the still, hot air. 'Some evidence has been uncovered that suggests Rooksley did not die in the manner you first thought.'

'How the devil…I mean, how on earth did you know that?' asked Ludd. 'Unless of course…'

'Unless of course, I had something to do with it?' asked Shaw slowly.

'Now look here, Mr Shaw,' said Ludd brusquely. 'I'm not suggesting anything of the kind. I know you too well from that business in Lower Addenham last year to think you'd have anything to do with something like this. But I'll come to the point. Did you see *anything* or *anyone* suspicious on North Beach this morning? I mean, of course, before you found Rooksley's body?'

Shaw paused. He decided it was time to reveal the reasons he had been walking on the beach. He explained about the Guru and the blackmail letters, taking care to keep Miss Sloan's name out of the matter.

After he had finished, Ludd pushed back his hat and mopped his brow with his handkerchief. 'Quite a tale. I do wish you'd mentioned this before.'

'I was told the matter in confidence, which is why I was urging the Guru to speak to the police. He gave me leave to inform you. Did you not, however, think it was peculiar that I should be going for a bathe at just that spot, early in the morning?' asked Shaw.

'The thought did cross my mind, but there's no harm in an early morning swim. I wouldn't mind one myself only I don't think I've been able to fit into my bathing costume since about 1919.'

'May I ask, what was it in the doctor's report that changed your mind about the case?' asked Shaw.

'Well...and this is strictly confidential, see, because you're a witness and this won't look good at the inquest if it comes out we've been chatting, but I trust you, Mr Shaw, and you were a great help on the Cokeley case. I've got nobody helping me on this apart from a few of the local lads who, though they try their best, are better suited to finding lost kiddies on the beach than this sort of thing. So here's the rub. It doesn't look like Rooksley died in a fall from that cliff.'

'I understood,' said Shaw, 'that there were signs of damage to the cliff edge, commensurate with someone having fallen over. They were pointed out by you when we recovered the body from the beach.'

'Yes,' said Ludd, wiping his forehead again and stuffing his handkerchief into his breast pocket where it hung like the corner of a wilted bed-sheet. 'But that damage looked to me like the same marks that were there after Prior went over. I checked myself during the search. I won't be able to make a proper comparison until I see the photographs and according to the local boys they have to wait until Boots' develops them, would you believe it? But I'm pretty sure he didn't fall off that cliff.'

'How can you be so certain?' asked Shaw, relighting his pipe.

'Firstly,' said Ludd, counting on his fingers, 'I couldn't see any evidence of the cliff edge being disturbed at any point where Rooksley could have fallen off and landed where you found him.'

'Perhaps he left no marks,' replied Shaw. 'The soil is not necessarily loose and crumbling along the entire cliff edge.'

'That was my thought as well. But there's something else. I assumed Rooksley fell off the cliff and landed slap bang on that wooden pillar thing on the beach, and that was what killed him, and he lay there like an unpaid bill on a metal spike until you found him at dawn.

'Now, Mr Dewynter says he was woken by Rooksley at around 1.00 a.m., and chased him out of the house about ten minutes later. It would take about ten more minutes to run from the vicarage to the cliff edge.'

'At least,' said Shaw. 'It was quite some way when we came back from recovering Rooksley's body.'

'Indeed. So if he fell off the cliff at, say, 1.30 a.m., he would have been dead for two and a half hours when you found him. But the doctor says rigor mortis hadn't set in when he first examined him. He's also found something to do with congealment of the blood—I don't understand it but I'm not a doctor— that makes him pretty certain Rooksley had only been dead about 30 minutes when you found him.'

Shaw puffed slowly on his pipe, so as not to overheat the bowl, as he was wont to do when thinking hard. 'Therefore he could not have died in a fall from the cliff some hours previously,' he said.

'No,' replied Ludd firmly. 'And there's something else. The cause of death was internal injuries caused by that wooden spike. But the doctor says he also had massive *external* injuries to his face and upper torso consistent with a blow or blows from an extremely large object. He didn't get that from falling on the pillar. That's why he was in a such a mess when you found him.'

Shaw shuddered as the image of Rooksley's corpse flashed before his eyes. He swallowed and willed it away. 'What sort of object?'

'Doctor has no idea,' sighed Ludd. 'A club, or a large hammer of some sort is all he could think of. Whoever did it must have been terrifically strong, both to inflict the damage on him and lift him up on to that spike.'

'Indeed,' said Shaw. 'It took three of the constables to get him down.'

'Exactly. And what puzzles me is, why weren't there any bally footprints on the sand if a person or persons unknown battered him to death and then stuck him up on a wooden post like Christ almigh…er, well, you see what I mean, Mr Shaw. The sand would have to be disturbed.'

'Yes, yes,' said Shaw, as he tapped out the ashes from his now cold pipe onto the flowerbed next to him. 'According to the tides, if he had died as close to 4.00 a.m. as the doctor says, anyone walking on that part of the beach would have left footprints, and yet there were none. There is something else I did not mention previously.'

'Oh yes?' replied Ludd, arching an eyebrow.

'When I told you there were no footprints around the body, that was true. But I *did* see some footprints further along the beach, with a pattern consistent to that of the sole of Rooksley's shoes. The prints disappeared.'

'What do you mean, disappeared?'

'Simply that. They stopped, and there were no further prints to be seen anywhere around.'

'Just upped and flew away, did he?'

'I think it is more likely that it was a fisherman of some sort who was picked up in a boat and a surge of tide, before the main influx of water, in some way erased the prints.'

'Hmm, possible I suppose,' mused Ludd. 'You said the prints matched Rooksley's shoes, though.'

'They were approximately the same size— about ten, I should say— with the marks of a metal segment on the heels.'

'Probably several million men with shoes like that,' said Ludd. 'I still wish you'd mentioned this earlier. Why didn't you?'

'I was concerned that I was drifting into the realms of amateur detection again, Chief Inspector, and that there was most likely no connection with the case.'

'Hmm, I suppose so,' said Ludd. 'But don't be keeping things like this from me again, will you? My next steps are going to be to speak to this Guru chappie, and redouble the efforts by the local boys to find someone— anyone— who might have seen what happened on that beach. I'm treating this as a murder enquiry now, and hopefully the Chief Constable will send me some assistance. Lord knows I need it.'

'It will be difficult to find witnesses that were about so early,' said Shaw. 'In addition, the cliffs slope upwards, making it impossible to see onto the beach unless one is on the cliff edge, and there are no buildings which overlook it either. I believe that is why Rooksley may have suggested it as the place at which the money should be left.'

'Don't I know it,' said Ludd, shaking his head. 'This thing's got me stumped, that's for sure.'

'Would it have been possible, do you think,' mused Shaw, 'for Rooksley to have been beaten elsewhere— on the cliffs perhaps, and then thrown over?'

'I thought of that,' said Ludd. 'Possible, but unlikely— as I said before, there's no signs of disturbance on the cliff edge apart from where Prior fell over. For someone to get *thrown* over, there would have to be twice the amount of scuffs and what-not, but there's nothing. No Mr Shaw, my best hope is finding someone who saw something at daybreak. I've got men asking down at the harbour as I'm hoping some fishermen might have seen something.'

'Let us hope so,' said Shaw. 'Will that be all, Chief Inspector? Time is getting on, and my wife will be wondering where I am.'

'Of course, of course,' said Ludd distractedly as the two men stood up. 'It's just…well I was wondering…'

Shaw looked at Ludd and sensed some reserve on the man's part in mentioning something.

'Yes, Chief Inspector?'

Ludd took a deep breath. 'I'm not much of a church-going man, Mr Shaw. I leave that sort of thing to Mrs Ludd. But I remember my lessons from Sunday School, and the story about when the devil took Him,'— here Ludd gave spoken emphasis to the capitalised pronoun— 'up the high mountain and offered Him all the kingdoms of the world.'

'The Temptation in the Wilderness,' replied Shaw.

'That's the one,' said Ludd. 'What I'm driving at, sir, is

197

this: that book of spells and what-not you found by the body…and now this Guru person and his Indian mysticism…it sounds fantastical, and I'm only mentioning it because I've heard such things in the bible like I told you, but do you think Rooksley might have been involved in, I don't know, something we don't understand? Demonic, I suppose is the word I'm looking for. You heard the way Rooksley talked on that dictaphone recording, Mr Shaw. Made your blood run cold, I'll wager.

'What was he mixed up in? That's what I'd like to know. For someone to do that to another human being and leave him up there on that post…I've never seen the like. Of course there was worse happened in the war, but that was because someone copped a packet from a whizz-bang or stepped on a land mine. It wasn't done *deliberate*, is what I mean. Even the Huns wouldn't have done something like that. And then there's the lack of footprints on the sand, as if he wasn't even put there by a human.'

Chapter Twelve

By Tuesday the news of the murder had spread across the country and the name of Eastburgh appeared even in the hallowed pages of *The Times* and on the BBC's wireless news programme. The little town was just large enough, fortunately, to absorb the inevitable influx of reporters and the various types of ghoulish camp-followers who appear on the scenes of recent murders, without causing too much concern for the locals or damaging trade.

The majority of holidaymakers, it seemed, were not overly troubled by a brutal slaying little more than a mile away from where they played on the sands or strolled along the promenade; the landlords and publicans spoke to one another of increased profits, and the two local charabanc hire companies vied with each other to take the curious out to the Wooden Witness, which was now protected by a paling fence and stern 'keep out' signs erected by the local council.

The murder had, it seemed, also boosted interest in Major Blair's aeroplane tours; tabloid news photographers were keen to get shots of the Wooden Witness from above in order that their dexterous technicians might paint in Rooksley's corpse to create artists' impressions of the murder scene.

At the little airfield outside Eastburgh, Nobby Finley,

Blair's mechanic, was sick to death of the whole thing already. He had already been disturbed several times by reporters wanting to go up, but Blair was nowhere to be seen. In fact, he was sick of Blair as well. A jumped-up little temporary gentleman was what he thought of him, half-cut most of the time and swanning around giving orders like he was still bossing the natives in the Black Hole of Calcutta or wherever it was he had come from.

Finley stretched and eased his painful back muscles, then returned to polishing the Sopwith Camel. He was too old for this caper, he decided, and too old to get another job. 53 years old, in the middle of a slump, and him not even a proper aircraft mechanic.

He had started out working in a bicycle shop, and then picked up the motor-cycle and motor-car trade when those had come along. When the war broke out he was considered too old to fight at first, but finally had got himself a cushy billet in the Royal Flying Corps and had been put to work on servicing aeroplanes— a specialist job, but if you knew one end of a spanner from the other you could pretty much get any job you wanted by 1916.

That was when the drinking had started in earnest; he had always enjoyed a drop, but during the long, tedious two years he had spent on that blasted airfield in France, there had only been two diversions in the local town when he got a pass; bottles of wine at a few centimes each, or women at not much more. He had never had much interest in tarts; especially not, he thought with a grimace, French tarts, so he had taken to the wine.

He took a swig from a bottle of brown ale, and tossed the cleaning rag into a heap in the corner of the shed. He had changed back to beer on his return to England from the war— French wine was far too expensive— and had been kicked out of a number of jobs until finally he had got this one, miles away from his native town of Coventry. Here he would most likely have to stay until he dropped dead from drink. That was one good thing about the Major, he thought. He was usually too drunk himself to notice that his 'batman' as he called him, was much the same way. Their drinking patterns were also similar. Both liked to work early in the morning so that they could have the afternoon free for boozing.

He looked up to see a stout party wearing a bowler hat and carrying a raincoat enter the shed.

'I told you lot we're closed,' said Finley, in his characteristic West Midlands whine. 'All enquiries to Major Blair, care of the Excelsior Hotel.'

'I'm not here for a jolly round the bay,' said the man. 'My name's Ludd. Chief Inspector Ludd.'

Finley instinctively braced himself up. He had had a few encounters with the law in his time, and knew that a surly attitude was the worst he could adopt. He tried, as best he could, to be charming instead.

'If it's about them library books I never give back in 1912, I'll come quietly,' he said quickly, with a grin which exposed nicotine-stained teeth.

'Spare me the music-hall act,' said Ludd, wiping his brow with his handkerchief. 'I've walked the length of these cliffs today and you're the last person I've come to and after this I'm going home, so I'll make it brief. Did you happen to see anything suspicious on the beach yesterday morning, at dawn?'

'This about that medium feller what got himself killed?'

'That's right.'

'People are saying him was killed by evil forces. That him were a devil worshipper.'

'Then people shouldn't be so bally silly. Did you see anything?'

'No.'

'Not here at that time?'

'No, but I couldn't have seen anything anyway, 'cos yow can't. North Beach in't visible from here.'

'I didn't say anything about North Beach. How do you know the body was found there?'

'Papers, innit. All over them. And on the wireless.'

'Hmm. So you didn't see anything at all? This would have been about 4.00 a.m. or thereabouts.'

'I didn't get here until five o'clock.'

'Bit early, isn't it?'

'Guvnor likes the plane to be out and ready for the first holidaymakers by 7.00 a.m., makes the most of the daylight. Takes me a couple of hours to work her over and get her spick and span like.'

'Guvnor?'

'Me boss. Major Blair. He was here afore I come, I know that much 'cos I saw him dash past me on the way home when I was coming here, all dressed up in his flying gear and with that blinking stupid scarf round his face. '

'Where do I find this Major Blair?'

'Care of Excelsior Hotel like I said. But he's laid up sick, I know 'cos I went round there and asked for him and they says he ain't come out of his room all day. But if you speak to him, tell him old Nobby's not happy. That's why I'm here late. Left it in a right state he did. I've had to waste valuable drinking time in getting the thing looking Bristol-fashion again. '

Chief Inspector Ludd, however, had already departed. Finley shrugged and opened another bottle of lukewarm brown ale.

'We have come to offer our thanks, Mr Shaw,' said the Guru as he walked with Miss Sloan across the hotel lawn to the terrace where Shaw was seated.

Shaw looked up from his bible. It was early evening and the shadows were just starting to lengthen; he had decided to have a moment of quiet reflection whilst his wife took Fraser for a walk along the beach.

'You have spoken to Chief Inspector Ludd?' asked Shaw cautiously.

'Indeed, indeed,' said the Guru. 'May I sit down?'

'Of course.' Shaw rose and pulled out the chair opposite. He looked around for another chair but the Guru laid a hand on his arm.

'No need, Mr Shaw. Shrutakirti will sit by me.'

Miss Sloan sat down cross-legged on the flagstone paving next to the Guru. Shaw looked at the pair with slight disquiet; there was something oppressively oriental in Miss Sloan's action of sitting on the ground, like the women who wore veils and walked two paces behind their husbands. In the bright, slanting afternoon light it could have been a scene from some sun-bleached Indian courtyard three thousand years ago.

'The Chief Inspector was most thorough,' said the Guru, 'and most respectful. Someone of my complexion would not receive such a polite interrogation from the British police in my homeland, as some of my Indian students will attest. They regard we brown fellows as mischievous. Beatings are not unknown.'

'I have met Ludd before,' said Shaw. 'He is, as far as I know, an exemplary officer.'

'The police here are based on a different model, Guru,' said Miss Sloan. 'On consent rather than coercion. They are civilians, just as we are. In India, however, the colonial oppressors…'

'Tsk, tsk, Shrutakirti,' said the Guru, raising a finger. Miss Sloan cut herself short and began again.

'The British administration, then,' continued Miss Sloan, 'feels it unwise to extend this model to the subject peoples, and the police in India are therefore a branch of the armed forces.'

'So I am led to believe,' said Shaw. He wished they would get to the point. He was still unsure of whether he could trust the Guru after what had happened.

'You were right to encourage me to reveal the blackmail plot to the police,' said the Guru, after looking around the terrace briefly to ensure they were not overheard. 'Chief Inspector Ludd is satisfied that I had no involvement. He assures me that I could not have assaulted Mr Rooksley since I was able to provide, what is the term, my alibi.'

'Oh yes?' asked Shaw.

'Yes,' replied the Guru. 'I was leading an early morning meditation session with Mr and Mrs Murray, before dawn, at the time the Chief Inspector thinks Rooksley was killed. We were engaged in Prahayana breathing exercises.'

'Er…quite,' said Shaw. 'I am glad to hear the matter is presumably over. But what of the other blackmailer? You said that you suspected another party was involved.'

'We have received no further communications,' said the Guru. 'It is my belief that the two were working in tandem, and following the death of Rooksley, the other has been frightened off.'

'You don't believe the other party may have been

involved in Rooksley's death?' asked Shaw.

'Who can say?' asked the Guru, shrugging his shoulders. 'It is a matter now for the police. At least I have been, as they say, "eliminated from enquiries".

'I feel also, Mr Shaw,' continued the Guru, 'that the universal forces that rule all things are working their purposes out. The Chief Inspector seems to think this fellow Rooksley was a thoroughly bad egg. Reports are coming through of his other crimes. The universal life force will not be altered in its course. As the uneducated might say, Rooksley had it coming to him. Fate, the wheel to which we are all bound, turns remorselessly and those who cannot rise above their earthly desires shall be chained to it for eternity, to return and suffer in innumerable reincarnations. Is that not so, Mr Shaw?'

Shaw cleared his throat. 'Something of that philosophy exists in Christianity,' he said carefully, 'but we are also granted the gift of grace and forgiveness. We are not doomed to eternal repetition of sin. I pray that Rooksley was forgiven at the last.'

'Perhaps, perhaps,' mused the Guru. 'You will forgive my oriental fatalism, Mr Shaw. That is something we Indians must learn to overcome if the new era of enlightenment is to dawn upon mankind, with all men as one. And on that note, we will say our farewells in case we do not meet again.'

'You are leaving?' asked Shaw.

'Miss Sloan has suggested, following the recent unfortunate events, that it would be better if we ended the lecture tour early, the day after tomorrow. It is likely that word will get out I was interviewed by the police; we cannot risk the adverse publicity. Mr Murray is also keen that no infamy be attached to the Church of Mental Magnetism before we begin our tour of his country.'

'I see,' said Shaw. 'Well, I wish you Godspeed, if we do not meet again before you leave.'

The Guru bowed as he and Miss Sloan stood up.
'Come, Shrutakirti,' he said. 'Let us walk in the gardens for a while.' They turned to go and walked slowly along the terrace where they momentarily disappeared from view as they walked down the steps to the lawn.

Shaw, having risen, sat back down, but before he could lapse back into reflection, he heard the scrape of boots on flagstones, and looked up to see a figure in front of him. It was Major Blair. The man looked terrible; his pallid face was unshaven and his eyes were bloodshot; his tousled hair was limp and greasy. His clothes had the appearance of being slept in.

'Padre,' he said huskily, looking about to ensure he was unheard. 'Padre, I'm afraid I've got myself in a bit of a pickle. That is…I've done something rather awful. Could we have a bit of a chat? Not here though. Up in my room.'

As Shaw rose to pull out the chair opposite, he caught sight of the Guru and Miss Sloan as they passed into view at the bottom of the stone steps. They were both looking up at him, and both wore worried frowns.

'Sorry about the subterfuge, Padre,' said Blair as he ushered Shaw into his hotel room. 'Too many people about on that terrace. Don't trust those Indian fellows, the ones in the pyjama trousers and All-India cricket blazers hanging around the place. Came across one too many of those types out east. Chucked stones at Britishers' cars and then sat there looking like butter wouldn't melt. Take a pew…I say, that's rather good isn't it, Padre? Take a pew. No pun intended, as they say.'

Shaw stepped back as the man stood a little too close to him while shutting the door. Blair reeked of stale alcohol, as did the room. Shaw sat down on an occasional chair and looked around the room; it had the half-hearted air of the permanent hotel resident about it, with too many personal effects in evidence for a holidaymaker, but not enough for someone's real home.

Rumpled clothes lay on the bed and spilled out of a steamer trunk on the floor; Blair's flying jacket, helmet, goggles and distinctive yellow scarf hung on the back of the door over a pair of grimy Royal Air Force overalls. Various pictures cut from magazines, mostly of aircraft, were pinned up on the walls. A framed photograph, a regimental one of some sort as far as Shaw could make out, was propped up on the dresser.

'Drink, Padre?' said Blair as he produced a bottle of cheap blended whisky from the wardrobe. 'You'll have to make shift with the toothbrush glass I'm afraid.'

'No thank you,' said Shaw. 'What is this about?'

Blair slumped down on the bed and poured a large shot of whisky into a grubby glass on the bedside table. He took a swig and looked at Shaw with rheumy eyes.

'Been a bad fellow, Padre. Need to make a sort of confession. Do you do those, or is that just the Romans?'

'Confession and absolution is a practice of the Church of England, Major Blair,' said Shaw firmly. 'But it is not something to be taken lightly over a drink. It requires genuine repentance.'

'Never been much of a believer, Padre,' said Blair. 'Perhaps I'm wasting your time.'

'No, no,' said Shaw. 'Perhaps we need not think in such strict theological terms. Would you rather simply just unburden yourself of something? Get something off your chest, so to speak?'

'That sounds a bit more my line,' said Blair, as he took another swig of whisky. 'But it mustn't go beyond this room.'

'Of course not. Anything you tell me will be in confidence.'

'Right-o,' said Blair. He then rubbed his eyes. 'Chri....I mean, by Jingo, I've got a headache. Never had such a head before. Must be coming down with something.'

'Perhaps a glass of water might help.'

'Good Lord no, never touch the stuff. I'll be all right. Look, the thing is, Padre, I've been a bad chap. Sent a letter. To that Indian fellow. Guru wallah. Wanders around here in his robes like he's in the Delhi Bazaar.'

'I know who you mean,' said Shaw. 'Why should there be any harm in sending him a letter?'

Blair looked worried, and took another swig of whisky.

'Look, all I did was send a little friendly note, telling the fellow I remembered him from my days in India, and if he could see his way clear to a little loan, I'd be much boliged…obliged to him, otherwise…'

'Otherwise what?' said Shaw sharply. He immediately regretted his harsh tone of voice, as it seemed to have had an effect on Blair.

'Stupid idea,' he said. 'Said far too much already.' He put his finger to his lips and made a shushing noise. 'Mum's the word from now on.'

'Major Blair, why are you telling me this? If you wish to make a sincere confession, God will hear you and forgive you. You do not require my presence.'

'I'm telling you because, damn it, I'm *scared*, Padre.'

'Scared of what?'

'Of what might happen to me. That fellow Rooksley...I've been laid up sick in here but I've read enough in the paper to know what happened to him. Chap was a rum cove, but still...he and I were sort of pals. He'd also tried to...well...ask the Guru for the loan of a few quid.'

'What of it?'

'Don't you see, Padre, whoever did that to him might do the same to me. For...asking for a loan, as it were.'

'Then you must go to the police.'

Blair drained the last of the whisky in his glass and poured himself another generous measure. 'Here's how,' he said, raising the glass half-heartedly. He then took a large swallow and sat forward on the bed, swaying slightly, his eyes unfocused.

'Don't think the police can do much,' he continued. 'Look, Padre, Rooksley was a shady character. Used to work with him out east when I ran a little flying service. Nasty temper. Once even beat up...one of the mechanics. Busted the chap's nose, just because he'd taken some popsie out in the plane on the quiet. Seemed to think he was some sort of wizard, or some such rot. Then he comes up against this Guru, who's also some sort of dabbler in the black arts, and ends up dead. Who's to say I won't be next?'

'The Guru is a spiritual teacher,' said Shaw. 'One that has the support of a well-regarded American organisation. He is hardly likely to be a dabbler in the black arts, as you call it.'

'That's what you think,' said Blair, conspiratorially. 'He might fool some Yankees, but not me. I know a thing or two about that chap. That's why I wrote Rooksley a little note. To check if he'd spotted what I'd spotted about the "Guru" as well.'

Of course, thought Shaw. That was the disintegrated note he had found on Rooksley's body. He pondered for a moment; was it right for him to turn what was originally intended as a pastoral consultation, into some sort of interrogation? Ought he to simply inform Chief Inspector Ludd? After some hesitation, he decided the present opportunity was too good to waste. If he stopped now, Blair might decide not to talk again.

'As I said, I'm not much of a lebiev…believer, Padre,' said Blair, who now looked on the verge of collapse. 'But these Indian fellows…seen them out there. Black magic. Heard of Kali?'

'The Hindu goddess of destruction, I believe,' said Shaw. 'She was the supposed inspiration for the murderous Thuggee cult of the last century.'

'S'right. Wrath and destruction. Seen statues of her in the temples. Horrible black staring eyes. Hordes of Indian blighters prostate…prostrating themselves in front of her in the dirt. Begging for help. Thought it was…lot of rubbish at the time but now…what if's true, eh? What if's true? He did for Rooksley and next it could…could be me. He's already done something to me.'

Blair closed his eyes and began to slump sideways on to the bed. Shaw stepped forwards and took him by the shoulders, gently shaking him.

'Major Blair…Major Blair, wake up. What do you mean, "he's already done something to me?"'

Blair opened his eyes and looked around, as if momentarily unsure of where he was.

'Don't know,' he whispered. 'Don't know how they work it. Pins in a wax doll, or something. Fact is, after I heard Rooksley had pushed that fellow off'cliff, I decided I didn't want any...anything more'do with him. Told the Guru meself, not in s'many words, but think he took the hint.'

'What do you mean, "took the hint"?,' urged Shaw.

'Sort of confessed to him,' replied Blair slowly. 'Not in s'many words, but mensh..mentioned there wouldn't be any more letters asking for money. Not from anyone in this hotel. Only telling all this as you're a clan of the moth, er, man of the cloth I mean, so-t'speak.'

'What has it to do with being a man of the cloth?' asked Shaw in exasperation. 'I have told you, this is a matter for the police.'

'Police...can't stop black magic,' whispered Blair. 'Guru's done something to me. Put a curse on me or whatever it is they do. After I spoke to him on Sunday night I was out like a light and didn't come to until nearly noon on Monday, with a blinding headache.'

Shaw sighed. He had met heavy drinkers who refused to accept they had a problem, but this seemed an extreme example. He wondered how to tactfully raise the subject of alcoholic blackouts, when Blair did it for him.

'I know what'thinking,' he said. 'Wasn't the booze. Only had one bally glass of champagne with the Guru...celebrate his new job in America...offered him a glass but he didn't want it. Next thing knew...woke up lunchtime...like a bally express train through my head. Told you. Pins 'n' dolls. Wax dolls. S'how they do it for....Kali.'

'Major Blair,' said Shaw insistently. 'You said you know "a thing or two" about the Guru. What is it you know? It is most important that...Major Blair, can you hear me?'

Blair's eyes opened momentarily and he put his finger to his lips theatrically.

'Wallsh have ears…' he slurred. 'Tell you about it tomorrow. Somewhere safer. Take you up in the kite again, eh? Man can think straight up there, in the heavens. "Nearer My God To Thee", what? Ha, ha! Nice 'n' early before the holi'makers start queueing. Seven o'clock. Meet you there.'

Blair put his finger to his lips again and made a shushing noise, then slumped sideways onto the bed. Shaw shook his shoulders but he was unresponsive. He made the man as comfortable as he could and was about to leave, when he caught sight again of the regimental photograph on the dresser.

He picked it up. On closer examination, it was not a regimental photograph, but a picture of some sort of aircraft crew in civilian clothing. A group of men stood on a dusty, sun-drenched field in front of an aeroplane, which he recognised as a Sopwith Camel, the same model that Blair owned. The photograph bore the title 'Simla Air Service 1923' in gilt letters, and the names of the men were listed.

In the front rank, squinting in the harsh sunlight with a topee held in his lap, was Major Blair, Pilot and Proprietor. Next to him were two other white men and on the end of the row was a slim man with a distrustful expression and a white streak in his hair, whom the caption listed as 'A. Rooksley, General Manager.' Shaw swallowed hard as he realised the only time he had seen that man, he had been a corpse.

It was the rear row that really caught Shaw's attention, however. Four Indian mechanics stood with arms folded; all except one had gaunt, dark faces, gleaming brilliantined hair and bristling moustaches, and the caption listed their names; A.A.T. Gunawaradena was the only one Shaw could pronounce. He then noticed the mechanic on the end of the row; taller, with a lighter complexion and more aquiline features than his fellows. He blinked, looked again and checked the name which, rather than Indian, appeared to be Greek: A. L. Kyriakides. The face, however, was unmistakeably that of the Guru, albeit without his distinctive broken nose.

What could it all mean? thought Shaw. He stood up to go, but as he turned to the door, he saw Blair roll off the bed on to the floor, hitting his head on the side of the night-table in the process. He groaned, and blood poured from a gash in his temple.

Shaw stepped forward and looked around vainly for something with which to staunch the blood flow; eventually he used the edge of the bed-sheet which was soon soaked. He decided that he must summon help, but did not think he ought to leave Blair unattended; one heard stories, he remembered, of drunken people choking when left alone. There was no telephone in the room, and he did not wish to alarm anyone by shouting for help.

He breathed a sigh of relief as he saw through the window the Guru and Miss Sloan far below on the lawn, accompanied by the usual gaggle of admirers, presumably following an outdoor lecture of some sort. He remembered that Miss Sloan had medical training; it would be quicker to summon her than to bother the hotel authorities.

Shaw shouted through the open window down to the gardens two stories below.

'Miss Sloan,' he shouted, 'might I trouble you to come up here, please? There has been an accident.'

A few moments later Miss Sloan was kneeling over Blair, while the Guru and Shaw watched with concern. A gaggle of Indian undergraduates jostled at the doorway to watch. One called out in a jocular tone.

'The British ruling class at leisure!' This was followed by

sounds of suppressed hilarity among his fellows.

The Guru turned and spoke sharply to them.

'Please, my brothers. Allow this poor man some privacy. Go, and meditate on his suffering that you might have compassion for all living beings.'

The young men hurried away and the Guru closed the bedroom door.

'Is he badly hurt, Shrutakirti?' he asked.

Miss Sloan looked up and Shaw saw a look of assured competence on her face as she patted Blair's temple with a damp towel. He could not help wishing she had been able to become a qualified doctor instead of playing second fiddle to the Guru.

'It is a little difficult to tell,' she said, 'with someone as inebriated as he is, but I think he will be all right. I have managed to staunch the blood-flow. The cut looks worse than it is. Help me get him into bed, please.'

Shaw and the Guru lifted the insensible Blair onto the bed, and, following Miss Sloan's instructions, put him on his side. As they did so, the man's eyes flicked open and he looked intently at Shaw. He seemed unaware of anyone else in the room.

'Shhh,' he said, in a stage whisper. 'Remember what I told you. About you-know-who. Tell you all about it tomorrow in the plane. Seven sharp.'

Then his eyes closed again and he began snoring heavily.

'I think we should leave him now,' said Miss Sloan. 'He just needs to sleep it off, and I've no doubt he's well practiced at that. Alcoholics who have reached his age generally have very robust constitutions; they have to in order to survive the daily punishment they give their bodies.'

'I am sorry to have troubled you, Miss Sloan,' said Shaw.

'I rather panicked at the sight of so much blood.'

'You did the right thing,' she said briskly. 'Always best to be on the safe side. I shall leave a glass of water for him, as he will be thirsty when he wakes up. I will also check in on him later, assuming the door is unlocked.'

Miss Sloan fetched a glass of water from the bathroom and placed it on the bedside cabinet next to Blair. She then turned to the Guru.

'We may go now, Guru, if you are willing,' she said. Shaw noticed the confident bedside manner had been replaced by the woman's habitual air of subservience.

'Of course, of course,' said the Guru distractedly, after a moment's hesitation. As they filed out of the room, Shaw noticed that the man's face wore a worried frown and that his gaze was fixed on the group photograph on the dresser.

Chapter Thirteen

'It's not you I want this time,' said Ludd as he met Shaw coming down the stairs of the hotel.

'Good afternoon, Chief Inspector,' said Shaw. 'Then I will not detain you.'

'Don't run off though, will you?' said the policeman. 'I'd like a word with you anyway a bit later on. There's been a new development in the case I think you ought to know about.'

The Guru and Miss Sloan appeared from around the corner on the staircase and Ludd started slightly, then nodded and touched the brim of his hat.

'Good afternoon, Miss Sloan, Mr…Vinda…sir.'

'Chief Inspector, what a pleasant surprise,' said the Guru. 'Do you wish to interview me again?'

'No sir,' said Ludd briskly. 'I'll let you get on with your lectures, or whatever it is you're doing. Good day to you.'

The Guru must have realised from the tone of Ludd's voice that he was not welcome, and so he politely bowed to the two men, and he and Miss Sloan rustled away down the staircase.

'I don't trust that fellow,' said Ludd, once the pair were out of earshot. 'Reminds me of some sort of music-hall mind-reader who's never been further east than Whitechapel.'

'I shall leave you to your business then, Chief Inspector,'

said Shaw, realising that he ought to see his wife. He was spending far too much time, he decided, on amateur investigations when he should be enjoying his holiday. 'I shall be in my room should you need to speak to me. Room 138.'

'Right you are,' said Ludd. 'I don't suppose you know where Room 109 is?'

'Why, I have just come from there,' said Shaw. 'That is Major Blair's room.'

'That's who I want to speak to.'

'I do not think that will be possible. The man is insensible.'

'What do you mean, insensible?'

'To put it bluntly, he is dead drunk. I was speaking to him earlier and he practically passed out.'

Shaw wondered if he had let slip too much. Would Ludd ask why he had been speaking with Blair? Fortunately, the man did not seem to notice, and Shaw continued speaking.

'Is it a matter of urgency that you speak with him?'

'No, I suppose not,' sighed Ludd. 'I'll call back in tomorrow when he's had a chance to sober up. That's another wasted walk up that hill.'

Shaw was intrigued by what Ludd might have discovered about Blair. 'Perhaps you have time for a glass of beer before you go?' he said.

'Well....' said Ludd, licking his lips, 'it's a little early, but I am supposed to be on holiday, not that you'd know it. I've requested help from the Chief Constable and he promised me a detective sergeant and a constable tomorrow but I'll believe that when I see it. So yes, offer accepted, although it's my turn to pay.'

Shaw smiled and led the way down the stairs through the lobby to the bar. A few moments later they were both seated in a shady corner of the terrace drinking beer.

Ludd let out a sigh of satisfaction as he held up his condensation-coated glass to the light, which twinkled through the golden bubbling liquid inside. 'That's good stuff, Mr Shaw,' he said. 'I believe that's what they call a lager beer. I haven't had that since the war— the Frenchies used to drink that stuff all the time. In heat like this it seems to satisfy better than a brown ale.'

'Quite so,' said Shaw. 'As a rule I do not drink it except in particularly hot weather. But I do not think you came here to discuss beer with me, Chief Inspector.'

'I'll get down to business then, Mr Shaw,' said Ludd, after taking another large swallow of his drink and smacking his lips. 'I'm telling you this because, well, I feel you're entitled to be kept informed, up to a point, following your unfortunate involvement with the case. And to tell the truth I've had it up to here with these local bobbies. They haven't the first idea of how to proceed in a case like this. It's a breath of fresh air to be able to talk to someone intelligent about it.'

'Thank you, Chief Inspector,' said Shaw. 'I appreciate your candour.'

'Very well then,' said Ludd. 'Thanks to the miracles of modern technology, I've been able to find out a little bit about this Rooksley fellow. Scotland Yard had something on him— involved in an extortion case a couple of years ago, though nothing was proven, it seems. Then the trail goes cold. The congregation at his chapel have closed ranks and won't tell me anything. But I did find out something in his living quarters. Seems he was out in India not so long ago— there were a few letters and papers about this, and the name of Simla came up. Know it?'

'The summer capital of India,' said Shaw. 'I have a cousin in the Civil who writes to me from time to time and so I have learned something of the place. I understand the whole administration decamps there every June to escape the heat of the plains.'

'That's right,' said Ludd. 'How they cope I don't know. It's 82 degrees here today and in India it can go well over 100. How do they stand it? Anyway, as I say, the miracle of modern technology enabled me to put through a telegram to the head of police in Simla.'

'What God hath wrought,' said Shaw with reverence.

'How's that?' said Ludd.

'It is a text from the Book of Numbers. It was the first message to be relayed by telegraph when the instrument was invented.'

'Was it really?' said Ludd. 'Well, it does seem a remarkable device, doesn't it? I'm used to it in England but never tried it to reach India before. Almost a miracle if you ask me. '

'Quite so,' said Shaw, trying to disguise his growing impatience. 'Did you find out anything?'

'I got a brief message back. Of course they can't say much in a telegram, as it costs a fortune and they have to keep the lines clear for more important matters, but the District Chief of Police in Simla told me Rooksley was cautioned for assault in '23. He's sending me the file by the new air-mail service. Should be with me in a few days.'

'Remarkable,' said Shaw.

'Oh I knew most of that already,' said Ludd, as he took another large gulp of beer. 'See, the thing about people like Rooksley is they always think they're one step ahead of people like me, and they get careless and that's when I nab 'em. Look at this. Rooksley left it amongst his things in the chapel.' He passed a small, yellowing newspaper cutting to Shaw. It bore a title written with a pencil: '*Times of India*, 12 June 1923.' Shaw read the brief article.

SIMLA BUSINESSMAN ARRESTED

Mr Aethelstan Rooksley of Gardenia Lodge, Church-Road, Simla, was arrested yesterday following allegations of assault by an employee in his service. He was later released without charge. Rooksley, 36, is general manager of Major Ronald Blair's well known Simla Air Service.

Ludd sat back and folded his arms. 'The Rooksley types like to show off a bit. They like the notoriety, you see. That's why he kept that, I'll wager. Not much in itself, I admit, but here's where it gets interesting. I've been walking along the coast here these last couple of days, trying to find anyone who might have seen what happened to Rooksley. Nobody did, it seems— not likely really at that hour of the morning. But one man *was* out and about that morning it seems, in his aeroplane.'

'You mean…Major Blair?'

'The very same. His mechanic said he saw him leaving the airfield in his car at about 5.00 am, with the plane still warm on the grass.'

'And you believe there may be a connection?'

'There must be. How many Major Ronald Blairs can there be flying aeroplanes around?'

'It is a common enough name and aeroplane pilots are increasingly common too.'

'Yes, but "Major" Blair? Major's an army rank, it's not what they use in the Royal Flying Corps, or the Royal Air Force as they call it now. I've been on to the War Office on the telephone and there's four Major Ronald Blairs on their records but only one was Indian Army— at least in living memory.'

'Living memory?' asked Shaw.

'Yes, the only other one was decorated in the Mutiny so he must be in a bath chair by now, not an aeroplane. No, the one in this hotel is the right chap I think. And that means he might be involved in the case in some way. That Guru fellow said he thought there was another blackmailer involved, though he wouldn't say who he thought it was. I'll find out soon enough, once Blair's finished his beauty sleep.

'He sounds a bit of a chancer to me; according to the War Office he was only commissioned in 1918 and was an acting Major just for the last two months of the show, in the Indian Defence Force, an outfit which as far as I can establish spent most of the war playing polo, so it's a bit rum of him to use that rank in civvie street.'

Shaw felt a pang of conscience, which he attempted to assuage with a large swallow of beer. He felt guilty about Ludd's willingness to share information, while he himself held something back. Should he, he wondered, tell the Chief Inspector of Blair's suspicion of the Guru? No, he decided. It was told him in confidence. He decided he would, however, impart something of use to the Chief Inspector.

'I have arranged with Major Blair to go in his aeroplane tomorrow morning at 7.00 a.m.,' said Shaw. 'Perhaps you will come to the airfield to meet us afterwards? I imagine we will be in flight for around 30 minutes or so.'

'You trust a man with a hangover to take you up in one of those things?' asked Ludd.

'He seems very competent, from what I can tell,' said Shaw. 'And strangely enough, I felt safer in the air than I have done in the fast motor cars of today. One forgets that one is only inches away from death on some roads.'

'Hmm, well, rather you than me,' said Ludd. 'I'll be there at 7.30 then.'

That evening, Shaw lay in bed unable to sleep, partly because of the heat and partly because his thoughts kept going round and round without reaching any kind of satisfactory conclusion. The sound of his wife's gentle breathing came from the bed next to him, as did the occasional contented sigh from Fraser as he shifted position on the floor between the beds.

After an hour of sleeplessness, he gave up and switched the little bedside lamp on, angling the shade towards him so that the light would not waken his wife. He picked up his pocket bible and opened it at random. It opened at the Psalms, as it usually did, since they are always in the centre of the book. He looked down to see Psalm 55, and remembered that that had been appointed for the previous Sunday. He read the words quietly to himself as he began to remember the tune to which they had been set in the parish church.

'Fearfulness and trembling are come upon me, and horror hath overwhelmed me/And I said, Oh that I had wings like a dove, for then I would fly away…'

Something was nagging at his brain; he decided to mentally review what he knew of the case so far. Rooksley had caused, at least indirectly, the death of Cotterill, but it was not murder; he had then done the same with Prior, which again was not murder. He had then attempted to rob Dewynter, and then Shaw had found his mangled corpse on the Wooden Witness, put there in some strange way that seemed to defy logic. Rooksley had been blackmailing the Guru, as had Blair. Had the Guru killed Rooksley? He had an alibi provided by the Murrays. Could they be trusted? Why was Blair out in his aeroplane so early on the morning of the murder— if indeed it was murder? Was there, as Blair had said, some kind of 'black magic' involved?

So many threads, he thought. Images from the past few days flashed across his brain like a cinematograph show. Shaw instinctively recoiled from the idea of there being some supernatural element to the killing…but then again, Dewynter had seemed convinced that such things were real. There was certainly evil in the world, Shaw knew, but did demons and evil spirits somehow conspire to brutally murder someone on a quiet English beach?

Shaw had always tried to tread the *via media*, the middle way between Protestant literalism and Catholic mysticism. His understanding was that the age of miracles had passed, or at least, that most things called miracles in ancient times now had a rational explanation. Did that also apply, he wondered, to 'evil spirits'? It would seem so. Evil no longer appeared in the forms of demons and goblins, those characters that preoccupied the mind of medieval man so much.

No, he concluded; the demons had gone, but the same evil manifested itself in new ways; in mustard gas and barbed wire; the machine gun and the bayonet, the Zeppelin and the bombing plane…

Shaw realised that he was on the brink of falling asleep, and had just enough time to switch off the bedside lamp before he spiralled down into a profound slumber, with the sure and certain knowledge of who had killed

Rooksley and how it had been done. He resisted for a moment, wondering if he should act, but the deep peace of sleep crept remorselessly over him. The last thought to pass through his mind was the twelfth verse of the psalm he had been reading. It was no demon he sought:

'But it was thou…my guide, and my acquaintance…'

Just before 7.00 a.m. the next day, after a brief conversation with the hotel chambermaid and night porter, Shaw strode up the hill to the little airfield. It was not as far away as it had seemed when he had travelled there in Major Blair's car, and he was able to take a short cut away from the road, which made the journey even quicker.

As he approached the airfield he heard in the distance the puttering sound of Blair's aeroplane engine, as the little red machine sat outside the shed. Shaw waved and increased his walking pace.

The figure seated in the cockpit, in flying helmet and goggles, with the face below obscured by a distinctive yellow scarf, pointed with a gloved hand to the passenger cockpit. Shaw climbed in and fastened his seatbelt. The figure turned, and pointed to the telephone headset atop the flying helmet; Shaw nodded and placed the headset over his ears.

Within seconds the plane was bumping along the

ground and then Shaw experienced for the second time the strange sense of elation and partial weightlessness as the craft left the ground. He looked down and saw what appeared to be a toy version of a sports car arrive at the shed, just before the plane banked steeply over the cliffs and the airfield was lost from view.

Shaw smiled and shouted through the mouthpiece. 'Good morning, Miss Sloan!'

The aircraft tilted suddenly and he saw the pilot's head turn briefly towards him; then the plane righted itself. Shaw heard Miss Sloan's voice clearly through the headphones, against a background of static and engine noise.

'How did you know?'

'Until last night I was not entirely sure, although I had my suspicions,' said Shaw.

'Of course, I knew you had found out something,' said Miss Sloan, 'which is the reason for the subterfuge. May I ask what you know?'

In for a penny, thought Shaw, and took a deep breath. 'It is my belief that you murdered Aethelstan Rooksley.'

There was a pause and a crackle of static. Shaw felt the wind rushing through the small gaps in the side of his flying helmet, and tightened the strap to block it out. He heard Miss Sloan laugh, a strange tinkling sound, which he realised he had not heard before.

'The man was brutally beaten and impaled on a wooden post, so the papers say,' she said. 'How could I have possibly done that?'

'With a rather unusual weapon,' said Shaw.

'Oh yes, and what might that be?'

'We are sitting in it.'

Miss Sloan laughed again and the plane banked sharply. Shaw clutched for support on the side of the cockpit and swallowed hard.

'My suspicions were aroused,' he said, 'by a set of disappearing footprints in the sand on North Beach. At first I thought they must have somehow been wiped out by a freak wave, but this did not account for how Rooksley was found impaled on the Wooden Witness. It took three men to get him down and would have been a very difficult task to put him there in the first place, unless of course he fell. The police believed he fell from the cliff, but this did not account for the injuries that he sustained which were not consistent with a fall. I believe that Rooksley took flight, quite literally.'

The plane banked again, then swooped down a hundred feet or so; Shaw felt his stomach churn, and breathed deeply to calm himself.

'Very clever, Mr Shaw,' said Miss Sloan. 'Go on.'

'It is my belief that somebody, who knew Rooksley would be on North Beach at dawn, dived down in this aircraft and caught him a severe blow, probably with the undercarriage. He was then somehow entangled in the wheels for a short distance and was dislodged, falling onto the Wooden Witness.'

'Well done, Mr Shaw,' said Miss Sloan. 'An admirable theory. But how could you know it was me?'

'I confess I thought it was another at first,' said Shaw. 'The most obvious answer was Major Blair, since it is his plane, and he was in cahoots with Rooksley in attempting to blackmail the Guru. But something did not add up. 'Firstly, he claimed he was in bed, with a terrible headache at the time of the murder, a fact which was verified by me following an interview with his chambermaid. However, his mechanic told the police that he had seen Blair on the airfield that morning. Either somebody was lying, or somebody was posing as Blair and taking his plane out. It would have been easy enough to do as with flying overalls, helmet, goggles, a scarf across the face, and so on, who would know the difference?'

'Fascinating, Mr Shaw,' said Miss Sloan. 'I was not aware you had such close relations with the police. Go on.'

She tilted the joystick and the plane's nose swung upward; they went into a steep climb and then plunged down again. Shaw looked down with some trepidation at the glassy blue sea thousands of feet below; they were now a long way out from the shore. The cliffs and sands of North Beach were just a hazy yellow strip in the distance.

'I then considered the possibility that the murder was carried out by the Guru,' said Shaw. 'But how could an Indian holy man have done such a thing? It was only by chance that I found out that he is not quite who he seems, your Guru. Or should I call him by his real name— Mr Kyriakides?'

Miss Sloan's head turned round sharply, and Shaw saw a flash of madness in the eyes behind the flying goggles.

'You leave him out of this,' she said. 'He *is* a holy man. More of one than *you* will ever be. And how could he possibly know how to fly a plane?'

'Because at some point, presumably before he took on his persona of the Guru, he was a humble aeroplane mechanic working for Major Blair in India. I know that because I recognised him from the company photograph in Blair's room. The Guru presumably picked up his knowledge of flying there. Blair also let slip that Rooksley had beaten up one of his mechanics so badly that his nose was broken— as is the Guru's— and the police in Simla confirmed via telegram that such an assault had taken place.'

'My, my, you have been busy,' said Miss Sloan.

'But I realised,' continued Shaw, 'that it could not have

227

been the Guru because at the time of Rooksley's death he had an alibi provided by Mr and Mrs Murray, who are pillars of their church and unlikely to be involved in a murder plot.'

'All very interesting,' said Miss Sloan, over a burst of static, 'but I still don't understand how you knew it was me.'

'The most obvious clue,' said Shaw, 'was when Major Blair told me that Rooksley had assaulted an employee— the Guru, or should I say Mr Kyriakides— because he had been caught taking out a girl-friend in the plane. I imagine that more than one such secret flight took place. I knew from my conversation with the Guru that you and he had had a…liaison…in India.'

'Liaison!' scoffed Miss Sloan. 'You make it sound sordid. It wasn't.'

'I make no judgement, Miss Sloan,' said Shaw firmly. 'I knew also that you had been taken out in this very plane by Major Blair, so you would know the location of it and so on; perhaps Blair even told you when his mechanic would not be working, such as today?'

'Very good,' said Miss Sloan. 'Anything else?'

'This model of aircraft— a Sopwith Camel I believe— was presumably the same as the one Kyriakides taught you how to fly in India, as that is the type shown in Blair's photograph. Blair said it was light enough for a mere girl to push it out from the shed, and it was modified by him so that it could take off and land without assistance. I noticed also that Blair is a slightly built man, around your height and build, so you could pass for him from a distance when wearing his flying overalls, helmet and so on. Not only did this subterfuge enable you to steal Blair's plane, it also made it likely that anyone who chanced to see the attack would blame it on him also. The first clue

228

however was a chance remark you made in the hotel.'

'Which was?'

'You said you had not flown before, but when about to go in Major Blair's plane you said that you would not feel cold at that altitude. How could you have known that unless you had prior experience of flying? Another thing I noticed was that the lecture tour was changed at short notice to Eastburgh,' said Shaw. 'I learned it from the hotel manager when discussing my own booking. It seemed strange that an organised person such as yourself would do such a thing. My guess is that you received a blackmail letter from Eastburgh, and wished to, as they say, "flush out" the culprit?'

'Very perceptive,' said Miss Sloan. 'Rooksley was stupid enough to send an anonymous blackmail letter with an Eastburgh post-mark on it. I thought if we stayed in the town he would soon show himself, and he did.'

'I also knew,' continued Shaw, 'that you had medical training, and that the Guru was taking some sort of sleeping draught. Blair said that on the night before the murder, he had passed out after just one glass of champagne he had drunk in your presence. I assume you drugged it using the Guru's medicine, in order that he should be unconscious in the morning and would not be at the airfield. I assume you did something similar with his drinking water when you attended him last night. But do not worry, I have instructed the hotel to check on him and call a doctor if he is unresponsive.'

'Think you're jolly clever, don't you?' hissed Miss Sloan. 'The only thing missing is my motive, but I suspect you have that all worked out too.'

'I confess not quite,' said Shaw. 'I discounted fairly quickly the "black magic" elements of the case which have been proposed by the newspapers and local gossip. I knew it must be something to do with Rooksley's blackmail attempts, but I also sensed the Guru was hiding something from me about his past, and that his affair with you was not the real reason for his fear of exposure.'

'You're damned right it's not,' said Miss Sloan angrily, and the plane's nose dipped down. Shaw felt his ears pop as the plane began to descend closer to the waves; he could now barely see the land at all, except for a tiny sliver in the far distance.

'I think,' said Shaw, 'it is more that he is afraid of his true identity being found out. A Greek surname, but too dark-skinned to be a Greek, and therefore likely to be of mixed race. Not, as he alludes at the hotel dinner table, a pure-blooded, high-caste Indian mystic who grew up in a monastery. In short, like Rooksley, he is an imposter.'

'How dare you,' said Miss Sloan, as the plane increased in speed in its descent towards the water. Shaw felt a slight sense of relief as he saw they were moving closer to the beach, although it was still a long way off.

'It is true,' she said, 'that he is the illegitimate son of a Greek sailor and an Indian prostitute. He was abandoned and grew up in an orphanage. It is true he worked as mechanic, and had no religious training. All that came later when he realised his calling, but nobody would have accepted him in his home country— or indeed the world— if they had known the truth. And once his reputation grew, it became impossible for him to let anyone find out.

'He is a true spiritual leader,' she continued, and her voice had the confidence of a fanatic. 'Some say he is the Second Coming. I don't believe that because I don't believe in the *first* coming, or at least not in the way your church teaches. But Guruji has a divine mission, to make all men one. To release the cosmic energy within all of us. Anything— and anyone— that jeopardises that mission

230

must be stopped.'

'And with the announcement of the American speaking tour,' said Shaw, 'you felt you had to get rid of Rooksley, permanently. He was too great a risk.'

'Exactly,' said Miss Sloan exultantly. 'The Guru may no longer love me, and our son may have died, but I still love him and always will. He. Must. Not. Be. Stopped.'

The plane began to wobble violently from side to side; Shaw heard Miss Sloan laugh again, louder this time, and he realised the woman had taken leave of her senses.

'I think we should go back now,' said Shaw. 'You ought to know that the police have been instructed to arrive at the airfield. They will be there by now.'

'No Mr Shaw,' said Miss Sloan, and laughed again. 'It's too late to go back. I told you, anyone who stands in the Guru's way will be stopped. I gave Blair enough of that sedative to knock him out, but when I get back, I shall make sure he takes enough to put him to sleep forever.'

'When *I* get back?' asked Shaw. 'Not *we*?'

Miss Sloan ignored the question, and countered with one of her own.

'Why on earth did you come up in this plane if you knew all this?'

'Because I had to be certain that you knew how to fly a plane, to make sure my theory was correct,' he said.

If truth be told, thought Shaw, he had perhaps been rather rash in putting himself in such a risky position, but he could not see how Miss Sloan could hurt him unless she intended to crash the plane and kill them both, and she did not strike him as the suicidal type.

'It was the same for me,' said Miss Sloan. 'I took a risk in taking this plane out again, but after I heard Blair speak to you last night I had to find out what you knew. To assess if you were a danger.'

'And am I?' asked Shaw cautiously.

'Most certainly,' said Miss Sloan airily. 'You gave away far too much. You would make a poor poker player, Mr Shaw…'

Miss Sloan was then interrupted by a roar of static; there was a sudden rise in engine noise as the plane went into a steep dive. Shaw felt his ears pop again and then a feeling of giddiness as the plane started to roll slowly over onto its side.

'One thing puzzles me, Miss Sloan,' said Shaw. 'How did you identify Rooksley when he was on the beach? He could have been an innocent man out for an early morning stroll.'

'He came to our first lecture here,' said Miss Sloan. 'Guruji recognised him immediately, and the wretched man made all sorts of insinuations without actually coming out and saying anything. I knew it was him when I saw him again.'

'And so you knocked him down,' said Shaw, 'and in the process he was dropped onto the Wooden Witness.'

'I didn't intend the second part, but it was a rather apt ending for him, don't you think? To die on a place dedicated to pagan sacrifices. I rather think he'd enjoy the irony.'

'Surely you were taking a big risk, stealing a plane?' asked Shaw.

'Yes, but with the potential for a large return,' replied Miss Sloan. 'You see, I intended that you should witness the attack on Rooksley. It was Guru's innocent idea to get you to identify him, but it was my idea to use it to greater advantage. As it was Blair's plane, suspicion would naturally fall on him. I would kill two birds with one stone, or two stones with one bird, if you prefer. However, you spoilt all that by turning up late. I only had one chance to dive on Rooksley because if I had kept circling he would have seen me and run for cover. I then had to get the plane back before anybody realised it was missing.'

Miss Sloan gave another empty laugh and Shaw felt fear rising in his throat. The woman was clearly deranged.

'I had hoped this would not be necessary,' she continued but you know too much. I can't possibly let you go now. I shall land somewhere up the coast and catch a train back to Eastburgh before anyone knows I have gone. But good news! You will be absorbed into the universal consciousness!'

The plane was now almost on its side, and Shaw felt rising panic. He fought it and held his voice steady as he spoke again through the intercom.

'I am not afraid to die, Miss Sloan,' said Shaw. 'But you will be found out.'

'I don't think so,' replied the pilot. 'The police clearly don't know as much as you or they would have arrested me by now. Who could possibly suspect me of being involved?'

'You have made the Guru a party to murder. How will that look when it comes out? He will hang for joint enterprise.'

'Impossible. He knows *nothing* of this,' said Miss Sloan. 'Nor of your "investigation". He thinks you worked purely to help him. I will ensure no guilt is attached to him.'

'How exactly do you propose to "get rid" of me, Miss Sloan?' asked Shaw. 'You cannot possibly leave the controls and attempt to eject me. I warn you I shall be forced to defend myself if you attempt it.'

Miss Sloan laughed again. 'Oh dear,' she said. 'The western mind is so blinded by the love of *force*. The eastern religions hold more with the concept of effortless action.'

Shaw felt the plane turn further on its axis until it was at

233

a right angle to the sea far below. He began to feel dizzy and fought back the feeling of nausea which rose in the pit of his stomach.

'I don't need to eject you,' said Miss Shaw. 'The force of nature— gravity— will do it for me. If you look at your seatbelt you will see I made a slight modification to it this morning. A precaution I hoped I would not need, but now I see that I do.'

Shaw looked down and saw that, tucked away almost out of sight, the end of the seatbelt where it was fixed to the cockpit was almost cut through in a ragged tear; barely half an inch of material remained.

'Once we have turned upside down, your weight will be sufficient to break the belt and dislodge you. You may be able to hang on for a while but eventually you'll fall. I can fly upside down quite easily— Guruji taught me when we used to take the plane out secretly in India.'

Shaw gripped the sides of the cockpit desperately as he felt the aircraft turn completely upside down; his head swam and his vision began to blur. He had no idea which way was up or down now, but could see the belt around his waist shredded now to almost a single thread of canvas webbing.

Over the sound of the blood singing in his ears, and the pounding of his heart which now seemed to have lodged itself in his throat, Shaw heard the faint voice of Miss Sloan on the intercom, which seemed as if she was a long, long way away. The voice sounded completely sincere, almost comforting.

'Don't worry— a fall from this height will kill you the moment you hit the water…remember, you are not a drop in the ocean, you are also the ocean in a drop…all is well…Goodbye, Mr Shaw!'

Ludd arrived at the airfield at 7.30 as planned, to find a small, red-faced man seething with anger next to a little sports car.

'If you're looking for a pleasure flight you're out of luck,' said the man angrily. 'Someone's pinched my bally plane! I'm just off now to telephone the police.'

'Let me save you the trouble,' said Ludd, showing his warrant card to the man. 'Chief Inspector Ludd. You're Major Blair, I assume?'

'Do you know something about this?' said Blair, in a slightly calmer, though still enraged, voice. 'Two people took off in the kite just as I arrived here. One of them was the fellow I was supposed to be meeting, parson called Shaw.'

'I know him,' said Ludd. 'Who was the other person?'

'I've a pretty shrewd idea,' said Blair. 'Mechanic I knew out east. Name of Kyriakides. Although now he calls himself Gurubaba, or some such rot.'

'You mean that Indian fellow is up in that plane with Reverend Shaw?' asked Ludd incredulously. 'What the devil for?'

'No idea, but he's had it in for me for a while. He got his, his…gangster's moll…to dope me up. Must have been her that pinched m'flying togs as well. I thought it was some sort of voodoo he was working at first but then she tried it again last night with a glass of water. Made me drink it down. Tasted foul. Did it while she played a Florence Nightingale act after I bumped m'head, but I was on to her. After she left I went into the bathroom and stuck my…'

'Yes, spare me the details,' said Ludd. 'Any idea where they might have gone?'

'Not a clue old chap,' said Blair. 'The kite's not got much juice in her so they'll have to ditch pretty soon.'

Ludd felt slightly bewildered at this new development, but it began to make sense. He knew from the press cutting that Blair had run an airfield in India; was there some connection with the Guru?

'If they don't come back here how far can they go?' he asked.

'Fifty, sixty miles or so I should think,' said Ludd. The Sop— that's the plane, Sopwith Camel— can land pretty much anywhere.'

'That means they could end up in any farmer's field from here to Norwich,' said Ludd. He thought quickly. Had Shaw, he wondered, got one step ahead of him, as he had done once before, and somehow found out the identity of Rooksley's killer? If so, was he in danger? His train of thought was interrupted by an excited shout from Blair, who was pointing out to sea.

'There she is!' he yelled. 'Out over the bay. What the devil are they doing? She's upside down!'

'Where?' asked Ludd as he squinted over the hazy blue expanse of the North Sea.

'Where are the blasted binocs?' asked Blair, and he rooted around hurriedly in his car. 'Not here. Of course, Shaw must have left them in the plane. Got another set in the shed.'

Blair ran into the open shed and emerged with a pair of binoculars. He held them up to his eyes and turned the focus wheel rapidly.

'Damned fool's doing aerobatics,' he shouted. 'He must know the Sop can't take much of that. He'll snap the ailerons.'

'Give me those,' said Ludd. He grabbed the binoculars before they were offered. Out over the bay he could make out the small red plane, shimmying and wobbling as it went into a steep dive. He handed the binoculars back to Blair.

'Got a telephone here?' he asked urgently.

'No,' said Blair, his gaze fixed on the plane out at sea. 'Nearest one's back at the hotel.'

'Take me down to the station,' said Ludd, as he sat down heavily in Blair's car.

'Look here old chap,' complained Blair, 'you can't just demand…'

'I'm commandeering this car,' replied Ludd. 'Either you drive it or I do. Whoever that lunatic is out there he's putting Mr Shaw in grave danger. We need to get down to the station and alert the coastguard and the lifeboat before a tragedy occurs.'

A mile or so out at sea, the Sopwith Camel continued its remorseless steep dive, upside down. Shaw felt a sudden lurch in his midriff as the last strands of the seatbelt gave way; he braced his legs and arms against the sides of the cockpit but the pull of gravity was enormous, and after

237

only a few seconds he felt his muscles quiver agonisingly as he fought to support his whole body weight. He kicked forward, trying to find some niche or ledge in which he could hold himself, but there was none. He thought of grabbing Miss Sloan, only two feet or so in front of him across the fuselage, but it was hopeless; it took all his strength simply to hold himself in place.

He heard a voice reciting the Lord's Prayer and thought at first it was somehow coming through the intercom, but he dimly realised it was in his head, his own voice playing back to him like a gramophone recording. Was he already dead, he wondered? Just then he felt a heavy object hit his shin, and as he glanced down, his eyes suddenly regained focus. It was the pair of heavy binoculars which he had left in the cockpit the last time he had flown in the plane.

All he could hear now was the roar of the engine and the howling of the wind. With his last vestige of strength he grabbed the leather strap of the binoculars and swung them forward towards Miss Sloan's head. They fell short by a few inches, and he tried again; this time the hard metal dealt her a heavy blow on the side of her head.

Shaw heard a gasp of pain over the intercom; Miss Sloan flung a gloved hand to her head and the plane lurched round to a less acute angle, relaxing the pull of gravity on Shaw's body. The craft then wobbled and shook alarmingly. Shaw pressed home his advantage and swung the binoculars once more. This time only a glancing blow was struck. Miss Sloan seemed unaffected, and began to tilt the plane upside-down again.

Shaw felt himself sliding out of the cockpit again; once again he tried to prevent himself from falling out, but it was no good; he felt his arms loosen their grip on the plane, and then he was scrabbling with his legs, finding only a tiny toehold which was not strong enough to hold him.

He began to prepare himself; he thought of Marion, whose benign face flashed briefly before his eyes, and then he saw a strange stone wall ahead. Were they about to hit the cliffs? No, thought Shaw, as his brain dimly registered he was viewing the tomb at Calvary. The stone wall rolled away, and his vision was dazzled by a light more intense than anything he could ever have imagined.

As he felt his legs give way, he heard Miss Sloan speak calmly over the intercom.

'I was a fool, Mr Shaw. I can't bring her round again, the stick's jammed and she won't correct. Try to forgive me. We're nearly at sea level now so you'll be all right. I don't want to kill you any more. Tell Guruji I love him.'

Shaw's headset was then ripped away as he fell from the cockpit, and less than a second later he was plunged deep, deep down into the green darkness of the North Sea.

For a moment Shaw had no idea where he was or which way was up; he seemed encased in a seething, broiling mass of water which buffeted and churned him from all sides; after a moment, he saw light far above him and kicked as hard as he could.

Gradually the light became brighter but the surface still seemed hundreds of feet above him; he felt his lungs bursting with the desire for oxygen; he held out as long as he could but his mouth involuntarily opened and he felt himself breath in seawater; at the same moment his head emerged from the water. He flailed around wildly and coughed hard until he felt air instead of water in his lungs. At least the sea was warm and still, he thought, and there appeared to be no strong currents here, as he trod water, kicking off his shoes and pulling off his jacket in the process.

Before he could begin to orientate himself to the land, he saw about fifty feet in front of him the wings of the Sopwith Camel floating on the water. They were mangled, and detached from the rest of the fuselage, which lay on its side in the water. He realised the plane must have crashed just moments after he fell out.

With the practised strokes of a regular swimmer he made his way to the wreckage, a process which seemed agonisingly slow. The fuselage hissed with steam and stank of the petrol which bubbled out on to the surface of the water in rainbow coloured waves.

He grabbed hold of the wreckage and felt it lurch under his fingers; Miss Sloan was still in her place in the cockpit, just visible a few inches under water; she scrabbled feebly at the belt around her waist. Before Shaw could do anything, the fuselage lurched again and tipped forward, then sank quickly beneath the water until it disappeared from view into the green darkness.

Shaw took a deep breath and prepared to dive, but then felt something dig into his back and lift him upwards. He thrashed wildly at his back, fearing he had become entangled in the wreckage. He then felt strong arms pull at him and seconds later he was lying on the deck of a boat next to the wooden boat-hook that had been used to fish him out of the water.

'Someone in there,' he gasped. 'Strapped in. Have to…get her out.'

'Sorry chum,' said a large, grey-bearded man in front him. 'It's ten fathoms deep here. She'll drop like a stone with the weight of the engine now the wings have gone.'

'A line…you must attach a line…' said Shaw huskily, as his vision darkened.

'Even if we'd had time for that,' said the man, 'she'd pull us down with her. This is only a small boat and we can't risk it. I'm sorry.'

Shaw felt himself falling into a deep, black pit. 'The ocean…in a drop…' he whispered.

'What's that?' said the man, then turned to his mate on the deck. 'Here, put that blanket on him. He's passed out.'

Epilogue

The tall, dark-skinned man appeared somewhat uncomfortable in a new-looking ready-made suit and a fawn raincoat, the shoulders of which were dappled with moisture; he turned a trilby hat awkwardly in his hands as he watched Shaw from the chair next to his bed.

Shaw blinked hard and looked again. The man was still there, and on seeing Shaw awake, he smiled slightly. Who on earth was he? thought Shaw.

'My dear Mr Shaw,' said the man, fingering his celluloid collar in apparent discomfort. 'It seems you do not recognise me.'

Suddenly Shaw remembered everything, albeit in a jumbled, confused way. The crash, the rescue, the admittance to some sort of hospital. Telling his story to Ludd before collapsing from exhaustion. He looked around the bright little ward with its flowers in vases and neatly made beds. He appeared to be the only occupant. He suddenly realised who the man was.

'Guru,' he said. 'What a surprise. But your clothes…'

'Please, Mr Shaw,' said the man. 'I have decided to wear only western garb from now on. And to use my real name. Antonio Kyriakides.'

'Miss Sloan…' said Shaw slowly, 'you know she is…'

'Yes, Mr Shaw,' said Kyriakides sadly. 'You have been asleep for the last 24 hours. The story is well known by

242

now.'

'Is Marion here…?'

'Your wife is just outside, sir. She was kind enough to allow me a few moments alone with you.'

'And Miss Sloan? Is she…?'

'A salvage company intends to attempt a recovery of the wreckage. There is no hope of her having survived.'

'She wanted me to tell you she loved you,' said Shaw.

'That is a comfort, Mr Shaw, thank you. I am so sorry that you had to suffer in this way. I should have been honest with you about my true origins.'

Shaw attempted to make a gesture of dismissal of the last remark, then winced as he felt pain shoot through his shoulder.

'You are in pain?' asked Kyriakides with a concerned expression. 'Shall I fetch the nurse?'

'No, no,' said Shaw. 'I am perfectly all right, thank you. But why have you changed your clothes, and your name?'

'You will not have seen the newspapers, Mr Shaw,' said Kyriakides with a sigh, 'but my secret, as they say, is out. I do not intend to continue as a guru.'

'But what of your mission to humanity?' asked Shaw. 'Miss Sloan…in her own way, acted as she did in order to protect that.'

'Oh Mr Shaw,' said Kyriakides. 'Your own bible warns against those that do evil so that good may come.'

Shaw thought for a moment. 'Romans…chapter three, verse…eight I think. Yes, I suppose you are right. What will you do now?'

'Mr and Mrs Murray have kindly agreed to continue to support me in the American lecture tour,' said Kyriakides. 'But I will do so as an ordinary man talking of matters of the spirit for other ordinary men, not as some sort of exalted idol. Mr Murray, with his infinite reserves of self-confidence, believes it may actually work to my advantage to "come clean", as they say.'

'Perhaps the time has come for the ordinary men to come to the fore,' said Shaw. 'I wish you well.'

'Thank you, Mr Shaw,' said Kyriakides. 'If India is to make her own way in the world, she will need men of all faiths to work together, especially men of mixed ancestry such as myself. There is much I can do, I think, to further this.'

There was a somewhat awkward pause, and Kyriakides was distracted momentarily by something happening outside the window.

'And now, Mr Shaw, I must take my leave,' he said. 'I see that most excellent officer of the law, Chief Inspector Ludd, is waiting outside with your wife to speak to you. He has advised me in no uncertain terms that although I have been cleared of any involvement in the death of Rooksley, he does not wish to set eyes on me again unless I am called to bear witness at a trial. Mr and Mrs Murray await me at the railway station from whence we shall begin our journey to America. Goodbye, sir.'

After briefly pressing both of Shaw's hands with his, the man was gone, leaving only a slight creaking sound behind him as the ward door swung shut.

Shaw lay back and then sat up again as he heard raised voices at the opposite end of the ward. The stentorian tones of the ward sister boomed across the polished linoleum floor.

'I have told you already, I cannot possibly allow that animal in here. This is a hospital, not a kennel.'

Shaw heard the rapid patter of canine feet on the linoleum and then felt a blow to his chest as Fraser jumped on the bed and began licking his face.

'Down, boy,' said Shaw, laughing. He immediately felt

better and sat up.

'Get off the bed, you ridiculous creature,' he said, rubbing the dog's ears, and then placed him on the floor beside him.

Mrs Shaw, along with the Chief Inspector, entered the ward. As his wife walked towards him he heard the sister call out angrily. 'Well I suppose if a policeman *orders* that dog to be in here, I have no choice.'

She then turned on her heels with a sharp squeak and was gone. Shaw embraced his wife, who sat down beside him on the chair. Ludd stood behind her.

'I'm so glad you're awake, Lucian,' said Mrs Shaw. 'You've been asleep for hours.'

'Where exactly am I?' asked Shaw.

'Eastburgh cottage hospital,' said his wife. 'Now don't worry, it's just a precaution. The doctors wanted to keep you under observation but they think you'll be well enough to go home tonight.'

'Home?' asked Shaw. 'Certainly not. We are on holiday.'

'That's the spirit sir,' said Ludd. 'You take it easy for the next few days in your hotel. You'll be in most of the time anyway, as the weather's turned and it's raining cats and dogs now.'

'That will be something of a relief,' said Shaw, 'and good news for the farmers.'

'Oh Lucian that's so typical of you,' said his wife. 'Always thinking of others. Well you just relax and think of yourself for a while.'

'I wouldn't mind a bit of rest and relaxation myself,' said Ludd, 'but not much chance of that now. The papers have gone wild over the story and I'm having to give something called a "press conference" today, would you believe it? Who do they think I am, Lord Rothermere? I told that Indian fellow he could have five minutes with you and

245

then to be on his way. I'm just glad he's decided to go incognito and dress normally now instead of like Gunga Din, as that would have brought the journalists down here like a plague of locusts.'

'I still don't understand how Miss Sloan fell in with someone like him,' said Mrs Shaw. 'She seemed as if she came from a respectable Anglo-Indian family.'

'I got the full story from the Guru, or rather, Mr Kyriakides today,' said Ludd. 'It tallies with what Mr Shaw here told me after we rescued him, though I tried to get him to rest. Mr Kyriakides and I had a little chat just to put my mind at rest that he wasn't involved. Turns out he was a mechanic at Major Blair's aeroplane taxi service in India. Miss Sloan's father, that's Major-General Sir James Winnington Sloan, Indian Army, DSO and bar, *if* you please, used to pop up to Viceregal Lodge all the time in Blair's plane.

'Kyriakides doubled as the driver who ferried people to the airfield, and Miss Sloan used to come along for the ride in the car sometimes. Got talking about spiritual matters, apparently, and that's how it all started. Before long he was taking out his boss's plane on the sly and not only that he was teaching Miss Sloan how to do it…fly a plane, I mean. When Rooksley, who was general manager, found out he beat the chap to a pulp, according to the file the police in Simla sent me. Nothing got done though.'

'How shocking,' said Mrs Shaw.

'Yes,' said Ludd. 'Kyriakides was what they call a Eurasian out there. Half-caste. They don't fit in with the British or the Indians, so he didn't get much in the way of justice I'm sorry to say. Neither fish nor fowl, as it were. Then General Sloan found out about his daughter carrying on with a half-Indian mechanic, and having a kiddie by him, who later died in an orphanage.'

'The poor, poor woman,' said Mrs Shaw.

'Yes, well,' continued Ludd, 'she was no good for the colonial marriage market after that, and somehow the medical school she attended got wind of it too and chucked her out, so she got packed off back to England quietly. After that, Kyriakides had a bellyful of the British, turned in his job and started all this Guru stuff, changed his name and pretended he was brought up in a monastery. Did surprisingly well. All sort of myths grew up about him in the Indian nationalist press and he got carried away with it all. Then when he was over here lecturing, Miss Sloan heard about him, realised who he was and tried to revive the old flame— although Kyriakides was no longer interested in romance— and the rest as they say is history.'

'But what,' said Shaw, 'of Major Blair? Will he be charged with blackmail?'

'Not much point,' said Ludd, shaking his head. 'He never in so many words demanded money, according to Kyriakides, who doesn't want to press charges anyway. I've given him a warning and he seemed to take it to heart. Says he learnt his lesson that crime doesn't pay. Claims he's stopped drinking and looking to have a change of business once the insurance money for his plane comes through.'

'"Joy shall be in heaven over one sinner that repenteth",' said Shaw. 'Let us hope it is true.'

'If you say so, sir,' said Ludd. 'I've heard such resolutions before from men like Major Blair, but we shall see. Well I'll be off now. Lots of things to do with this case, and Mrs Ludd keeps asking me to go on charabanc trips and attend pier concerts and the like. It's hard work, this holiday business. Good day to you both.'

After Ludd had left, Mrs Shaw chattered about events surrounding the case, and how clever the Chief Inspector had been about keeping Shaw's location unknown to the press. Shaw's heart sank, therefore, when he heard an altercation behind the ward door; he assumed the journalists had tracked him down.

'Your hands and face are filthy,' he heard the ward sister say. 'And you— what on earth is in that parcel? It is making *noises*.'

The sister's tone of voice then changed to something approaching, if not exactly warmth, then a certain degree of defrosting. 'Oh, vicar, I did not realise these…persons were with you. I dare say that is acceptable. Go in, but not too long please, you will tire him out.'

Shaw looked up to see Dewynter, Prior and Billy. Fraser jumped up to meet Billy, who petted him enthusiastically.

'Dewynter, my dear chap, what a pleasant surprise,' Shaw said to the other clergyman as they warmly shook hands. 'Billy, how good of you to come. And Mr Prior. We meet under slightly more pleasant circumstances this time.'

Prior merely nodded and stood awkwardly by the bed, clutching a parcel wrapped in brown paper to his chest.

'Your whereabouts are supposed to be a secret,' said Dewynter. 'The town is crawling with the most reprehensible scandal-sheet-mongers and I have been turning them away from the vicarage all day. I only found out your whereabouts from Sam Perkins, the fisherman.'

'A large, bearded man?' asked Shaw.

'That's right. Hooked you out of the drink. I was down at the quayside when they bought you in because I heard the maroon go up and thought they might need another oarsman.'

Shaw smiled at Dewynter's implacable enthusiasm, and chastised himself for wondering, albeit only momentarily the previous day, whether the man had had some involvement in Rooksley's death.

'Les and me's got you something, Fa…I mean, vicar.' Give it to him, Les.'

'Got you this,' said Prior, who thrust the parcel at Shaw.

'What on earth is it?' asked Shaw, as he unwrapped the layers of brown paper to reveal a small wooden box covered in dials and wires, together with a headset similar to the one he had worn in Blair's plane. The faint, tinny sound of a radio announcer's voice could be heard from the headphones.

'It's a crystal radio set,' said Prior. 'So's you won't get bored. It's already on because I just tested it. You can listen to all sorts…it uses a half-wave rectifier, so only needs an amplitude modulation of thirty per cent at….'

'Yes, yes, thank you Leslie,' said Dewynter, 'let's not tire Mr Shaw with the finer details of radio technology.'

Prior fell silent and Shaw smiled at Dewynter's tact.

'And I brought you these, vicar,' said Billy. 'Seeing as you're sort of a detective. I've read 'em so I don't want them no more.'

Shaw smiled as Billy placed a pile of dog-eared little booklets with lurid covers on the bedside table. They were the Sexton Blake detective stories he had seen on sale at the railway station bookstall when they first arrived, which now seemed an age ago.

After a few minutes the visitors left, with Billy cheerfully announcing that he would take Mr and Mrs Shaw's suitcases back to the station for nothing when they left.

Shaw suddenly felt tired, and with his wife beside him holding his hand, he lay back on the pillows and fell contentedly asleep to the rhythmic sound of Fraser's tail beating against the linoleum floor.

The rain intensified outside Shaw's hospital window,

and the following day, when he was safely returned to his room at the Excelsior Hotel, a terrible storm battered the east coast of Britain from the Straits of Dover all the way to the Moray Firth. It was one of the worst anyone could remember. The cliffs above North Beach crumbled, perhaps because of the rain, and perhaps because of the curious onlookers and journalists having trampled the area in their hundreds to look down at the Wooden Witness.

Heaps of rock fell on the ancient wooden circle in the night, rending the central post in twain, then a freak combination of tide and wind the next morning swirled thousands of tons of silt onto the beach, burying the site from view once more. It was hopeless, a local archaeologist stated, to try to rescue it.

With the death of Aethelstan Rooksley, the Wooden Witness had claimed its final victim.

Other books by Hugh Morrison

A Third Class Murder (Reverend Shaw's first case)

An antiques dealer is found robbed and murdered in a third class train compartment on a remote Suffolk branch line. The Reverend Lucian Shaw, who was travelling on the same train, is concerned that the police have arrested the wrong man, and begins an investigation of his own.

The King is Dead

An exiled Balkan king is shot dead in his secluded mansion following a meeting with the local vicar, Reverend Lucian Shaw. Shaw believes that the culprit is closer than the police think, and before long is on the trail of a desperate killer who will stop at nothing to evade capture.

The Secret of the Shelter

In modern-day London, two children dare each other to explore the garden of an abandoned suburban house. They enter a half-buried bomb shelter, untouched since the Second World War, which holds a strange power that is to change their lives forever.

Published by Montpelier Publishing
Available from Amazon or your local bookshop

Printed in Great Britain
by Amazon

20514570R00150